IDYLLS OF THE SOUTH SEAS

Idylls

UNIVERSIT

of the
South Seas

William S. Stone

F HAWAII PRESS   HONOLULU 1970

Library of Congress Catalog Card Number 73-128083
Standard Book Number 87022-775-0
Copyright© 1970 by University of Hawaii Press
Manufactured in the United States of America

*To my wife Barbara
whose enthusiasm
helped so greatly*

Contents

Preface

AMONG the widely scattered Polynesian peoples, many variants of their legends are to be found. As one travels from island group to island group he may observe that the names of characters in a given tale, the relationships of the actors, even story incidents have become changed. Of such modifications the story of Tafai affords an example. In Tahiti and Samoa the great hero is still known as Tafai. Hawaiians call him Kahai. To the Maoris he is Tawhaki, and to the Mangarevans, Tahaki. In the Tahitian account Tafai is killed by his cousins and restored to life by his mother, whereas in the New Zealand Maori version he is killed by his brothers, and it is his wife who brings him back to life. Tahitians told of Tafai's descent to the underworld in search of his father, Hema. But in Hawaii this passage was replaced by an adventure in which Hema was carried off by a great bird from whom he was later rescued by his son.

It will be seen, then, that a Polynesian legend bearing the name Tafai may be any one of a number of differing tales. I have seen fit to permit my narrator, Tetua, to borrow on occasion from the renditions of those of his countrymen who settled on distant islands; but for the most part the legends in this book follow, in their main outlines, the versions of his own Tahiti.

Legends such as those of Nona and of Tafai had their origin in Tahiti, and it may therefore be said that the patterns on which Tetua's tales are based are the oldest. When his ancestors set out in their canoes for such far-separated islands as Hawaii and New Zealand, Mangareva and Rarotonga, they carried with them the rituals and the chanted legends that had grown upon Tahiti. But though the chants became altered in the new lands to which they were taken—sometimes slightly, sometimes radically—the Tahitian place names remained identifiable. The names of valleys, mountains, and streams indicate clearly the island on which the heroic sagas were first sung; and they show as well that Tahiti and neighboring Raiatea were the Pacific homelands from which great voyages were begun.

It must not be thought, however, that because their framework is taken at the Tahitian source the stories as they appear in this volume are literal translations of ancient song and myth. Students seeking such material will find it elsewhere. The intention here has been to present a group of legends in such a way that they might have living reality for a reader who has little or perhaps no personal familiarity with Polynesian peoples or Polynesian islands. I have wanted such a reader to see the tales taking place in the settings where they are said to have happened; I have wanted him to see the youths and maidens and men and women, not as so many strange names, but as real human beings. Finally, I have wanted him to feel himself on and of Tahiti or whatever other island was concerned. If I have succeeded, it is because I have not restricted Tetua to simple quotation of the words of his forebears. Yet to whatever extent he has elaborated upon the original narratives, setting his stage, painting his characters and his island's moods, he has only supplied for his foreign listeners what was intimately known to those who composed the tales and to those for whom, generation after generation, they were repeated.

To make full acknowledgment to all who have helped me in the writing of this book I should be obliged to list the names of the many Tahitian friends and acquaintances who, over a period of more than thirty years, have given me some understanding of themselves, and through whose eyes I have been permitted to look upon their island world. To every one of them I am more than grateful.

For the actual materials of which the stories are made I am especially indebted to ethnologist J. Frank Stimson, most of whose working life was spent in French Polynesia; to Temarii Ninau, former chief of the village of Haapu, Huahine; and to the late Louis Drollet of Papeete. For several of the tales I have also relied heavily on Teuira Henry's *Ancient Tahiti*, Bishop Museum Bulletin 48.

Honolulu, Hawaii
August, 1969

IDYLLS OF THE SOUTH SEAS

Of Tetua the Teller of Tales

OLD Tetua's visitors are few and are likely to be those who, however well they may love the South Sea islands of today, would give almost anything in life to have come upon the curving, palm-grown shores before progress-busied white men first arrived. Tetua's conversation is not of copra and vanilla markets, nor of island politics or world affairs. Yet for all that, he is a practical man. He tends the patch of taro growing close to the stream which flows into the sea before his bamboo house; he gathers the coconuts which fall from his trees, dries their meats, and sells them to the district Chinaman; he fishes with hooks of steel. One must eat, and in order to do so Tetua comports himself as a man of modern Tahiti. But his thoughts are often elsewhere, and his dark brown eyes look inward where his astounding memory holds stored the fast-disappearing lore of his forefathers. There, in Tetua's mind, are the customs of earlier days, the rituals, the sacred chants, the dances, the wondrous tales of kings and queens and youths and maids who breathed the warm, flower-scented tropic air, who loved and fought and laughed and sang, treading the jungly trails and sailing the blue seas many long centuries ago.

Some to whom Tetua's island is now home—Frenchmen, Americans, and even Tahitians—think him silent and eccentric. They sense his unconcern with their present-day affairs, and if they take slight umbrage they must not be blamed; for everyone, whatever the color of his skin, likes to imagine his own interests important and significant. But neither must Tetua be blamed if he prefers to walk with seeing eyes through his verdant countryside rather than to rush blindly past its changing beauty in a brightly painted car. Not for a minute does he begrudge others their pleasure in such things, but his own satisfactions and delights he finds elsewhere. Between him and many of his fellows there lies a gulf that can hardly be bridged. It is as difficult for them to converse as if they inhabited different planets. And so, in a sense, they do. Tetua's world is one in which the wind and sea, the sun and moon and stars are man's close companions. His airy house stands upon stilts sunk in the dark sand of a mile-long, bow-shaped beach, facing a bay of deep blue water and almost directly in front of the pass which leads through the barrier reef to the outer sea. It stands alone. No other human habitation is in sight. There is only the backdrop of high mountains, the clouds, the vaulted sky.

Tetua has his friends, for even now there are those who envy him his simple, wholesome way of living; and if the number of like-thinking folk upon the globe were known, it might be found surprisingly large. Happily, some of them are near and ask nothing better than to join him in his walks into the hills where he goes for fruit and firewood, or to ride with him in a canoe when he sets out for the reef to place his traps for fish, to wield his harpoon, or to set his lines. At such times, and with such friends, Tetua is far from silent. Then, with little urging, speaking in his deep, musically resonant voice, he will tell the wonders of the Tahitian past. To a sympathetic listener he will pour out his stories from dawn to dark—stories of fabulous fish and beasts, of mighty rulers, of brave and daring men and women to whom Tahiti was native land. Perhaps you who hold this book are such a listener, in which case, if you could be here on this island, you would certainly find yourself his welcome, close companion. He would insist that his house is yours and that, in visiting him, you must not think to stay brief hours, but rather days or weeks.

Often he has said as much to me. And it was not lack of inclination that so long kept me from paying him a visit on the shores of the Bay of Matavai. It was simply the warm-country habit of mañana that causes one to postpone even those things which promise to be pleasant. The day came, however, when I wrapped a few belongings in a length of cotton print and, with a similar cloth bound about my waist, set off by canoe for Tetua's beach.

It was early morning and the month was April, which in these southern latitudes is the beginning of winter. True, the seasons here bring little change, but in April and May the days are shorter and the sun disappears into the sea far to the north. With darkness the downdrafts from the mountains carry a decided chill, and during the first morning hours there is a tang and crispness in the air. It is a time of year to remind a transplanted white man of the energy and ambition that filled him in his youth. "Come," he says to himself, "you have been half asleep through the long, dreamy days of summer. The things you planned—why not do them now?"

So I paddled on over the calm, bright lagoons, keeping close to the shore, which fell away to north and east. Here and there small islands of mist hung low on the water; the bow of the canoe parted them, and in slow whorls they floated away to either side. As I rounded the last, jutting point of land which separated me from Tetua's bay, the breeze sprang up, ruffling all the great half-moon of Matavai and causing it to dance and sparkle in the sun.

4   However often I may happen upon the magnificent harbor where Captain Wallis in the stout English ship *Dolphin* dropped anchor, I think the effect upon me always will be the same. For a time I am left near breathless, and the paddle is forgotten.

The canoe drifts on a little way under its own momentum, and then its forward movement ceases. But it does not stand still. So wide is the pass that the whole bay stirs in sympathy with the sea beyond, and the little craft rises and falls as, with steady, measured pulse, the swells slide under it and roll on to foam at last upon the beach at the foot of Tetua's house. I gaze up at the towering mountains and at Orohena, the greatest peak of all, which loses itself in clouds; I stare down the dim, winding, green-clad valleys; my eyes sweep the deserted, sun-drenched shore. And at that moment, invariably, I am subject to a fascinating illusion —an illusion for which Tetua and his often repeated stories of the first coming of white men to Tahiti are, of course, responsible. As I sit drinking in the beauty of Matavai, the scene before me seems to come to sudden life. The lonely strand is no longer empty. I imagine that I see not only Tetua's solitary dwelling, but others by the many score. They line the shore, they dot the hillsides, their soft brown roofs of thatch peer out from between the grey-white boles of the coconuts farther inland. It is a village, a city, a capital—the seat of a government of kings and chieftains. From all directions the people come running, and the air is filled with cries and shouts, with the yelping of dogs, the squeals of startled pigs, the squawking of frightened fowls. Where the populace converges to stand gesticulating, massed together on the beach, there is the flash of spears and the color—bright red and yellow—of feathered ornaments. A fleet of canoes now rides the shimmering surface of the bay, and in them paddle a thousand brown-skinned men of matchless physique, warriors all, hurrying out to the harbor's center where floats the cause of all the shouting, all the astonishment and excitement. It is the weather-beaten *Dolphin* resting upon the blue water, her sails furled and her anchors gripping tenaciously the sandy bottom.

Amazed but unafraid, the Tahitians swarm about her. "See," they call back and forth, "there is no outrigger; it has but a single hull and yet does not capsize!" Can less than magic, they wonder, account for such a thing? And there are other marvels: "Behold the color of the creatures that line her rails—their bodies are white, their faces pale! Do not the gods alone have skins of white?" Trustingly, unhesitatingly, they clamber aboard, bearing their gifts of coconuts, bananas, fish, and shells.

At this point the mental picture fades. Perhaps it is because I wish to see no more, because I would willingly forget all those who followed so close in the wake of the trailblazing *Dolphin*. In square-riggers out of Salem and New Bedford they came, in men-of-war from London and Marseilles, in merchantmen from Amsterdam and Cadiz—the brawling tars, the whalers, the soldiers, the traders. Was there ever more tragic error than that which caused such as these to be looked upon as deities? Better, one is inclined to think, if they had been taken for children

5

of the devil and met with stones and spears. That they were not is hard to understand, for the Tahitians had had recent warning from their own high priest of what the white invasion was to mean.

The warning had come but a short time before the arrival of the first foreign vessel. Solemn religious ceremonies were in progress at the holiest of all the ancient shrines. Taputapuatea was its name, and a multitude had assembled there, coming from many islands to witness the sacrifices, to join in the chants and time-honored rites. Close to the massive stone monument which was the center of the place of worship there grew a mighty, spreading *tamanu* tree in whose thick shade stood the king, his chiefs, and his foremost warriors. It was evening. The air was still, and all eyes were turned on Vaita, the high priest, whose voice rose clear as he intoned a prayer to the ruling gods. Suddenly a strange and terrible thing occurred. A great whirlwind rushed in from the sea and fell upon the rugged *tamanu*. For a brief moment the wind roared in the heavy, lashing branches. Then the top of the tree was wrenched up and borne away. Again the air was calm, and the frightened people stared dazedly at the leafless trunk.

Slowly Vaita made his way to the side of the king, and on his face there was a look of deep concern.

"Is it a sign?" the king demanded. "Can you read its meaning?"

The priest nodded gravely. "It is an omen of great change. There are those coming to our islands who are like us in shape, yet in some ways very different. In a ship without outrigger they will come, and they will put an end to all our present customs. They will possess our lands, they will possess our people, and the sacred birds of the sea will come to mourn all that has been taught beneath this mutilated tree."

Such were the dire, cold words of Vaita as Tetua has repeated them to me. "You were warned, Tahitians," I find myself thinking. "Why did you not fight the invaders?" But perhaps I am wrong; perhaps the Polynesian rulers who have been dust these two hundred years were wise. Possibly they sensed that they could as little hope to resist the blond men whose ships were beginning to crawl the seven seas as to bind the *tamanu*-destroying whirlwind.

"Well, enough," I told myself on that April morning. "Have done with such gloomy thoughts. Push on. Ahead lies a house whose doorway leads to an untarnished past, to happier days when Tetua's forebears still walked free, their minds filled with the wonder and the glory of their island kingdoms."

I had taken but a few strokes more when I made out the tall figure of Tetua himself striding down to the water's edge to stand where the waves creamed about his feet. He raised a brown arm, swinging it in an arc above his head, beckoning; and I put my back into the paddling so that the canoe passed swiftly over the gently rolling swells.

6

"*Ia ora na!*" he cried when I was still some distance off. "May you live, Viriamu!" Because the Tahitian language has no sounds approximating either "w" or "l," the name William has its difficulties for Tetua. But he has done his best and has added a final vowel to conform to his ideas of what is proper. Viriamu is the result.

There are times when a high sea crashes on Tetua's beach, running up the smooth, shaded slope to lick the grass roots and the wooden stilts upon which his dwelling perches. On such days even an islander may have serious trouble in beaching his canoe. Fortunately, my visits have coincided with mild weather, and this time was no exception. Nevertheless, my friend waded out to meet me till he was waist deep in white water. As he grasped the bow I leaped over the side, and together we ran the light dugout up to dry ground beneath a *purau* tree whose dark green foliage was at that season spangled with large, bell-shaped, yellow blossoms.

"Ah," Tetua exclaimed, snatching up the small bundle wrapped in a blue and white *pareu* and holding it happily aloft. "At last you have come to stay. It is true, eh? You will not take to your canoe as soon as the sun is low?"

"No, this time there is no need."

"You will remain long with old Tetua?"

"As long as you will have me."

He laughed and led the way to the house. "In that case your wanderings are over, and we may spend the rest of our days beneath this roof." Nimbly he mounted the upended sections of a coco trunk that formed the steps. He placed my things on the lid of a chest which stood in a corner and then, turning to me, asked suddenly, "Would you be willing to do so?"

He still smiled as he spoke, and yet I was quick to sense that he was in earnest. We seated ourselves tailor fashion upon the white matting which was spread over the board floor, close to the wide doorway. Tetua opened his tin of native tobacco, placed it between us, and held out a pandanus leaf from which I tore a small strip, and together we began to roll cigarettes. Meanwhile, my eyes roamed the simple dwelling that I had come to love so well. Nothing had changed since the last time I was there, several months before, when he had told me the story of the conquering Rata and his Ship of Flame. Whatever might have been happening in the crowded countries of the outside world, Tetua's domain was untouched, unaltered, and so, I felt sure, it would always be. I glanced up at the steeply pitched roof with its symmetrical crisscross of neatly plaited fronds, at the evenly spaced ribbons of bark with which the leafy covering was secured to the straight, slender rafters of ironwood. At one end, very near the peak, and hanging quietly in the center of its ingenious web, was a grey spider—the same, I did not doubt, which had inhabited that spot since my first acquaintance with Tetua. Enclosing the single room were walls made of bamboo that had first been soaked in the sea, then split into narrow lengths no wider than a pencil, and finally woven in six-foot squares to make a tapestry of softest yellow, through whose minute chinks the breeze now stirred with a lazy whispering. All was the work of Tetua, all was done with the materials that grew about him; nowhere was there nail or hinge or any other bit of metal. In such a house his father had lived, his grandfather, and his great-grandfather, who had been chief of that entire region.

"You do not answer my question," said Tetua. "Is it that you are not sure you could be content with such a life as mine? Possibly you are not, after all, so very different from other white men, Viriamu. I have seen your house with its many books, its electric icebox, its talking machine. I have seen the white cloths and the knives and forks you put upon your table. Such things you do not find here, and I think it may be that, in time, you would miss them."

"Perhaps," I admitted. "But at the moment, I feel a contentment such that the number of our days seems far too little time in which to savor the beauty and peace in which you live."

"I have had the same thought," Tetua replied, "and it has made me wonder if it is so with men of other lands, if to them also a life span seems as fleeting." He was silent for a while, and there was no sound in the house but the soothing voice of the wind, the swish of the sea on the beach, and the lively chatter of a bird in the nearby *purau* tree. Then he smiled.

"Do you hear the laughter?" he asked.

"Laughter?"

"Yes, the bird—the *manu-iti*. We have him to thank for the fact that we are but mortal and that death, all too soon, comes to every one of us. If it were not for those mischievous and irrepressible little birds—for one of them in particular—we might have all eternity before us in which to chat and smoke and watch the shifting shadows on the lagoon. But for the *manu-iti* we might look upon the swift revolving seasons with unconcern. Summers with their warm rains and hot suns, winters with their cold south winds could come and go, and come and go; we should remain the same, ageless and in our prime." Tetua sat with his elbows resting on his outspread knees, his eyes bent upon the cigarette which he turned in his long, brown fingers. An ash fell to the floor and was whisked by the breeze out the open door. He sighed and repeated: "It is all the fault of the *manu-iti*. But surely that is known to you?"

"No," I replied, "I do not think you have spoken of it before."

"Such things," Tetua stated, "should be heard and remembered, for they explain the world we live in. You must at least recall the name of Maui. Your friends in Hawaii will have kept you in mind of him."

"Maui, who snared the sun and compelled it to travel more slowly through the skies?"

"And who first raised numbers of our islands from the bottom of the sea. Seven great deeds he accomplished, as is commonly accepted. But there was an eighth task to which he set himself, a task to dwarf all others by comparison. Here in Tahiti the tale is now rarely told, although in Aotea—in New Zealand—it is still often on the lips of our brother Maoris."

I settled myself more comfortably. "Let me hear it, Tetua," I said, well pleased to see him launched upon the adventurous early days.

He nodded and began.

The Eighth Great Quest of Maui

THERE came a time when all the islands Maui had brought to light were richly clothed in green. Fruits hung ripe and heavy on the trees, fish were thick in all the bright lagoons, and upon the land the pigs and fowls multiplied and were most plentiful. Maui observed these things, and he saw the sun moving across the heavens with such slow obedience that his mother had ample time between dawn and dark to beat out and dry her tapa cloth. It seemed to him that, both above and below, all was ordered and fair and as it should be. But in the next minute the idea struck him—even as it has you and me—that such beauty as everywhere met his eye, such happiness as he saw upon the faces of his people, should be not brief and transient, but everlasting. And in so thinking he realized that there was still one thing in the world which needed correction. Death, he decided, had no place amid such loveliness; the goddess of darkness, who was responsible for this final evil, must be overcome.

Wishing for companions on so dangerous an adventure, Maui went first to his relatives and, addressing himself to the young men among them, said: "I go to the far horizon seeking the abode of the goddess Hine-te-po. Who will join me and help me put an end to her grim domination of us all?"

Not one of them raised his voice, not one of them stepped forward. Instead they averted their eyes and turned away, for not even the bravest desired to face the dark goddess who draws men so easily into oblivion.

Maui therefore left them and sought out those who were his friends but not his kinsmen, and to these also he said: "Come with me, and we shall travel to the hazy distance where Hine has her home; for not till I have found and destroyed her shall I be content to rest." But they, too, were reluctant to voyage to the land of darkness and preferred to sit quietly waiting for Hine, in her own good time, to come to them.

Seeing their fear, Maui said no more but walked to the drum which stood in the place of assembly and beat upon it with his hands. When the entire populace had gathered he spoke to them, saying: "Men of the islands, who will share with me my quest? Who will risk Hine's cold embrace to rid us of her tyranny?"

There was a long silence while the people shifted uneasily from foot to foot with their eyes bent on the ground, and no one replied. Then, at last, one among them who was a warrior of much prowess asked: "Are you not content, Maui, with your seven deeds? They have made you great in the eyes of your fellows, and great you will remain as long as men have voices with which to sing your praise. Why must you again seek out danger? You are no longer young and have earned repose. Take it, and find pleasure in what you have won."

"Am I so different from other men?" Maui demanded. "After many years I still find contentment and pleasure unattainable. Nor do I understand how it can be otherwise with you. Does not the goddess Hine haunt your thoughts as she does mine, robbing you of satisfaction? When you taste the sweet waters of the springs and rivers, when you fish and swim in the warm light of the leisured sun, when you hunt on the cool mountain slopes or skirt the coral beds in your fleet canoes—does not the shadow of Hine cross your minds? When you look into the faces of those you love are you not reminded that they, like all the other blessings of this earth, are given to us but for the passing moment, only to be snatched away whenever it suits Hine's inscrutable purpose? She amuses herself, this goddess of enveloping night, with one hand dangling before our eyes all life holds that is fond and dear, while with the other she grasps her voluminous garments of cloud-dark tapa with which she may, tomorrow or the day after, enfold any one of us in unwaking slumber. Do you ask me to take repose, to stretch myself under a shading tree with a drinking nut beside me, there to wait, meek and submissive, for the end? Is such a course proper for a man to whom the sun itself has bowed? Ah, no! Speak, then. Who goes with me?"

There was no reply, for, though among those who had listened to Maui's words there stood many a warrior who would gladly have met any mortal foe in battle, none would deliberately look for Death.

Maui waited for some time, then called upon them by name, singling out here and there a man known for especial valor. "You, Tu, and you, Moro, will you not ride with me in my canoe? You, Niua, and you, Popoti, will you not come to help me win the boon of lasting life?" But as before, the eyes of each one turned away, and at last Maui saw that if he was to succeed in his eighth and last great deed it must be without the aid of other hands. Like many a man whom fame has set apart, Maui's path was from the first destined to be a lonely one; yet his love of companionship was no less than yours or mine, and sadness now filled his heart.

"My people," he said, "we have parted before, but never have I found the leave-taking as difficult as I do now. I cannot be sure that I shall again return, and it is possible that I look upon you for the last time. Let my love for you linger on behind me, speaking to you in the murmuring sea and wind and reminding you, now and then, that I sought to make enduring the happiness of our islands. If I fail, your lot will remain unchanged, neither worse nor better; If I succeed, you will see my canoe again, for I shall come back to share with you the days that will stretch ahead of us without an end."

Maui walked to his house, and as he went there were many who attempted to detain him, to reason with him and turn him from his perilous undertaking. But he brushed them gently aside. Still they followed, and when he went into his dwelling they pressed in behind him, gazing anxiously to see in what manner he would arm himself. Spears and battle-axes rested against the walls, but all these Maui ignored. From a calabash standing in the corner he took the jawbone of his grand-mother—that same jawbone, great with *mana*, with which he had grappled the sunken islands. Carefully he wrapped it in the folds of a length of beaten bark cloth; then, carrying no other weapon, he went down to the shore where his canoe rested upon two crotched branches driven into the sands of the shallows. There, seeing clearly that he was not to be discouraged, several youths lifted the outrigger from its supports and placed it upon the water. Maui took his seat upon a thwart and grasped the paddle.

"*Haere 'oe!* Go then!" cried the watchers on the shore in the ancient farewell.

"*Parahi 'outou,*" Maui responded. "Remain, all." And then he impelled his small craft toward the sea. So, with nothing more than the tapa-covered jawbone and a few drinking nuts which someone had thoughtfully placed aboard, Maui set out for the dim land that lies below the vague horizon where the sea slopes down-ward and where Hine-te-po was known to dwell.

The southeast trade blew steadily, and as soon as he was some distance offshore, Maui turned his canoe so that the bow pointed for his destination, with the wind fanning refreshingly at his back. All appeared to favor his mission and to make swift his progress. How much better had he met head winds, adverse currents, and battering waves; how much better had the elements risen to force him back to the land from which he came. But, as often happens in the affairs of men, the path to ruin was made smooth, and the gods of both wind and sea lured him on.

It was not till the sun was almost directly overhead that he paused and looked behind. Only the highest, shattered peak of the mountain at whose base he had built his home reached above the waters. "Well," thought he, "I have covered a great distance in a short time; surely a compelling current bears me to my meeting with Hine-te-po." Then, feeling a sudden thirst, he bent and picked up one of the ready-husked drinking nuts at his feet. With a stone he split off the top of the brittle shell and raised the nut to his lips. He drained the brimming, natural cup and with a finger scooped out the soft, white meat. He sighed with satisfaction and tossed the empty shell into the sea.

"There," he said aloud, "is one of life's greatest blessings. What can compare with the cool tang of coconut juice when a man's mouth is parched and dry? The delight of it never wanes, and it is a pleasure of which Hine shall not rob me."

Brave words. But in Maui's ears his voice sounded strangely small and, as his eyes wandered over the desolate sea which stretched away before him, he wished again that one man, at least, had had the courage to voyage with him. He would have been glad to have someone to talk with; but, lacking any companion, he picked up his paddle in silence and, swinging it vigorously, pushed on his way. He had taken fewer than a dozen strokes, however, when he heard a fluttering in the air above and looking up saw a flock of birds winging toward him from his now far-off island. Several large frigate birds were in the lead, and trailing them in a long, wavering line were other birds of various size and species of both land and sea—terns and boobies, gulls and cranes, parakeets and pigeons, thrushes and owls. Last of all, lagging at some distance behind the others and chirping excitedly as it beat furiously with its tiny wings, came a little fellow hardly larger than a hermit crab. It was the manu-iti.

At sight of the birds Maui's spirits rose. "Here," he said to himself, "is company lively enough for any man." Tilting back his head, he called up to them. "Come down, friends, and rest on my canoe."

Without a pause, and as if it had been their original intention, the leaders swerved downward, and in a narrowing spiral the others followed. The crimson-feathered ducks, the gulls and boobies, alighted upon the waters close beside the dugout where they paddled along, easily keeping pace with Maui's strokes. The land birds came one after another to roost upon the gunwales till they completely lined both sides. Only then, when the last inch of space appeared taken, did Maui become aware of the insistent scolding of the single little bird that still hovered overhead, vainly seeking a place to rest.

"Hmm," said Maui, eyeing the two rows of feathered folk, "this is very unfortunate. Someone will have to move over." But the larger birds were all contentedly preening themselves, and none attempted to make room. "Here!" Maui insisted more loudly. "Can you not give way a little and provide a perch for the manu-iti?" Not one of the birds complied and, although Maui was puzzled by their behavior, he did not stop to consider what it might mean. Instead, seeing that the manu-iti was nearly exhausted, he cried, "Take your place upon the bow!"

The bow of Maui's canoe rose to a point higher than the gunwales, and there, taking his advice, the tardy one alighted facing him and, in spite of the breeze, managed to keep its perch. It was in truth at this moment that Maui failed in his last great enterprise; but, far from realizing that the seed of his destruction now rode with him, he took up his paddle with renewed confidence and sent the crowded canoe forward with long, sweeping strokes.

As everyone knows, the manu-iti is not an evil bird, but merely a silly one. There are times, however, when a foolish companion is more dangerous than a bad one. This Maui was soon to learn. Yet for the time being his frame of mind was a happy one, and he listened with pleasure to the chatter of the birds. Even the incessant, twittering laughter of the manu-iti seemed to him far preferable to the silence in which he had ridden so long, and he viewed them one and all with affection.

"My fellow voyagers," said he after they had gone some distance, "this is a serious adventure upon which you have seen fit to embark, for I seek the resting place of the goddess of night in order to destroy her and win eternal life for us all." Maui paused, waiting for their applause of so noble a purpose, but none came. It looked a little as if the birds were no more interested than had been his own people. "Perhaps," he suggested, "you are not aware of the risks involved. In trying to gain lasting life it is possible that I shall succeed only in losing it altogether."

At the sound of Maui's voice the birds, both those escorting him in the water and those on the gunwales, had ceased their talk, and now they looked at him solemnly, first with one unblinking eye and then, by a quick twist of the head, with the other. But the manu-iti stood on one leg and laughed as though Maui had said something either ridiculous or witty.

The performer of the seven great deeds gave the little bird a stern glance. "Can it be," he asked, "that you do not know who I am? I am Maui-of-the-Great-Deeds, and this is the eighth and last task that I have set myself."

The manu-iti lifted its tiny head, and the laughter trilled from its throat in such a torrent that its entire body shook and it came near to losing its hold on the bow-peak.

Maui's eyebrows rose at such a display of bad manners. "This is truly astonishing," he remarked. "Who would ever think so loud and idiotic a laugh could come from a thing no bigger than a *mape* nut? But then, I have often been brought to wonder for what reason the gods made many of the creatures with whom we share the earth." He stared the offending mite directly in the eye. "If I had better known your character, manu-iti, I should have thought twice before asking you aboard."

Despite the severity of Maui's tone the bird would not be stilled, but after a while Maui succeeded in directing his attention elsewhere. He watched the terns and gulls darting here and there after stray minnows; he studied with interest the small, round-eyed owl which walks the island beaches in the night; and gradually he forgot about the manu-iti. Yet though forgotten, the insignificant feathered thing remained noisily present, and the time was not far off when it would assume an importance out of all proportion to its size.

The sun went down, the breeze died away, and the stars appeared; yet Maui paddled on. The land birds peeped drowsily and, one after another, closed their eyes. The sea birds stopped their feeding and swam silently over the dark water. Even the manu-iti seemed at times to doze, but always, just when Maui had decided the bird would not be heard from again till morning, a shrill peal of outrageous laughter would shatter the peaceful quiet. At last Maui's annoyance mounted till he could contain himself no longer. "*Mamu!*" he exclaimed. "Be quiet! Can you not respect your sleeping fellows?" It was to no avail. Manu-iti, it appeared, had respect for neither man nor fowl.

At break of day the trade wind sprang up once more and blew coolly on Maui's brown, muscular back. He looked ahead and saw an island of blue mountains rising from the sea and knew it for the home of the goddess Hine-te-po. With a sigh of satisfaction he rested his paddle on his knees and reached for another drinking nut. When he had quenched his thirst he scattered the coconut meat in the bottom of the canoe, whereupon with much hopping and squawking and fluttering of wings his passengers made a hasty breakfast.

"Friends," said Maui as soon as they had finished, "I have been very happy to have you on this voyage. But our journey is almost done. Within another hour I shall step ashore on that island which now appears so blue, but which, when the sun is a little higher, will turn to green. From the minute my foot touches dry land I shall be in mortal danger; for it is into the home of the dread Hine that I force my way. She is, as you have heard, goddess of night and of death as well. This is the hour when she sleeps. No doubt she has earned her rest, for who can say how many souls she has busily gathered to her cold bosom in the night just past? But she sleeps lightly, warily, and uneasily. So I must warn you: let no one utter a sound. Let there be no chirp nor caw nor hoot among you. I have noted," he added gravely, "that there is one of your company who is prone to unreasonable laughter. There is one" —and here he fixed the manu-iti with a stern gaze—"who finds cause for unbridled merriment in almost anything he sees. But on this journey let none make the slightest sound. It would mean the death of Maui, who sits before you, and with him would go the last hope of mankind for life without end. And the same is true of birds. Have I made myself quite clear?" No denial came from the birds, and even the manu-iti was silent. So, tossing away the empty coconut, Maui again drove his canoe forward.

As he went, the island rose ever larger and higher before him, and the color of its hills slowly changed to a lustrous green. Soon he was able to distinguish the individual plants and trees which drank so greedily of the sun's light: there was wild *fe'i* or mountain plantain, there was breadfruit and sweet banana, all growing in the greatest profusion. Never, he thought, had he seen an island in which food of all sorts appeared more plentiful. But there was no sign of human life. No plumes of smoke rose into the clear morning air to betray the presence of village cooking fires; no small boys scurried up the slanting boles of coco palms to stare at the strange, bird-laden canoe of Maui and to shout the news from tree to tree; no single figure walked the skirting reefs in search of shellfish or sea porcupine. The sun shone bright, the lagoons sparkled clear, but despite the beauty, despite the richness of growing things, Maui felt a sadness as he scanned the lonely island from end to end. He saw neither man nor woman nor child in all its length, and he knew that this land, so deceptively fair, nurtured not life, but death—that it was Hine's kingdom and no other's.

When the bow of Maui's canoe at last touched the strand, his feathered crew, understanding that the ride was over, took to the air. He was not, however, to be without company during the last and most dangerous stage of his journey. The birds did not desert him but hovered above his head while he carefully removed from the bottom of the canoe the tapa cloth package in which was wrapped the miracle-working jawbone of his grandmother. They waited while he tucked it securely beneath his arm and followed when he struck off inland.

From far at sea Maui had seen that Hine's island was cleft almost in two by a large valley which penetrated deep into the interior. He had remarked that though the sun dappled the surrounding hills its light failed to reach the steep-walled canyon. There dense shadow hung persistently, giving the impression of night but half dispelled. With a sure instinct he set out toward this region, moving soundlessly on bare feet and keeping his eyes wide for any untoward sign. For long there was none. He walked on, leaving the shore behind; and had it not been for the unnatural still-ness and his own certain knowledge to the contrary, he might have thought he was treading the familiar ground of his homeland. Here grew the same flowers, the same hibiscus and *tiare,* the same shrubs and trees. For a moment he paused to watch a giant crab making its slow, sure way up the bole of a coco palm, where it would snip the stem of a nut, then return to earth to tear apart the tough husk with its enormous claws. And in that, too, there was nothing unusual: the robber crab was to be found on many a populated island. Maui went on. From time to time he looked above where his bird friends circled and noted with relief that, either because of their consuming curiosity in his mission or because of his warning, they flew silently. The manu-iti flitted erratically here and there and it also, for a wonder, emitted no cry. The last time Maui glanced up he saw that the light was fading. He had entered the mouth of the valley.

In the days of his vigorous youth, when he was drawing up the South Sea islands and distinguishing himself by other accomplishments, Maui would have thought nothing of a voyage such as he had just made. For a day and a night he had traveled in his canoe and, though helped by favorable winds and currents, he had never ceased to raise and dip his heavy paddle the whole, long way. There had been a day when lack of sleep and food for such a period would have caused him only slight discomfort. But that day was gone, and now Maui was no longer young. He felt a weariness such as he had not known before. Perhaps it would be well to pluck a

few ripe bananas, to stretch himself for a while on the grass and renew his strength with food and rest. He paused in momentary indecision. Yes, he was unquestionably very tired, and the task ahead seemed increasingly beyond his powers. In all the world could anything possibly be as pleasant as sleep—as long, long sleep?

Suddenly he brought himself up sharply. What had he been thinking? Rest was not for him. He must keep on. The goddess Hine might sleep—he prayed she did, and soundly—but he would not sleep. This was the hour of opportunity: while she slumbered he must strike the blow. He went forward again, still picking his way carefully, parting noiselessly the clumps of fern which barred his path, stepping cautiously over moss-grown stones and fallen logs, penetrating ever farther into the shadowed gloom, leaving ever farther behind the world of light which he loved so well, the world where children laughed, where bards lifted their voices in song of his own conquests, where maidens danced to joyous drums and all was life and merriment.

Maui came then into a large clearing rimmed by gnarled old trees of a kind he had never seen. In uncanny symmetry, spaced at regular intervals, the sentinel trunks formed a vast circle over which the reaching branches spread an impenetrable, leafy canopy. "Is it possible," he wondered as he strained his eyes, "that it is mid-morning while I stand here in dusk which dims the sight? And what is it that I see in the center of this tree-ringed cavern, like a shapeless thunder cloud which hugs the ground, like a frozen wave of the midnight sea, like a giant and forgotten fragment of night itself?

"That," his senses told him, "is the nub of darkness, the portal to the underworld, Te Po; and it is the goddess Hine lying outstretched, unconscious, upon her bed of fallen and decaying leaves where the ancient forest trees stand silent watch upon her fitful slumbers. Take care! Go warily, as when you stalked elusive fish beneath the sea. Go silently, as when with readied snare you waited on your mountaintop to seize the rising sun. But go quickly, while yet she sleeps!"

He started forward, half crouched, swiftly running, his feet making the slightest rustling on the withered, once-green carpet. Swiftly—but with what unaccustomed effort! His legs felt as if weighted with great stones, and his breath came in the labored gasps of an old, old man who struggles up a steeply sloping hill. "How is this?" his mind questioned wildly. "Where is your strength, Maui? Where is the strength with which formerly your limbs were bursting? And what means this pounding of your heart, which never before so much as faltered under the most superhuman strain?" It was confusing, bewildering, this unwonted weakness, this feeling that his blood had turned to water; but he kept on doggedly and did not stop till he stood at the brink of darkness where Hine lay unmoving, wrapped in the billowing folds of her somber robes. Only then, when he took the tapa cloth package from beneath his arm, did the reason for the trembling of his hands strike him with sudden impact.

"Why," he thought, "there is no mystery in your enfeeblement. You are not betrayed, unless it be by time itself. It is that you are grown old, Maui. Yes, old. You have done much, much in your life, but all the while the years were hastening

17

by. And you are tired, tired almost unto death. You have taken pleasure in your islands and in their warm, surrounding seas, but could anything be so sweet as long, enduring rest?"

Wearily Maui shook his head and roused himself. There was still a task to do. Slowly now, he began to unfold the tapa, but a fluttering above his head caused him to pause. He looked up to find the lower branches of the trees crowded with the birds who had from the outset been his constant companions. In quick alarm his hand went to his mouth in a gesture of silence, but it seemed unnecessary, for no sound came from any one of them. He turned his attention back to the sleeping goddess. Her face was hidden from him, as it has been from all men till she goes to meet them, and Maui could only guess the appearance of her terrible countenance. Suddenly, feverishly, with fumbling hands, he tore away the last of the cloth. Let him but succeed and never again should mortal man be forced to look on Hine's frightful features! He whipped out the jawbone, raised it high—then froze, as immobile as an idol carved in stone. A shrill peal of laughter rang through the shadowy grove, and the manu-iti rocked delightedly back and forth upon its perch.

Hine-te-po rose slowly from her couch. She spoke no word. But the veils fell from about her face; and Maui gazed, spellbound, in amazement and relief. Hine was not as he and all his people had always imagined. She was beautiful—beautiful with a calm serenity that told of peace and repose. He felt one fleeting pang of regret, wishing that he might tell his loved ones in the homeland of his great discovery. Then the strange weapon fell from Maui's hand, and he slipped forward gratefully, trustfully, into the arms of darkness.

The Sacred Blue Shark of Taunoa

How we came to be speaking of sharks I do not recall, but it was some time after noon and we were still seated in the cookhouse, where we had had our midday meal. The cookhouse, or *fare tutu*, was a near replica of the main building as to materials and general shape, but was little more than a quarter as large. Adjacent to Tetua's dwelling, it was set back a short distance from the beach, and its three walls rose from the sandy soil which formed the floor. On the sea side there was no wall whatever, so that the breeze from the lagoon entered freely beneath the low-drooping fronds at the eaves. We often lingered in the *fare tutu* long after the last wisp of smoke from the cooking fire had filtered out through the thatch overhead, and even after the stones on which the fire had burned were cold.

The preparation of food is surely one of the most pleasant of mankind's arts, and the places where it is done seem invariably to hold a warmth and cheer, a friendliness hardly to be found elsewhere. Especially is it so in Polynesia. In the very fruits and vegetables standing here and there in small, neat mounds, or hanging in wide-meshed *purau* nets from the darkened rafters, there is a sort of genial companionship. And there was much of such company in Tetua's cookhouse. To one side lay a pile of taro and *uhi* roots—the potatoes of the South Seas—and suspended just above them was a heavy stalk of red-skinned mountain bananas. There were yams and breadfruit and pineapple, and strings of ripe oranges with coats of glossy green. Even the few utensils hanging upon their wooden pegs seemed to speak of pleasant talk and of food shared in friendship.

Since Tetua was moved to speak of sharks, I was glad that he had selected the homely security of the *fare tutu* in which to tell his tale rather than waiting for a day when we might chance to be in his canoe. As if he had read my thoughts and wished at the outset to clear up any misunderstandings, Tetua said: "You have been in these islands some years, Viriamu, and you must know by now that there are good sharks as well as bad. More than that, some are even sacred."

This, of course, I knew. Many times I had heard of the guardian sharks that haunt the seas close to former temple sites. Such as they were most sacred, *tapu*, and an islander would no more think of attacking one than he would deliberately desecrate the grounds they so jealously watch. Often I had heard, even from the lips of skeptical white men, of the terrible fate which pursued those who were brave enough, or foolish enough, to flout the shark-gods. At various times in the past, collectors or mere vandals have evaded the grim patrol of the deep, entered the hallowed shrines and thrown down or carried away ancient idols. But if one may believe the accounts, their flight was never swift enough to escape a terrible retribution. I was quite ready to agree with Tetua that sharks who made life unpleasant or impossible for such individuals could be called good; but, either divining my agreement or holding it unnecessary, he went on without pause.

I am going to tell you of the great blue shark of Taunoa and of how he brought happiness to a boy and a girl who lived upon this island many, many years ago. The story has its beginning far from the sea, deep within the majestic valley of Fautaua. There are those who say that in all the world there is no valley so beautiful as that through which the Fautaua River makes its twisting, tumbling way. Certain it is that in Tahiti, at least, there is no other to compare. It does not appear likely that so vast a gorge can have been formed by the slender, though rapid, stream which it now guides seaward. Possibly a cataclysm once rocked the island, splitting the mountains apart. Or did monstrous toil of giants create that enduring beauty? This last appears most reasonable. For who can doubt that the beckoning, citadel-like cluster of peaks framed at the valley's distant end, those crowning basalt prongs which men now call the Diadem and to which so many of Tahiti's valleys thrust, are the work of knowing brains and hands?

It is curious that today men hug closely the fringes of our island. Their villages skirt the calm lagoons, and in all the wide interior no human voice is heard. Formerly it was not so. Many tribes lived far from the sound of the breakers, and one, of whom Vao was both high priest and king, was established on a tableland in Fautaua Valley, high in the mountains and close to the foot of the Diadem. Whether it was because of the cool, bracing quality of the air on the heights, or because the region was much frequented by moisture-laden clouds, I do not know, but Vao's clan was famed not only for bravery in warfare, but for the uncommon physical beauty of its men and women—and for their extraordinary appetites.

More comely than all others, and excelling all whenever feast was spread, was the king's seventeen-year-old son, Taru. This young man stood well over six feet tall—our race in general was taller in those days than now—and his face was handsome and appealing. His dark eyes were large and widely spaced, his mouth generous and full lipped. He had the luxuriant black hair common to his people, but his skin was such that he stood out from the others wherever he went. It was lighter than that of his fellows, even approaching the golden color of the sands on certain of our beaches. More often than not, conspicuous beauty is a dubious blessing to a youth, yet it left Taru untroubled; he was supremely unconscious of it, and his character was as pleasing as his appearance.

Up to the time of which I speak, Taru's thoughts had been largely occupied with hunting and swimming and also, it must be added, with good things to eat. He had never experienced troubles other than the fleeting ones of childhood; he had never seen bloodshed; he had never known love. Yet within the compass of a single day and night, all of these things were to crowd into his life.

There was warning of what was to befall, and it came in the early morning. With his parents Taru had climbed to the mountainside terrace on which stood his people's temple—the *marae*, as we say. Here, according to custom, each one had placed an offering of fruits on the shark-god's altar. After a moment of silent prayer, Taru and Queen Rai—such was his mother's name—were about to turn away when the king raised an arresting hand.

"Stay," he commanded. "Ma'o, god of sharks and men, Ma'o, in whose great body lies the spirit of our first ancestor, speaks to me."

Neither Taru nor the queen was unduly surprised at this, for it will be remembered that Vao was not only king of his clan but high priest also, and as such he held frequent communion with the strange deity to whom the *marae* was consecrated. From the shark-god he learned many things: when to expect droughts, storms, sickness, death; when it was best to hunt for the wild pig; on what night of the moon to search for crabs; when to dance, or feast, or make war. Now it was of a different matter to which he listened with some inner ear of his mind. His face blanched perceptibly and his eyes turned quickly to his son.

"You must hide," he warned. "At this minute, men of the lowlands are seeking you."

Taru smiled. "Have I ever shown fear of the men of the lowlands? You are jesting, my father."

"Is it my habit to jest when I stand within the *marae*?" the older man inquired sternly. "I do not altogether understand what I have learned, and I believe those who come intend no harm. But if you should follow them, I see that either carelessly or wittingly they will lead you to great danger. I am told that if you go with them you will be tempted to tarry on the way, and that in so doing you will come to grievous harm. Do not think to disregard the warning of the shark-god unless you would bring great misfortune on us all."

Taru could not do otherwise than consent, especially when Queen Rai's entreaties were added; but it was with a feeling of disappointment and in a somewhat rebellious frame of mind that he followed his father along the paved courtyard of the temple to a large flagstone which covered a secret vault below. For what reason, he wondered, was he hunted? And what exciting adventure might it mean if he were free to seize it?

Vao lifted the heavy slab and Taru stepped within. The lid closed down and

21

Taru stood in darkness. "It will not be long," came his father's voice faintly from above. "Even now I see runners coming up the trail. I shall be quick in sending them on their way."

Soon the sound of voices again penetrated the hidden chamber, and Taru knew that the king had received his visitors within the *marae*. But although the speakers must have been near, their words ran together in an indistinguishable jumble, and, strain his ears as he would, the young man could make out nothing. At last he put his back against the cold flagstone overhead and cautiously raised it so that a narrow bar of light slanted in. With it came his father's deep tones: "You have traveled a long distance, friends, and all in vain. He is not here."

"Tell us then," said one of the strangers, "where we must seek him, because we dare not face our king till we have seen your son and given him our message."

"You may give me the message," Vao replied.

There was a pause as the emissaries briefly conferred; then the spokesman made answer. "Very well. I see no objection, and it is simply done. Our ruler, Teri-tini of Taunoa, has prepared a great feast which is to be held this evening. Princes and chiefs and other men of high station have come in large numbers from over the seas, and the king desires to impress these visitors with Tahiti's finest manhood. In the night a dream came to Teri-tini, and in the dream, while he sought the man who might stand for our island's best, both in beauty and in talent for the feast, there came to him the name of Taru, your son. We have come for Taru in order that he may be honored in our village by the sea."

Vao appeared to hesitate, and it is possible that for a moment he was irresolute, his pride in Taru being not untouched by the neighboring king's invitation. He had not, however, forgotten the shark-god's warning. "I am sorry," he said quietly. "You must return to Taunoa with the thanks of my queen and myself but without our son. You will not find him, believe me, not if you search all the lands touched by the light of day."

"*Aue!*" the two men exclaimed in unison, both of them genuinely grieved, and both jumping to the mistaken conclusion that Taru was no longer among the living. "How sad, and he so young! He has departed to Te Po?"

"In all truth," the father replied gravely, "Taru now lies in darkness."

"*Aue te mauiui e!*" the messengers cried again and again. "What sorrow, what pain!"

"And to think," said the first, "of all he has missed by dying at this particular time."

"Yes," the second agreed mournfully, "the feast of Teri-tini can be of little interest to him now. It is a shame that he will never see the earth-oven we have made which is of a size before unheard of and which extends"—and here the man waved his arms as if to include the entire *marae*—"all the way from here to there.

At this very moment there lie on the bed of heated stones within the great trench all kinds of savory foods that our island affords, and already so delicious an aroma seeps through the covering leaves that I can almost imagine it to reach my nostrils at this distance."

At these words Taru of the prodigious appetite stirred uneasily in his confinement. Young as the day was, he had not so much as broken his fast, and the visions which the stranger's account caused to leap before his eyes so agitated him that the slab lying upon his back shook in a way that threatened to betray him. But neither the messengers nor the king and queen appeared to notice, and soon the two from the lowlands were outdoing each other in extravagant descriptions of the feast which was so soon to be spread.

"Would you believe it, King Vao, more than two hundred breadfruit are now slowly roasting within the *ahima'a*."

"There are," stated the second proudly, "fifty strings of new-caught fish: *ono, ava, iihi, ature,* and many little *tarao,* than which there are no sweeter."

"With my own eyes," the other continued, "I saw four turtles laid upon the stones, and any one of them could well feed an entire village."

"Did you not also see, Tu," demanded his companion, "the bananas and *fe'i* and sweet potatoes, all in such number that they could not possibly be counted?"

"Indeed I did, Hoa. And likewise not to be counted were the crabs, lobsters, mussels, and sea centipedes."

By this time the unfortunate Taru could hardly contain himself, and it seemed to him bitterly unjust that the shark-god should deny him the right to assist at such a superlative feast. Had his long-dead ancestor Ma'o, the shark-god, never felt the pangs of hunger? Furthermore, were not sharks themselves known to have huge appetites, and therefore should they not take pity on him? But Taru's trials were not over.

"O my friends of the highlands," exclaimed Tu, "when I think of this I am brought near to tears, so sad it is that Taru will never look upon nor sink his teeth into the crowning glory of all the feast. For imagine! Forty boars were slain and stuffed with fragrant ti leaves, and at this very instant they lie side by side in the deep oven, turning to a luscious, tender brown. Is it not enough, almost, to raise the dead? I should say . . . ."

Just what he would have said will never be known, for at that moment he was interrupted by a sudden upheaval of a section of the *marae* paving as Taru flung back the flagstone and leaped out into the light. "Take me with you!" he cried, running up to the two envoys of King Teri-tini and ignoring his father's frown. "I can hear no more. Let us go immediately, for, whatever befalls me, I must be present when the mats of *purau* leaves are torn from the *ahima'a*."

It was some time before the men from Taunoa succeeded in recovering from their

23

astonishment at seeing Taru, far from dead, standing before them in all the strength and beauty of his youth, clearly eager and impatient to set out. Slowly, smiles spread across their faces and finally they burst into laughter.

"Ah, Vao," said the leader, when he could sufficiently control his mirth, "this is a priceless jest you have played upon us, and how our ruler will enjoy it when we recount it to him! 'You will not find him in the light of day'—was that not what you said? Ha, ha, ha! That is very good, very good, and I see that you are not only a bold warrior-king but a clever one as well."

The anger which Vao had at first felt at his son's unexpected appearance gradually subsided, and he made no denial that all had not turned out as he intended. As is often the case with those in·exalted position, the king was not. averse to being thought clever, even if his so appearing was the result of accident. He had long ago discovered that the world is not run for man's especial benefit and that it is full of surprises, many of them unpleasant. He had learned also that when events came about other than as hoped for or foreseen, it was less trouble to accept them quietly than to struggle endlessly to shape all creation to fit his own notions of what was good. Anything, therefore, which went wrong—whether a canoe that stubbornly developed a crooked keel beneath the adz, or a daughter who as stubbornly chose an undistinguished mate—was the will of the gods and should be dismissed with a shrug of the shoulders. So now, if Vao felt any further fear for his son's safety, he put it aside with the reflection that it was very likely none other than the blue shark who was responsible for Taru's abrupt decision to disclose himself; and who would dare oppose the will of his ancient ancestor?

"Go, if you must," he said to his son, "and may you do full justice to my friend Teri-tini's feast." He started to turn away; then, having himself been much impressed with all he had heard of the celebration, he thought to add, "It is possible your mother and I will join you later in the day."

So it happened that within the hour Taru, having stopped only long enough to bathe and to rub his handsomely tattooed arms and legs and chest with scented oil, had put the Diadem at his back and, with the Taunoans on either side, was making his way down the valley toward the sea. About his middle was wrapped a strip of pure white tapa which his mother's servants had beaten thin and fine from bark of the paper mulberry; tucked behind his left ear against his dark, curling hair was a large red hibiscus blossom; and gripped in his right hand was a stout spear. He was very happy and he whistled as he went. The two runners were also in a pleasant frame of mind. Each time they glanced at Taru they were struck the more by the perfection of his body and the nobility of his features; surely Teri-tini would be overjoyed at such an example of Tahitian manhood and proud to display him to his guests from other lands. Because the morning was still cool and because the path led steadily down, all three had breath to spare for banter and idle talk, and they were soon on very friendly terms.

"I see," said the man called Tu with a meaningful smile, "that you wear your flower on the left, Taru. It tells me that you have not yet found a sweetheart."

"No," Taru replied casually, "I have not. May I ask a favor of you?"

"Of course!" the older man generously agreed, it being a characteristic of his that he always enjoyed being asked advice or help in matters of love.

"It is this," said Taru. "Would you be so good as to enumerate once again the things Teri-tini in his bounty has had placed in the great oven?"

"Yes," said Tu, a little crestfallen but still not to be turned from the theme on which he had embarked, "I will be glad to do so. But first, tell me. Of all that grows and blooms and ripens on our island, surely nothing surpasses the grace and charm of Tahiti's young women. Have you never happened upon one who caused your head to whirl and your heart to do strange things within you?"

"I find all the girls very pretty," Taru admitted equably. "Especially when they dance with flower wreaths about their throats and in their hair."

"Yet you have never had such feelings as . . ."

"Oh, yes indeed," the young man interrupted. "I have experienced sensations such as you describe. And never so strongly, I believe, as when I lay hidden just now listening to your conversation with my father. Then, in all truth, my head became dizzy, and deep within me I felt a great anguish and longing. About those lobsters, sea centipedes, and crabs, Tu—in what quantities did you say they had been gathered?"

Tu raised his hands in a gesture of resignation and with a sigh began anew his account of the impending feast. In this manner the time went quickly. They passed the natural stronghold in the hills where, in time to come, their descendants were to fight a losing battle for three long years with the invading French; they passed the cascade where the Fautaua River leaps into space to fall four hundred feet into the rocky basin beneath; and they passed the tranquil pool where, in a still later day, another man of France—Pierre Loti, as he called himself—was to swim and dally with an obliging Tahitian maid. A little farther on, at a place where the valley widened broad and fertile, where the stream wandered placidly through beds of taro, dark mango trees, and quick-sprouting papaya, they came into a small hamlet. Although he had never before had occasion to stop there on his trips to the sea, Taru knew well that it was the village of Princess Tuihana, sister to King Teri-tini. On this morning all three of the travelers suddenly discovered that they were very thirsty.

"We will not disturb the princess," Tu decided, "for she is doubtless preparing to leave for the feast. Did I tell you that she is to dance for the guests? No? Well,

25

so it is, and I can assure you, Taru, it will be a thing to remember. Now let us see if at this humble dwelling by the riverbank we can find refreshment."

Tu approached a little thatch house which was clearly in need of a new roof, and he called politely, "Is anyone at home?"

"There are people here," came a thin but friendly voice, and an old woman appeared in the doorway.

"Ah," Tu exclaimed, "it is you, Grandmother." He turned to Taru. "This is Tuihana's grandmother."

"I am the son of King Vao of the highlands," Taru explained, "and with these good men I go to the glorious feast prepared by Teri-tini. We are very thirsty, Grandmother."

The old woman laughed quietly. "I am accustomed to young men stopping at my door when my granddaughter is here. But if thirst is all that troubles you it is easily remedied." She disappeared inside momentarily, then returned with three opened drinking nuts.

Like his companions, Taru gratefully accepted one of the nuts. He tipped it up and let the cool liquid run down his throat. As he lowered it he sighed. "Nothing," he observed judicially, "can compare with the water of the coconut." His eyes wandered seaward where the village of Teri-tini lay hidden beyond the groves of palms. "Nothing except, perhaps," he added, "good food which has cooked long and slowly on the hot stones."

It was then that, for the first time, he became aware of a muffled, steady tapping sound coming from within the house. "That is very curious," thought he. "I hear the rhythm, the unmistakable pulse of fish-skin drums which play for festival dances. But surely it is no pedestaled drum which makes that gentle sound?" He glanced past the old woman into the dim, windowless interior and there made out a little boy seated on the hard-packed, earthen floor. Between his knees he held an empty gourd nearly as large as he, and over its smooth, rounded sides his small hands fluttered in short, caressive movements, the tips of his fingers touching lightly the thin-shelled instrument and coaxing from it the soft, blood-quickening beat which had attracted Taru's attention. This was interesting and amusing, and the youngster played well—but what child of a race in whom the sense of perfect rhythm is inborn does not? Taru started to turn away, but as he did so his eye, now more accustomed to the faint light within, caught a fleeting shadow at the far end of the room, and wheeling quickly, he peered once more over the old woman's shoulder. It was, after all, a private dwelling into which he pried, and Taru's first glance had been casual and discreet. Now, however, he stared openly. He took a step forward and, placing both hands on the door post, put his head inside. In the next instant he had brushed past the old woman as if she were no more than a harmless and slightly withered plant.

Far from taking offense, Tuihana's grandmother, long accustomed to similar distracted behavior on the part of whatever young man laid eyes upon her charge, did no more than look from Tu to Hoa, at the same time screwing her wrinkled face into an expression which said, "You see how it is?"

Tu saw how it was, and he experienced a certain satisfaction that Taru, who by his own confession had always taken the women of Tahiti very much as a matter of course, should suddenly find himself toppled from so comfortable a condition by the mere sight of Tuihana practicing her dance. But it was unfortunate, Tu considered, that it had happened at this particular time. He was anxious to be on his way and to carry his prize before Teri-tini.

"Taru," he called through the flimsy wall of bamboo. "Shall we start along?"

But no word came from within.

"My friend, they wait for us by the sea."

There was no sound save the soft beating of the gourd.

"Dear, good Taru," called Tu. "Let us go!"

He heard no answering voice.

"O noble son of King Vao," the messenger implored in growing concern, "tear yourself away!"

Silence.

Tu frowned. Then a crafty smile came to his lips. He put his mouth close to the thin partition. "If we do not immediately take to the trail," said he with measured distinctness, "we shall be late for the opening of the *ahima'a.*"

From inside the house there came a sudden, surprising bellow of exasperation. "*Aue!* Cast your oven into the sea!"

The two men from Taunoa looked at each other in astonishment, and Tuihana's grandmother chuckled quietly. "I am afraid it is useless for you to wait. Tell Teri-tini that Taru will come with the princess," she said and then went in, leaving them to continue disconsolately on their way.

Taru stood close to the door with his back pressed against the wall. He did not notice the old woman when she passed before him and seated herself unobtrusively on her mat; he gave no thought to the departing envoys, Tu and Hoa; and it is doubtful if the warning of the blue shark that to tarry on the path to the coast would place him in grave danger entered his head at all. His eyes were filled with the vision which swayed before him, and his mind could contain no more. He was conscious of a hunger such as he had never felt before, a hunger which not even the lauded bounty of Teri-tini might satisfy. One thing alone, he thought, could ease the peculiar and unimagined pangs in which were both yearning and a strange sense of emptiness—and that was the nearness of Tuihana. 27

From about the princess's slender waist fell the waving, shimmering strands of an *ahu more,* the ancient costume of the island hula, made of many fine ribbons of bark stripped from the *purau* tree. There were flowers in her hair, garlands circled her wrists and ankles, and a *hei* of delicate, star-shaped gardenias hung from about her throat to lie lightly upon her small, firm breasts. These things Taru saw, but only as part of a picture in which all was lithe movement and sinuous grace. His eyes never left her as Tuihana's feet wove their nimble pattern over the earthen floor, and although he followed every slightest gesture, still it seemed to him as if the girl continually escaped, allowing him but isolated glimpses, mere fragments of beauty when he wished the whole. He would catch the flash of dark eyes, the shadow of flowing hair, cool slim legs parting the veiling *ahu more*, hands which had the grace of birds. Could one ever hope to hold anything so volatile, so light, so airily free? Taru had the feeling that what he beheld could not be real. It was the image of delight a man carries in his mind, and as illusive.

Until Taru arrived, Tuihana had been dancing with little spirit and more than a trace of boredom. But the moment the uninvited spectator entered, there came a change. It was not simply that, like any artist, she performed better when observed. It was something more, as her grandmother quickly detected, something more and different. At one minute she had been merely a very pretty girl of sixteen such as might be found in the fold of almost any of Tahiti's many valleys, but in the next, as if Taru's steady gaze touched and kindled some hidden fire within, she seemed to glow with a living, radiant beauty which made of her, for that day at least, a being unique in all the island kingdoms. Gradually her dance lost its dreamy listlessness; her body, no longer languid, became knit and firm, and, taking to herself the hurrying, hollow-noted music of her tiny drummer, she whirled into the age-old hula. No word had passed between the two young people, nor was there need of any. The girl's every motion spoke a powerful language which Taru was quick to understand. It was a dance of love, and the story it told was for him alone.

Tuihana's grandmother smiled in sympathy, gently clapping time with the palms of her hands and perhaps remembering a day when she, also, was slender and filled with such vibrant, overflowing life. To her old eyes what was taking place beneath the weathered thatch of her small house was clear. She had seen it before, and might well again, yet it was always new with fresh mystery and wonder. A pleasant warmth stole through her veins, and her head slowly, sagely nodded. "This is your hour, Tuihana," she murmured. "And yours, Taru. I know how the world now seems shrunk till it is of shape and size with your beloved; but it holds more, much more than your two selves, and not all is laughter. So cling to the happy oblivion which folds you away from all others; cling to it while you may."

28   Motionless, Taru watched as Tuihana glided from end to end of the narrowly confining room, passing him again and again, always a little nearer, a little nearer, till at last the flowers swinging from her throat grazed his chest, leaving his nostrils filled with their heady perfume. Suddenly he was lifted on the wings of the same

intoxicating rhythm, his body, no less agile than her own, drawn into the same primitive convolutions, his feet pressing the earth where hers had touched but the instant before.

"*A 'ori!*" cried the little drummer, delighted at the success of his efforts. "Dance, Tuihana, dance!"

The girl needed no urging. Her smile was now wide and exultant. She made a single turn of the palm frond cottage and at the center of the room wheeled with head thrown back, to face her chosen man. There, so close to Taru that they seemed to merge into one, Tuihana danced—danced as she had never done before. Then, with legs slowly bending she sank lower, lower, till at the final beat her knees brushed the dark earth.

The child put aside the gourd and trotted out. Taru put his cheek to Tuihana's in the caress of the olden days, lifted her in his arms, and carried her to the mat where her grandmother sat patiently. He put her down, and the old woman gathered her close, making soft, soothing sounds. After a moment she looked out at the pools of shadow beneath the palm trees which told her it was high noon, then up at Taru, who was still obviously in a daze.

"Leave us," she said, "while we prepare ourselves for the journey to Teri-tini. We shall go together; and it appears to me it will be a marriage feast to which we make our way." Gently the old woman repeated what she had said, and Taru unsteadily went out.

He took up his spear, which was resting against the outer wall, walked about aimlessly for some time, and at last seated himself to wait on a fallen log near the village outskirts. It is practically certain that nothing was then farther from his thoughts than the words of the shark-god, but even if he had recalled the warning, it is doubtful he could have averted the disaster which was even then overtaking him. How it came about that Taru was so soon to be struck down, trussed like a dead hog, and thrown to perish in the sea, is in itself very curious.

His ruin began in this way. Because she wished to borrow a fishhook, Piti, a girl of that village, picked up her baby, set him astride her hip, and went over to Tuihana's house. No one was there. But the shiny shell hooks hung in a cluster on one of the posts, so she helped herself. On her way home Piti passed Rupe's dwelling, and Rupe, the mother of seven, was seated in the doorway combing the hair of Una, her oldest girl, who was on the step just below.

"*Mea maitai oe?*" said Piti. "How do you do, Rupe?"

The older woman looked up from her task. "*Eaha te huru?*" she replied. "What news is there?"

Piti put down the baby and squatted on the ground, drawing her tapa between her legs as she did so. "I have been to Tuihana's," she said, and might well have let the matter go at that; but Piti had imagination. "There were," she added with the air of imparting news of consequence, "three hens scratching in the house." This was not so, but Piti considered that it might have been.

"And in the *fare tutu*," she continued, "a fire was burning under some *fe'i* that had burned to a crisp. I think," she summed up, "Tuihana must have left hurriedly. Could it be a *tane?*"

"A man?" said Rupe, her interest caught, and she pushed her daughter away. "Tuihana has never paid much attention to the young men hereabouts. But there was a stranger in the village this morning. He came with two of Teri-tini's messengers. But he did not leave with them."

Rupe's daughter stopped scratching her head long enough to point and say, "He is there. If you look through the trees you will see him sitting on a log by himself."

The women were disappointed, for there is nothing of special interest in a man sitting alone on a log. Curtly Rupe said, "Mind your own affairs, Una, when I am speaking."

Una pouted but then, as quickly, brightened. "I walked quite near him a little while ago. He just stared straight ahead as if—as if he had seen a ghost!"

"Well!" exclaimed Piti and Rupe together.

"And there was blood," the girl added.

"What's that you say?" her mother demanded. "Where?"

"Everywhere," said Una blandly. "On the ground and on his big, long spear and on his face and hands." There was, she told herself, pigs' blood in the area where the village contribution to the feast had been prepared.

The two women looked at each other and their eyes rolled in their heads. Tuihana not at home? A bloody stranger? They put two and two together and obtained, not the customary result, but a nightmare. Tuihana was dead—killed by the devil of a highlander who sat brazenly in the midst of his carnage!

Screaming the awful news, they rushed to the house of the chief, and the chief quickly dispatched his son, who was very fleet, to the coast to inform Teri-tini of his sister's death, and to demand armed men to deal with the culprit.

It was not long after that two of Teri-tini's warriors leaped upon the unsuspecting Taru from behind, one dealing him such a blow with a war club that he was laid prostrate beside the log, and the other kicking him energetically in the stomach. When they had quieted King Vao's son they bound strands of tough coconut cordage about his wrists and ankles, then slung him on a pole which they carried between them.

Now at last Taru had time to think of the entreaties of his father and mother, who had begged him not to leave that day. He thought also of the prophecy of the family god, but now it was too late. The path which his captors followed was familiar to him, and he knew that it led to Teri-tini's temple. He knew as well that once there the priest would promptly put him to death and place him beneath the flagstones of the *marae*, and that this time it would take a great deal more than mention of a feast to bring him forth. Taru admitted that he had been foolhardy and that he had in some inexplicable manner blundered into serious trouble. But even in his present straits he could not regret having left the security of his home. If he had not come down from the mountains, he might never have found Tuihana. Better to die than never to have seen her. So thinking, he faced his approaching end with a fortitude sure to make his ancestors proud of him.

Taru's first ancestor, the blue shark, was more proud than any others from beyond the grave who may have been watching what was going on. And he put words in Taru's head and Taru spoke them.

"My friends," he remarked, "I am glad to see that you do not intend to weight my body with stones and cast me into the ocean, for there I should certainly remain dead forever. But since you are going to bury me in the *marae* I shall take pleasure in arising every night to haunt each one of you."

The two warriors halted and looked at him dubiously. "You would do a thing like that?" one asked in a voice which shook a little.

"I would," Taru replied.

"What do you think?" the first man to speak inquired of his companion.

"I am thinking the same as yourself," he said quickly. "Let us turn around."

This they did and set off for the sea. Too many ghosts already wandered the night winds to have still another especially devoted to haunting them. At the shore, with heavy stones attached to his feet, Taru was placed in a canoe, and the two men paddled out to the deep pass of Taunoa. There they rolled him over the side and remained watching as he sank through the clear waters, slowly turning over and over till he came to rest on a jutting coral ledge in an attitude of sleep. Hardly a moment passed before the great shadow of a blue shark swam between Taru and themselves, and without waiting to see more, Teri-tini's men went away in much haste.

There was, understandably, considerable astonishment when, a few hours later, Tuihana presented herself at the feast, her grandmother at her side. Had not all those present been so much taken aback to see the princess alive, there would have been interested comment on the red flower she wore over her right ear as does any girl who has found a sweetheart. But as it was, no one noticed either the flower or the troubled look in Tuihana's eyes as she scanned the crowd searchingly.

Young King Teri-tini broke away from his guests to rush up to her and demand in astonishment, "From where have you come, beloved little sister?" *31*

"From home," she replied simply. "Why do you ask?"

Teri-tini then saw that somehow a mistake had been made.

It is best not to dwell on the scene which followed when Tuihana learned the truth. But at last she dried her tears and asked to be taken to the spot where Taru had been committed to the sea and where surely, according to the miserable warriors, he had been subsequently devoured by an enormous shark. Somewhat reluctantly these same men accompanied the princess and brought her to the place where they had disposed of Taru. There all three looked down and were surprised to see the young man, now freed of his bonds, lying peacefully upon the dim coral ledge with his head resting on a pillow of ocean ferns. Close beside him watched the great shark of dully gleaming blue.

At sight of her lover an agonized cry escaped from Tuihana and, so quickly that no hand could stop her, she threw herself into the sea. Once again Teri-tini's henchmen watched a body drift slowly down into the depths where it came finally to rest at Taru's side. And the longer they stared, the more it seemed to them that while the shark kept silent vigil both the girl and the man lay, not in death, but in sweet slumber. At last, in terror of so unnatural a thing, they broke away and made off, with paddles flashing.

As light faded from the sky Taru and Tuihana remained in each other's arms, fathoms deep beneath the sea, where lazy currents ran soft fingers through the long tresses of Tuihana's hair, and schools of little fish curiously explored their unmoving forms. There was an hour of darkness; then the light of the rising moon filtered down to the coral couch. With its coming the blue shark of Taru's people gathered them both gently in his great jaws and swam slowly toward the shore. In the shallows he released them from his grasp and from the enchanted sleep in which they had been held. Hand in hand they walked up from the lagoon to the sand of the shelving beach. The waters behind them boiled as the shark whirled with a lash of his huge tail and returned to his home in Taunoa's pass, from which, for years to come, he would continue to guide and advise the clan of King Vao on their tableland high in Fautaua Valley. Taru and Tuihana watched till the upright, darkly glinting dorsal fin was lost to sight, and then they set forth along the shore toward the village of Teri-tini. Before they reached the settlement the sound of women's voices raised in a wailing dirge came to their ears, and they stopped, listening.

"The song of the dead," said Taru.

Tuihana looked up at him smiling. "Of course. It is for you and me. Let us hurry to put an end to their sadness."

Together they ran down the beach and did not stop till they burst upon the startled assembly which had come to feast and stayed to mourn. Past the glowing red flares and past the wide-eyed, half-fearful, upturned faces Tuihana raced straight into the arms of her brother.

Unable at first to believe his eyes, Teri-tini ran his hands over her brine-drenched clothing, over the damp locks of her hair and the firm flesh of her arms and legs, as if trying to assure himself that it was no spirit he held, but Tuihana in the warm flush of her youth, more alive than she had ever seemed before. And when he turned his eyes to Taru, who stood straight and tall and solid before him, they told him with surety that this man, too, was no ghost, but a fitting mate for his sister.

Suddenly Teri-tini found his voice. "O my people," he cried, "you have generously shared my grief when I believed my little sister, the most dear, was forever lost. The reason for which you came fled from our minds, and the great oven lies forgotten, still guarding warmly the bounty of our lands. Now we are greatly blessed. Tuihana is returned to us unharmed, and with her she brings her chosen *tane*. So have done with sorrow, and let rejoicing take its place! Fling off the coverings of the *ahima'a* and prepare to feast and dance and sing!"

The cheers of the guests rent the night. By the score men leaped to their feet and rushed to tear away with eager hands the blanket of leaves which sealed the mighty oven. And Taru and Tuihana stood, still hand in hand, smiling and breathing appreciatively, happily, the delicious odors which rose to fill the air.

Nona-of-the-Long-Teeth

"YOU could make the circuit of Tahiti and not find finer fishing ground than this," Tetua said and then added casually, "It was the favored place of Nona-of-the-Long-Teeth."

"Nona?"

Tetua broke a shrimp in two and baited his hook. He nodded. "The most voracious man-eater who ever lived upon our island."

"And he came here seeking an occasional change of diet, I suppose?"

"Although possessed of the strength of a man, Viriamu, Nona was a woman."

I do not know why I should have found this fact disconcerting, for cannibalism is surely horrible enough in any form; but somehow it had never occurred to me that it was practiced by women as well as men, and, despite the tranquil beauty of our surroundings, the knowledge sent a chill up my spine.

The canoe in which we rode, facing each other and seated upon a thwart at either end, was anchored far from shore in the meagerly protective lee of the broken chain of slightly submerged reefs that separate the Bay of Matavai from the outer ocean. Had the day not been of such a calm that, to the very horizon, the sea appeared but a continuation of untroubled lagoon, we should have been obliged to go elsewhere to cast our lines. As it was, our small craft rested confidently upon water of the same blue as beyond. All about, it was deep, and the fathoms-long rope of *purau* bark which carried a mooring stone fell away till it was lost to sight in submarine darkness. Tetua's house was distant on our right, and on the left, much nearer, were the somber cliffs of Taharaa. I must have been gazing at that harsh and inhospitable section of coastline when Tetua, noticing the direction of my glance, spoke again.

"You are looking," he informed me, "at the very spot where Nona lay in wait to snare her victims—Taharaa. Have you walked around it?"

"Never."

"On a day like this it can be done, by leaping from one boulder to another, but such days are rare. There have been those who tried to reach the beach on the other side when the sea was running. I know of none who succeeded; all were ground to death upon the rocks. But there is a way through the surf-sprayed mountain we call Taharaa. I can show you the tunnel, and you may pass in perfect safety. Not so in the time of Nona. One path then led to death as certainly as did the other."

Feeling sure that my friend would need no prompting to tell the tale, I waited patiently while he swung his first catch over the side, jerked the hook from its mouth, and dropped it between us. As soon as the fish had ceased to flap its loud tattoo on the canoe bottom, Tetua drew a long breath:

You must have noticed how frequently the characters of men resemble the places in which they live. Whether they are drawn to seek out regions which harmonize with their own natures, or become what they are because of the soils and climes which fate has imposed upon them, I will not venture to say. The fact of the strange affinity remains. Look at you Americans. You come from a country where the air is brisk and invigorating, where the mountains dwarf our own, and where distances are so great that we of Tahiti can hardly conceive of them. And what is the result? As a people you are filled with restless energy; nothing appears to you too difficult to be attempted, and you must be forever active. I am speaking of Americans in general, understand, for in you personally, Viriamu, I detect a tendency to take your ease. It has made me wonder more than once if you have not in some mysterious way acquired a drop or two of our own blood. But there, again, we Tahitians bear out the point I am making: our land gives us all that is necessary to life, and with little effort. Is it remarkable, then, that we are sunny of disposition and that we appreciate leisure? Yet you have only to travel to the nearby Tuamotus to find men of our race—men whose skins are the same brown and whose features have the same contours—who are, nevertheless, different from us in habits, in way of life, in thoughts and speech. Tahiti is rich; the insignificant circlets which form the lonely atolls are unproductive coral dust. Tahiti has fruits and vegetables, game and fowl; the atolls have next to none. The Tuamotu man has had to struggle for his livelihood, wresting the greater part of it from the often angry sea, and for the rest contenting himself with coconuts and the tough, un-savory kind of taro which reaches a stunted growth in brackish water. In consequence, his muscles are harder than ours, his temper sharper and perhaps a little sullen. He does not mind the solitude, but it has tinged his character. His music carries a strain of sadness; yet in it there is the pounding vigor of the sea. Even his language differs, though we can understand it, for it has come to mirror his more strenuously daring life.

By all this I have hoped to prepare you to understand exactly what I mean when I say it is inconceivable that long-toothed Nona should have lived elsewhere than close under the cold, brooding bulk of Taharaa. I could take you to the damp, miasmic glen in which she had her hut and where perpetual moisture dripped from

35

the *niau* fronds of her moldering roof. As far as I know, the place has been deserted ever since Nona met her violent end, and it may well remain so till Tahiti again sinks beneath the sea. Certainly no man goes willingly where the horror of ancient crime hangs so heavy, so palpable in the very air. My path rarely leads that way, and for that I am glad to thank the gods, because I cannot repress a shudder when I walk in the footsteps of the dread cannibal woman, with the story of her last, solitary feast always in my memory. So much a part of her gloomy environment was Nona that in Taharaa she seems to go on living even now. It is as if she were embodied in the few tortured, wind-whipped trees with scraggly arms, in the dark, bald-faced cliffs, and in the foam-swept rocks which lie jumbled at their feet. From Mangareva to Hawaii and from Easter to Rurutu there is no island fairer than Tahiti, no island more filled with light, with changing color, with friendliness and warmth. Still, like the flaw in an otherwise perfect pearl, stands the ugly promontory of Taharaa. Perhaps it was created so that, by its contrast, we might more deeply appreciate the rest. However that may be, it is a place which cries aloud of death and horrible deeds.

No one knows the number of men who trustingly entered the long, dim tunnel which afforded so convenient a bypass of the mountain-clawing sea. Into the humid dark they walked, feeling their way through the winding passage with a hand to the slime-clothed walls, confidently facing the gloom in order to reach more quickly the relatives and friends living in the district just beyond. Did nothing tell them of Nona's lurking, evil presence? Did nothing warn of the voracious creature crouching where the mountain weighed most heavily overhead, where the blackness was most intense and the outside world was lost to sight both before and behind? Apparently not; and many a man went unsuspecting till Nona's long, cold fingers twined round his throat to shut off the precious breath of life. For it was there, hidden from all humankind, deep in the bowels of Taharaa, that this fiendish woman indulged in her hideous repasts.

It may be difficult to believe that such a being could ever have known the meaning of affection, or of any other of the emotions which distinguish man from beast. But in Tahiti, as elsewhere, there has probably never lived a character of so unrelieved a blackness as not to contain some ray of light, some suggestion of what the person might have been had not a warping blight deformed the soul. We have no explanation for Nona's terrible depravity. But that once, at least, she gave way to a generous impulse is well established. She adopted—though the story does not disclose how or whence—a beautiful baby girl. Hina was the name she gave the child, and through the years she reared it with a tenderness which, in any other woman, would have been touching. Hina developed into a very lovely young girl. Like a single exquisite flower in a dismal swamp, she grew to maturity, and the more beautiful she became the more jealously the foster mother guarded her from any possible contact with others of her race. This was not so difficult as it may sound, because as the years passed, men came to shun the region of Taharaa. Though Nona succeeded in keeping Hina in ignorance, rumor of the fiend's awful practices eventually escaped to spread across the island. More and more she was obliged to resort to this fishing ground where we now try our luck, and if it had not been for Hina, Nona's appetite for human flesh might have gone unsatisfied.

But Hina proved a potent lure. The rumor of her beauty passed like a whispering wind through the coconut groves, ran the circuit of Tahiti-*nui*, leaping the Isthmus of Taravao, and continuing on to the farthest headlands of Taiarapu. And while the story of such a girl will set men crossing oceans in search of her, the attraction in Hina's case was doubly great because of the danger which surrounded her. From scattered, distant villages came young men of courage, hoping for her favors. They never saw her face; they never returned.

Of all Tahitian youths probably none had paid less attention to the tales of Hina's charms than had Noatu, son of the chief of Mahina, on the border of whose domain Taharaa was planted. He might have continued to disregard her existence indefinitely if his father had not said to him one day: "Son, the time will come when I shall be chief no longer, and you will take my place. Because of that, and because you are of suitable age, it is fitting that you should take a wife."

"A wife?" said Noatu. "What should I do with a wife?"

"You will share your mat and your catch of fish with her," the chief replied, "and you will raise a family. Have you seen no one in our village with whom you would like to do these things?"

"No," said Noatu after slight deliberation, "I believe not."

"What is the matter with the girls of Mahina?"

"Since you ask, Father," he replied, "I will tell you. I find them ugly and would have none of them."

"Well!" said the chief, somewhat taken aback. "You are very hard to please. I have seen many who look attractive to me. But the point is this: it is my wish that you should marry, and without loss of time."

It was then the name of Hina came into Noatu's mind. He had always enjoyed having his cool sleeping mat to himself, and there was no one in the village with whom he felt impelled to share it. Was it possible, he wondered, that with Hina it would be different? Might it, just conceivably, be a pleasure to divide his fish with such a girl as she was said to be? Noatu decided he would go and see.

Saying nothing of his intention to his father or to others, he took up his spear and set out on the trail to Taharaa. Those who had followed the same path were undone at the outset. One and all, they had become so entranced by their visions of the fabled Hina that their minds held little else. Lost in pleasant reverie, they walked heedless into Nona's lair. But Noatu was a wise and cautious youth and gave thought to his safety. When Taharaa loomed up between him and the westering sun he looked well to his spear, striking it upon a rock and listening for the ring that told of a solid, flawless shaft. Then he went on and did not stop again till he stood by the mouth of the tunnel leading into the fortress-like mass of the mountain. He took a step forward, then paused. To take this natural shortcut was certainly the easy thing to do. Yet in such close confines a spear would be of little use. And the darkness was intense. He considered making a torch of a coconut frond. But that would serve only the better to disclose himself to an enemy. Noatu shook his head and turned his attention to the sea. The rumbling of waves dashing against the cliffs came clearly to his ears, and he knew no man could go that way. So he looked above.

Taharaa presents a grim visage to the district of Mahina, and it was at this face of the mountain Noatu stared. From narrow crevices in the almost perpendicular rock, from slippery clefts that held a handful of poor soil, a few scrub trees and bushes grew. There was possible, but most precarious, foothold. No wonder others had chosen the tunnel road. Noatu, however, preferred obvious danger to the unknown. He tied his spear across his back and started up. After a slow, difficult, and often perilous climb, he gained the summit. And although Nona, crouching spiderlike in her black hole below, was ignorant of the fact, in so doing he determined the number of her days. He crossed the narrow crest and started cautiously down the other side. He had covered half the distance to the level of the sea when he chanced to glance over his shoulder into the shadowed glen which lay at his feet. There the half-rotted rooftop of Nona's dwelling showed. But it was not this which caused Noatu to halt motionless with his body pressed close against the cliff. Not far from the house was a small clearing into which slipped a few of the sun's rays, throwing mottled light over the surface of a spring. In the circular pool a young girl bathed. Noatu had no need to be told that it was Hina. He had come to see for himself what this half-mythical person might be. So now he gazed. And, doing so, he felt a quickening of his heart. To share with this girl might not be hard. Ah, no. With her he would be willing to do more than share. She might, without the asking, have all his catch of fish, all of anything he possessed.

Hina came out of the pool, wrapped herself in her *pareu* and walked to the house. And Noatu, more hurriedly than before, continued his descent, convinced at last that his father was entirely right: it was high time he had a wife. The moment his feet touched level ground he was running lightly, soundlessly, past the pool and along the path the girl had taken. Close beneath the eaves of the house he stopped and softly called.

"Hina! Come quickly, my beloved; come quickly, and together we shall fly from this dismal place. You shall see my father's kingdom, and there you will find sunshine and gaiety and many friends."

At the sound of Noatu's voice—the first man's voice she had ever heard—Hina appeared in the doorway to stare at him with her brown eyes large and round. "From where do you come?" she asked slowly in great wonder. "Can you be of this world?"

"I am," Noatu replied smiling. "I am a mortal man like any other, and one who will love you well."

"Love?" she repeated.

"Yes. Do you not know its meaning?"

She shook her head and at the same time, in frank curiosity, came nearer.

"It means," he explained, "that I shall build a house for you and me, and within its walls we shall live together through many years. We shall take a name, a marriage name, and to all Tahiti it will mean not Hina, not Noatu, but Hina-and-Noatu—a single thing, a family. But it will not be in name alone that we become one. You will see; with passing time each will resemble more the other, in speech, in thought— in everything."

"I think I should like that," said Hina, and with a fingertip she touched his dark, straight brows, his lips, his cheeks, examining, still with the air of happy wonder, his every feature. "Are other men as beautiful?" she inquired.

Noatu flushed at her open scrutiny and at the simplicity of her question. "It is for strength and bravery men are admired, and in those things I hope I am the equal of others."

"And would other men cause me to feel as you?"

"How do you feel, Hina?"

"I cannot say. It is strange."

"A small thing?"

"No, it is big."

Noatu laughed aloud. "That is good, and it tells me we were intended for each other. Now hurry. Wrap what you would carry with you in a *pareu* and let us flee before Nona-of-the-Long-Teeth learns I have come to steal the single lovely thing which lights her evil life. Hurry, for if Nona finds me here, either she or I will surely die."

"Why do you speak of death?" Hina asked. "Though I have a longing to follow you I cannot go without first taking leave of my mother."

"Your mother!" he exclaimed. "You must have looked at your own reflection in the spring in which you bathe. Having seen it, can you imagine yourself the child of that creature sprung from dragon's blood?"

"You are harsh," she said, shrinking back. "Why should you hate her? She has been kind to me."

Noatu stared in astonishment. "Is it possible Nona has kept her secret from you who are so near? Do you not know she feasts on human flesh, gnawing the bones

39

of the unfortunates who come within her grasp, then flinging them to the hiding sea?"

"*Aue!*" the girl cried in sudden horror. "It cannot be! She is not like me. She is cold and never laughs, as did you just now; no, nor even smiles. But the awful thing you say—it cannot be!"

"Yet I speak true words," he protested. "Many a wife and mother mourns a man who set his foot to the Taharaa trail. Do you think the sea has claimed them all? A few, perhaps. Most have died in the embrace of the cannibal witch who keeps you an unknowing prisoner."

"No, no! I would willingly have gone once Nona was returned, but now you try to frighten me."

"And would she let you go? Has she ever let you step beyond this dark mountain of gloom? Has she?" he insisted when Hina did not answer.

"No," she said slowly. "I have been told great dangers lie beyond Taharaa. Is it not true?"

"Not great dangers, Hina, but great happiness. The danger is here, close beside you, so close, so ever-present that you have never learned to see it. Trust me, believe me, and let us go."

"No," she repeated, although there were now clouding shadows of doubt in her eyes, "I cannot believe; I could not believe unless . . . ."

"Unless you saw the fearful thing itself," he finished. "Very well; you shall." He freed his spear and sat at Hina's feet. "I shall wait for Nona."

"Not that," she cried, dropping to his side, betraying her mounting fear. "Oh, not that!"

The young man stared stolidly before him toward the yawning mouth of the tunnel which was visible through the foliage. He made no move.

Hina threw her arms about him and pressed her face to his. "Go," she implored. "Go now. Do not wait, Noatu!"

"But why, if Nona bears no man ill will?"

"I do not know," exclaimed the girl distractedly as tears started down her cheeks. "I no longer know what to think, but your words have filled me with unnamed fears. My eyes are opened; scenes and events of my childhood which then seemed innocent now flash before me fraught with suspicion, with sinister meaning which is new. And yet I must be sure. I cannot go before I know. But you, Noatu, do not stay longer in this place where, for the first time, it seems to me the air holds the clammy touch of death. Perhaps the day will come when I shall join you, because if I look upon a hundred men, I shall wish to live in no other house than yours. Leave me; leave me now. Already the hour is passed for Nona's return."

At last the chief's son yielded to her entreaties. He rose to his feet. "I will go," he said quietly. "But each day at evening I shall be by the tunnel where it opens on

Taharaa's other side. Do not keep me waiting long, Hina, for the passing hours are a treasure we throw away."

Still seated on the damp earth before the dilapidated dwelling, she watched him climb the mountain in the gathering dusk and disappear from sight.

Remarkable events have a way of hastening, one upon the heels of another. After the many years of solitude during which she saw no other soul than Nona, Hina was to confront another man on the day immediately following Noatu's departure.

Mono'i was no more than nineteen years of age and he came from the village of Tautira which lies not far from the isthmus connecting Big-Tahiti and Little-Tahiti. The word *mono'i* has the meaning "sweet perfume," and the parents who gave this young man such a name must have been gifted with rare foresight because, although Tahitians in general are fond of flower scents, Mono'i was pleased to anoint himself in such fashion that he reeked. Despite his somewhat mincing gait and gestures, he had proved himself so successful with the girls of Tautira that the fateful notion came to him that it would be amusing to see if Hina's affection could as easily be won.

With the unaccountable luck which frequently accompanies the vain and self-inflated, he passed safely through the tunnel at a time when Nona was absent from her post, and he sauntered up to Hina, who sat outside the house with her head bent over the coconut she was grating on a pointed stick.

"Is this the little dove of whom everyone speaks?" Mono'i inquired, and he smiled down upon her in the manner others had found so attractive.

Hina dropped the coconut and looked up, hardly less startled than when Noatu had first appeared. But as she gazed at the young dandy she experienced no strange feeling. Quickly she demanded, "How have you come here, foolish boy?"

"I neither flew nor swam," replied Mono'i cockily. "Hence, my love, I came by the tunnel."

"Did you meet no one on your way?"

"Neither Nona nor anyone else."

"Ah. Then you have heard of her."

"Who has not?"

"And you have no fear?"

Mono'i laughed, and it was the second time Hina had heard such a sound, but this time it was different and held an empty, idiotic ring. "No," he answered, "I know of her cruel appetite. But she is a woman, is she not? I have never found one who would not prefer me alive rather than dead."

Hina shook her head. "Can the outside world hold many as stupid as you?"

"Stupid?" Mono'i echoed, his jaw slightly sagging.

She rose and stood before him. "I, too, am a woman," she said coldly, "but I find that whether you live or die is of no importance to me. Do you think Nona-of-the-Long-Teeth is likely to be more impressed? It is only recently I have been warned, but the danger may well be real and deadly."

Mono'i now looked at her with mouth agape, his eyes reflecting both his incredulity and a growing uneasiness. "Do you feel no desire to walk with me through the woods?"

"None."

Suddenly all Mono'i's confidence left him, and he became a badly frightened young man. He peered quickly from side to side through the shadowy glen. "When will Nona come?" he asked abruptly.

"At any minute."

"*Aue!*" Without another word he turned and made off on the run for the tunnel.

"Not that way!" Hina called after him. "It is the path by which she will return."

Mono'i halted. "What am I to do?"

"You must climb the mountain."

He looked above. "I am the first of Tahiti's climbers," said he in a last attempt at bravado, though in a voice which quavered, "but no man could hope to scale the face of Taharaa."

"There is no other choice."

In rising terror Mono'i looked first at the tunnel, then at the cliffs above. Finally he sat down where he was and, burying his face in his hands, burst into loud sobs.

Hina watched this performance with a certain pity, but with greater interest. Her understanding of the world which lay beyond Taharaa's boundaries was fast progressing. Clearly, not all mankind was made in the same mold; clearly not all men were possessed of rugged courage, and some were even weak. This knowledge colored her thoughts of Noatu. As she recalled his readiness to remain and face the dreaded Nona, then his unhesitant ascent of the mountain, he appeared in a new and still more favorable light.

She walked to the great lover of Tautira and touched his shoulder. "Come," she said, "I will help you. But what I can do will only postpone the danger, for in the end you must make your way out by your own efforts. Follow me and waste no time."

Hina led the way along a narrow trail where the vines and shrubs crowded close, and which skirted the mountain. After a short time she turned from the path and began to force her way through the tangled underbrush.

Mono'i paused and looked doubtfully into the semidarkness of the jungle. "Where are you taking me?" he asked.

42   "Do not stop to ask questions," she said. "I shall show you a place to hide, a place known to no one but me, not even to Nona. There you will be safe—for a while."

Mono'i stumbled after her, and they had gone but a short distance when a small, steeply rising hill blocked their way. At its base was a cave of a size a man might enter without stooping. To one side of the arched opening, and of similar shape, there hung like a massive door a heavy slab of native rock.

"Go within," Hina directed, "and draw the rock behind you. Its outer face is of such smoothness that it cannot be opened from this side."

"It will be dark," Mono'i faltered.

"Very dark," she agreed.

"And I shall be alone."

"Therein lies your safety."

"Stay with me, Hina," he burst out. "I am afraid!"

"I shall come back," she said, trying to keep her contempt for the miserable man from her voice. "I shall bring you food. When you hear me say, 'Pillar of rock, break open!' push the door ajar, but not before."

Mono'i went in. Together they worked the great slab into place behind him, and Hina went back to the house.

The next morning, as soon as Nona had left, Hina wrapped some fish, some plantains, and some baked breadfruit in *purau* leaves and went again to the cave. Standing before the entrance she called, "O pillar of rock . . . ." But before she could finish, Mono'i pushed ajar the heavy barrier and leaped out.

"Beautiful creature," he exclaimed, "you have brought food for Mono'i of Tautira, and it must be that you care for me after all!"

It was apparent that he had recovered his composure and also his conceit. "I have indeed brought food," she replied, "but only that it may give you sufficient strength to climb the mountain and be gone."

Mono'i took the package of fish and seated himself with his back to the door of the cave, his legs comfortably outstretched before him. He began to eat. "You must think me very foolish if you imagine I intend to break my neck on Taharaa," said he. "I am very content here. What more could a man ask than a soft bed of leaves, a lovely girl to wait upon him, and nothing to do from dawn to dark but take his ease? Come, sit beside me."

Hina made no move.

"You will find me very charming," he remarked arrogantly.

"You may keep your charms to yourself, and if you are wise you will leave at once. This morning I think I was unseen, but Nona's eyes are as sharp as her teeth are long. You must go."

"No, Hina. I shall stay, and in time you, who have no other man, will grow to love me. You are a strange girl and shy, but I am willing to wait."

Hina was at a loss to know what to do with the impossible fellow. She left him by the mouth of the cave and returned to her home, undecided as to how she might be rid of him. On the following day she had still found no solution. But she could

43

not allow the man to starve, and again she gathered up the remnants of the breakfast she had shared with Nona and set out for the cave.

The moment Hina had passed beyond a turn in the trail a tall, angular woman whose muscular hands swung at the end of long, bony arms stepped quietly into the house. Nona had detected a strangeness, a tenseness in Hina's behavior, and now she sought the reason. She brushed aside the damp, black locks which straggled over her cruel face, and peered about the room. Ah! Two fish which had been left were gone. So was a banana stalk with its cluster of ripe fruit. To whom could Hina be carrying food? To whom, if not a man? Nona's lips curled back from her protruding teeth. A man hidden somewhere in the very shadow of Taharaa! Hunting had been poor of late, and Nona had spent many hours in the tunnel's darkness without success. For long she had dined on unexciting fish, and the craving for meat was strong upon her. Noiselessly she slipped out and ran down the trail in pursuit of Hina. When she heard the girl making her way through the brush Nona slackened her pace and, keeping always carefully from sight, followed till Hina's voice brought her to a stop. "Pillar of rock," she heard, "break open!" Inch by inch Nona crept forward. She parted the leaves before her and saw the door of the cave move back. A man stepped jauntily forth, a man of only moderate size, but young and seemingly tender. The cannibal woman of Taharaa waited to see no more. Soundlessly as she had come she retreated, and only at some distance did she begin to mutter the password. A savage light came into Nona's eyes and her strong, clawlike hands opened and closed as if they yearned for the soft feel of a human throat.

Evening had come, and the shadows stretched long and dark over all the region of Taharaa when Hina again prepared to visit the obstinate Mono'i. In the morning she had tried as before to induce him to go away, but without success. Secure in his appalling vanity, he was sure he had only to wait a little, and Hina would fall submissively into his arms. Nona had eaten very little for supper and had lingered long afterward about the house. But now at last she was gone, and Hina hurriedly gathered what food was left. Was there time to go and come back before Nona would return to lie down for the night on the mat across the doorway? A glance at the fading sky told Hina that there might be time if she ran, but none to spare. Reckless of the noise she made, heedless too of concealment, she raced over the trail and plunged into the jungle. Brambles and coiling vines tore at her *pareu*, at the tresses of her hair, and left deep scratches on her arms and legs. Could Nona fail to hear her crashing progress? And where had Nona gone? Perhaps she was on the short reef, the long reef, the near reef or the far. Perhaps she still wandered the darkening trails of Taharaa.

Hina came breathless upon the small, steep hill where dusk was thickening. She went to the door of the cave and called softly, "Pillar of rock, break open!" Mono'i did not answer. There was silence, a silence that was in some way grim, and the stone portal did not move. She called more loudly. "Mono'i is the man; Hina is the woman. Great sealing rock, break open!" There was no sound save the whirring of a cricket somewhere in the underbrush and the occasional sleepy conversation of birds in their jungle roosts. Throwing all caution aside, Hina cried out in sudden terror, "Mono'i, where are you?" and rushed to the heavy door of cold, grey stone. It stood ajar! With frantic hands she seized it and forced it back. The cave gaped wide, exposing to the fading light a sight so hideous that Hina's senses reeled. Staining the earthen floor were the remains of what had once been a human being— a human being who had been both arrogant and foolish but who must, nevertheless, have relished his carefree life. Mono'i would never again enjoy the attentions of Tautira's maidens nor of any others; for Nona, craftily mimicking Hina's voice, had brought him forth to die in the merciless hands so adept at strangulation.

For minutes Hina stood rigid, unable to stir. Then, slow step by slow step, she retreated, her eyes still fastened in awful fascination on the cave. At last she broke away, wheeled, and ran more swiftly than before. She hardly knew the direction she took, and for the moment nothing seemed of importance except to put the frightful scene of recent crime behind her. Blindly she ran, heedless now of the clawing creepers, stumbling and falling, picking herself up again to rush on as if the thing she fled had the power to follow. And so it had; it pursued her into the deepening night. Only when she found that her steps had led her to the still-deserted house was she able to pause and think: "Escape now, this minute! All these years you have lived on the brink of horror. Go now!" She listened for footsteps and heard none. Even the birds had fallen silent, and in all Taharaa nothing breathed. "Quickly, quickly, Hina, run! Yet who can hope to outrun Nona? And will Noatu be waiting? Each evening, he said. Already it is night; you must gain time," her thoughts cried, "time, time."

Her eyes lighted on a long knife of polished wood lying just inside the door. She snatched it up and raced to the nearest banana tree. With a few slashes she severed a length of the soft, porous trunk and carried it hurriedly into the house. Hastily she laid it on her sleeping mat, placed a coconut at its head, and over the improvised dummy drew a strip of tapa cloth. Hina gave one glance at her handiwork. If Nona did not immediately make a fire it might serve to gain a few precious moments, it might give her time to make her way through the dark tunnel which had always been mysteriously forbidden her. It was a mystery no longer. All that Noatu had said was true, true. Oh, if she could only reach Noatu, if she could only feel his arms about her, then she would be safe.

She darted out and fled away from Nona's house with its moisture-sodden roof and its smell of damp decay, away from the narrow, confining glen in which the sun so rarely shone. On flying feet she ran toward the mountainous rock of Taharaa

45

with its twisting tunnel. She had not so much as reached the opening when watchful, suspicious Nona entered her dwelling, walked straight to the sleeping mat and whipped away the covering which hid the pitiful effigy. Hina heard clearly the cry of rage which long-toothed Nona gave, and a sob of despair came from her lips.

"Noatu," she called, "Noatu, I tried to come to you, I tried!"

Then she was in the tunnel and could run no more. Frantically she groped her way through the unfamiliar dark, desperately feeling for the bends and turns with outstretched hands. Jutting rocks reached out like diabolical, animated things, to wound and bruise her; crawling roots and unseen pits seized her feet, sending her prostrate on the slime-wet floor. Yet always she struggled up to stagger on, sometimes colliding with a hard, blank wall, sometimes wondering if, in her fear and confusion, she went backward toward the pursuing Nona and not forward to an ever more distant and impossible freedom. Was there no end to the maddening, bewildering labyrinth, no end to the black corridor's serpentine writhings? Could it lead to the fresh night air, or did it but make its tortuous, gravelike way to the final darkness called Te Po?

"Hina!" Nona's frenzied scream echoed in the low-roofed caverns. "Hina!" The chilling cry came nearer, rapidly nearer. With sure instinct the crazed woman sped through the tunnel, each foot of which was as well known to her as the contours of her own rapacious hands.

Why do you not go faster, Hina? Why does your pace become more slow, your blind stumblings more wild and your progress near halted when so few precious moments still remain? Must your legs fail you, your young strength desert when all depends on this last effort? See—the darkness lessens there ahead! The lightening is very slight and it is still far away; it is only the faint bluish lucency of veiled and distant stars, but it could beckon no more hopefully if it were the rising sun itself. Hurry, hurry, for the beat of Nona's running steps is close behind, and her hoarse breathing fills your ears!

But Hina could do no more, and her tired body cried for rest. The terrible weariness rose to her brain and there drummed its despairing counsel: it is no use to struggle, there is no escape; lie down and the end will quickly come. The pain is brief, the sweet forgetfulness long. Noatu? He must have been a dream which your loneliness conceived, which your imagination touched with fancied life. And Noatu's country, Mahina, where the trade winds rush joyously through the fluttering palms, where children play and people share each other's simple lives—had all that happy picture been nothing but illusion? No, no, she thought in a last burst of rebellion. It was no fantasy. It was all true, and she was not meant to die! The promise was there before her eyes.

She staggered out from the mountain of Taharaa, and Nona's clutching fingers closed upon her naked shoulder. For a moment Hina felt the breath which hissed through the older woman's long, bared teeth; then she was crushed to the ground by Nona's greater weight. She cried out once before consciousness left her, a feeble cry, but one that reached the ears of him for whom it was intended. "Noatu . . . !"

The history of Tahiti would have been very different if Noatu had failed to hear that cry. It would have been very different if he had never set foot on Taharaa. The days of the cannibal woman first were numbered when he scaled the mountain to her especial hunting ground. But he did far more than determine her fate when he made his way into Nona's valley. He found Hina there, and he fell in love. Had this not been so, one of the South Seas' greatest heroes would never have been born.

Each evening, as he had promised, Noatu had come to Taharaa, there to wait hopefully while the hours passed, while the sun set and darkness settled over the island. Each time he had gone home heavy hearted. And so it was on this final day. But he was not far on his way when a sound came to him which caused him to stop. He listened. It had come faintly on the night air, and at first he thought it was no more than the raucous cry of some solitary bird of the sea. But it came again, stronger, clearer, and Noatu recognized the distant screech for what it was: it came, in truth, from the throat of a long-clawed bird of prey, and the throat was Nona's! Noatu whirled. Swiftly, between the dim, grey boles of the coco palms, leaping clear of fallen fronds, he raced back toward the black, lowering mountain.

Hina's eyes could have closed for no more than seconds. When she opened them she remained for a moment unmoving, bewildered. Her hands brushed the soft earth which still held a little of the sun's warmth. This was not the cold soil of Nona's glen. Where was she? Where, how . . . ? Suddenly the answers came to her, and she remembered all that had happened in a night that had just begun. But immediately other questions flooded her brain. Why did the sweet air continue to fill her lungs, and where were Nona's grasping hands? Where was the weight that had brought her to the ground? Hina turned on her side and then lay rigid, staring, unable to move.

Starlight trembled palely on the stone heights of Taharaa, and vaguely silhouetted against the sheer cliff, close to the tunnel's mouth, were two swaying human figures. The bodies of Nona and Noatu merged into one as they bent together, locked in silent, mortal combat. It was said, in the olden days, that in eating the heart of an enemy one took to himself the victim's strength and courage. If this were true, Nona's strength would surely have been that of scores of brave though hapless men, and so for a time it seemed. She fought with the fury of desperation, with all the unleashed venom of her wicked soul. Noatu was forced down. He sank slowly to his knees while the witch of Taharaa crouched above him, her face so close to his that the tangle of her locks brushed his cheeks, and her eyes, burning with the fire of hate and madness, bored into his own. No word passed between them, and there was no sound in all the night except that of their labored breathing and the beat of waves against the mountain's seaward slopes.

When life hangs most delicately in the balance, time seems to stop its steady march as if the gods, momentarily distracted from their duties, pause to watch and to await the outcome. Who is to live and who to die? This they ask themselves, and look down with interest upon the sea in which Tahiti lies, while the wheeling heavens come to an expectant stand. So it was now as Noatu was pressed slowly back, closer and closer to the earth. Twice he tried to rise but could not fling off Nona's rigid, sinewy frame. Was he to perish like all the others who had vanished on the road to Taharaa? Was Hina to be next?

"No," he thought with a terrible rush of anger, "not that—not Hina!" In a supreme effort he threw himself backward and to one side, and so wrenched free. His hands stabbed for Nona's throat. They found their mark, then tightened about the gaunt and corded neck, tightened till fiery pain shot up his arms. Like a snared wild beast she lashed and fought and clawed, but Noatu's grip fastened upon her only the more mercilessly. Gradually her writhings lessened, and when at last she lay quite still he rose, leaving a huddled shape upon the ground. A breath of wind stirred the night air as the gods sighed and turned back to their own concerns. Time went on again and they had their answer: Noatu would live, Hina would live, and between them they would hand life on to a child destined to become still more famed than they.

Noatu lifted the fiend's body and walked with it to the sea. Standing on the spray-drenched rocks which litter the base of Taharaa he lifted long-toothed Nona high above his head. With a heave of his powerful arms he sent her hurtling into the crashing waves below.

Then he went back to Hina and drew her up beside him. "I have built our house," he said. "It is a very fine house. Come, it waits for us."

Tafai

To look upon Tahiti's smaller sister from Tetua's beach one faces west. There she stands at the other side of a channel in which swift currents often twist through turbulent seas, the most breathtaking and endlessly surprising of all the South Sea islands—Moorea, once known as Eimeo. I say "she" advisedly and rightly, I believe, because Moorea has an infinity of moods. There are days when she is proud and haughty, with spired peaks thrusting disdainfully into the blue tropic sky. There are others when, with a festive air, she wreathes her brow with small white clouds like garlands of flowers. She may lie dreamily languorous in slowly swirling haze or frown while storms hover and lightnings flash in the deep valleys. This most volatile of islands does not even remain stationary—or so, at least, it seems. Eleven miles are said to stretch between Tahiti and Moorea; it is so stated on the charts. But who was rash enough to make such a flat and uncompromising assertion? And when did he make his measure? Was it during clear weather and calm, when the air and the green lagoons are limpid, one as the other? If so, he caught the capricious queen at a time when she swims serenely through the bridging waters toward Tahiti to cut the distance easily in half. Or perhaps this man who loved to imagine each bit of land throughout the world as fixed and stable made his computations when the trade wind played briskly on a live and leaping sea, when the sun reflected blindingly from each dancing whitecap and Moorea sailed, aloof and distant, with wind whistling in her highest pinnacles. I am obliged to smile when I imagine the cartographer's plight if he tried to read his log on a day of grey overcast, when the elusive island had retreated to the far horizon behind a bank of clouds. Surely he would have been forced to conclude that it did not then exist. So what is eleven miles? I do not know, exactly; all I can say is that it is never twice the same. And I am tempted to add a warning to mariners: beware of charts, good people, lest your ship join many others which lie wave-washed and rotting on Moorea's unexpected shores.

Such were the thoughts that were running through my mind as I sat on the beach before Tetua's house the evening following our fishing expedition to the chain of reefs at the entrance to Matavai Bay. I was not aware of Tetua's approach until he spoke, bringing me suddenly out of my reverie.

"Of course," he said, "Moorea traveled a great distance across the sea to become Tahiti's satellite. Once it was joined to Raiatea, more than a hundred miles away."

I suppose Tetua must have noticed the direction of my gaze. But was that material from which to read my mind? It was not the first time he had surprised me in similar fashion; yet it was always slightly disconcerting.

Tetua had his hands full. One after another he deposited beside me a glass pitcher of cool spring water, two tumblers, a little plaited basket filled with limes, a bowl of native red sugar, and a liter of rum in which floated several dark brown vanilla beans. "This is the hour, Viriamu," said he as he seated himself, "when a small punch is an excellent thing."

"Yes," I agreed readily, "even two might be acceptable."

He laughed. "*Parau mau.* That's true. But no more, lest you think Tahiti itself is in motion." He cut a few limes, squeezed their juice into the glasses, then re-marked, with the laughter quite gone from his voice: "In former times it might easily have been fact and not imagination. The gods, in those days, had an eye for beauty and experiment. They were continually shifting the islands about, trying them here and there, in this arrangement and that, sliding them over the Pacific as you might push checkers over a board; grouping them in clusters, strewing them in chains, and occasionally misplacing a bit of land altogether, as is the case with Rapa-nui or Easter Island. I find their interest in the world's pattern a cheering and heartening sort of thing—a reminder, as it were, that the gods were near and that man was not alone on the boundless seas. Nowadays the old gods are deposed; Oro and Tu and Tane have not a temple standing. But with all due respect, Viriamu, it seems to me that the missionary god who has supplanted them takes peculiarly little interest in our affairs. Naturally his temperament is different. Our own deities were of our shape and character; they were fond of coconut sauce and of beautiful women and of winds which carried the taste of the briny oceans; they had their faults and sometimes they did foolish things. But they were like us and we could understand them. You will know that I am not complaining, that I merely express my thoughts with a frankness you have encouraged. And I am thinking that it is not surprising that this one called Jehovah should not have very much to do with us. How should it occur to him to transplant Moorea or Bora Bora to a more favorable or attractive location when the parched desert land which was, and still must be, his primary concern holds hardly enough water—or so I'm told—to float an out-rigger canoe, let alone an island? No, we cannot wonder that he pays little attention to our brown-skinned, seafaring people who are so different in every way from the nomadic tribes of Israel. I do not deny that I mourn the old gods and that I wish it were still possible to expect that we might wake some morning to see a fragment of the island of Raiatea bearing down to join the soil on which we live. I have told you, have I not, that it was from there—from Raiatea—that Tahiti also came?"

I shook my head.

Having added the sugar and a measure of rum, Tetua now filled the glasses with water and handed one to me. We sipped our drinks in silence for some few minutes while the soft darkness grew about us. What light still remained of the day just past clung to the edges of a few slow-moving clouds and the tremulous surface of the lagoons beneath them. It was the hour when enchantment is most palpable, when the air quivers in a brief, unreal twilight, thick with memories of the Tahitian past.

"I forget sometimes," Tetua resumed, "that you are a *popa'a*—a foreigner and that the origins of our lands are not as familiar to you as they are to me.

"There was a time when this southern ocean held but one great island, and its name was Havai'i. A small segment of it still exists, and that segment is now called Raiatea. In old Havai'i our ancient customs grew. There were laboriously raised the first majestic temples, the same which today lie strewn as so much pitiful rubble on weed-grown, once *tapu* ground. There, in the shadow of Mount Temehani's volcanic cone, the first of the sacred chants were sung, the same which now echo down to us so faintly, haltingly, on the tongues of a few lonely men even older than I. From the holiest *marae* of all, at Opoa in Havai'i, our religion stemmed; within its walls of stone the exacting rituals developed. For many years Opoa's priests held sway over the entire island; the people never failed to bring regularly their offerings of fish and game and fowl to the temple altars, and the gods rewarded them with great prosperity. Eventually, however, there came a change. Perhaps it was brought about by too long security in easy living. Men became less conscious of their dependence on the gods and more arrogant in their own imagined importance. Priestly laws were broken and the old *tapu* was flouted. It must have come about most gradually, but the day came when those who ruled the world from the skies above and the seas below could no longer close their eyes to what was happening.

"Some say that a young girl brought about the final downfall and humiliation of Havai'i, and it is true that she caused the offended deities to take action; yet it should be remembered that her crime was only one heaped upon many others that had gone before. Tere-he was young and comely; she was also contemptuous of restraint and was possessed with the irresponsibility which was then rife. On a day of especial sacredness at Opoa, when it was forbidden any cock to crow or dog to bark, and when it was also *tapu* for any man or woman to walk abroad, Tere-he went brazenly to swim in the river that passed her home. She threw aside her *pareu*, slipped into the cool water, and swam slowly to midstream where she turned on

51

her back, letting the lazy current carry her where it would. Little time could have passed before she looked up again and cried out in fright. At first she thought she had drifted into the ocean, but, glancing over her shoulder, she saw that the thatch house in which she had been born was still standing at the edge of the stream only a short distance away. The river's other bank was moving, was already far away, and the water between was widening, widening to the size of an inland sea! Tere-he, who had always been occupied with the most trivial things, was unable to grasp the terrible catastrophe that was taking place before her eyes. Havai'i was sundered in two, robbed of more than half her land! The girl swam frantically back to shore, where already the stricken populace crowded, crying aloud their grief and tardy penitence. But nothing halted the slow, irrevocable passage of the larger part of the island out to sea, and the people observed that the hills and valleys and mountains which they had accepted so casually as their very own were now quickening with mysterious life. The great mass of rock and soil and coral, no longer merely land, assumed the shape of an enormous fish. Tahiti-the-Fish, destined to be mightier than all Havai'i, swam majestically away and finally passed out of sight."

Tetua paused briefly to fill our glasses and then went on. "There are some who claim it was intended to sail Tahiti and its offshoot Moorea into the lagoons of the atolls Rangiroa and Tikehau. This is said mostly by the boastful folk who inhabit those two places, and I think it unlikely. Admitted that their far-flung ribbons of land are of a shape and size to enclose Tahiti and Moorea very perfectly, it does not seem reasonable to me that the gods failed of their purpose simply because they ran upon a shoal in the place where we now sit. Could the all-seeing ones have been such poor navigators? At all events, here Tahiti-the-Fish stopped and here it took root. It became land again, sprouting banana trees and palms and banyans. But you have only to look at a map to see that it retains the shape of a fish. You have only to look up to the greatest mountain, Orohena, to see what was once the tremendous dorsal fin; you have but to travel to the cliffs of Pari to find the head, or to the district of Punaavia to discover the tail. The twin caves of Ana-reia are the gills, the tumbled rocks of Po-fatu-ra'a are the teeth, and if you have any further doubts of the truth of this account you can go to now denuded Opoa on Raiatea and see the great, gaping cavity in the shore which this newer land once occupied."

Tetua looked at me as if he would appreciate an affirmation of faith in his recital, so I said promptly, "I have been to Opoa and have already seen the great wound in the shoreline, but of course I should have been willing to accept your word for it in any case."

"I know," he replied. "But you would be surprised at the number, even of Tahitians, who scoff at this explanation of the island on which they live. Their smug stupidity annoys me. Why is it so hard for them to believe? Nothing was impossible for the gods. And as for the matter of transplanting Tahiti, a mortal man once very nearly accomplished as much. Would you care to hear of it?"

"Very much," I said honestly. "But first, can you not satisfy my curiosity about one point? This afternoon, when you were telling of the cannibal woman, you mentioned that in escaping her, Hina and Noatu were to bring into the world one who would be more famous than either one of them. Who was that, Tetua?"

His white teeth flashed as he smiled in the darkness. "Tafai was his name—the same of whom I was just about to speak." This is his story:

Hina and Noatu did, as I intimated before, pass the gift of life along to the great and intrepid Tafai, although this they did as grandparents and not as mother and father. Two sons were born to Hina; one she called Pu and the younger, Hema. Hema it was who fathered the famous hero and had many other glorious descendants, while those who claim Pu as ancestor are people of little importance. Hina foresaw that this would be the case on a certain day when both her sons had reached young manhood.

She was seated before the house which her husband had built for her when Pu strolled past and she said to him, "My arms grow heavy with the years, Pu; be so good as to come and braid my hair."

"I am on my way to play in the breakers," replied Pu, "and have no time to waste."

Then Hina said, "Your character saddens me, my son, and I fear you will have but a common and undistinguished woman for a mate."

A few moments later Hema passed, carrying his fishing pole and a basket of minnows for bait, and Hina called to him. "Hema, will you not put off your fishing and first braid your mother's hair?"

"Gladly," Hema replied, and seating himself beside her he deftly plaited two long braids which Hina then wound about her head.

"Thank you," she smiled. "Your thoughtfulness lightens my old age. You deserve an exceptional wife, and such you shall have. Come to me tomorrow, and you shall learn how she may be won."

The next morning Hema again took his mother's hair in his hands, and while he wove the strands, Hina said to him: "Go to the hollow river, Vai-po, and hide yourself by the banyan tree which grows on the bank where the stream is most deep and tranquil. There, as I have seen, the river goddess Tahu comes each day to bathe. No man has ever possessed a water nymph, but if you are clever and strong, Tahu will be your wife. You must seize her by the hair and carry her. Under no circumstances must you set her down before you have passed four houses, or she will be lost to you. Now go quickly, Hema, and find your bride."

Hema ceased braiding his mother's hair and jumped to his feet, and, taking tender leave of his mother, he started for Vai-po. As soon as he had reached the stream he lay down beside the banyan tree and prepared for a long wait. But he had no more than settled himself when the quiet waters before him parted and a beautiful girl with long, flowing hair rose to the surface to play in the deep pool shaded by

53

the ancient tree. Hema's fancy had been greatly stirred by the few words his mother had spoken concerning the goddess Tahu, but he had hardly expected anything so ravishingly lovely as the nymph who now slid up on the river bank and lay upon the soft moss, wringing the water from tresses so long that they completely covered her.

Mindful of his mother's instructions, Hema crept silently closer, then suddenly leaped forward and wrapped his right hand firmly in Tahu's long, dark locks. With the suppleness of youth, with the slippery agility of fish or eel, the nymph struggled in his grasp, but Hema held her fast and, lifting her up, set out for home.

They had come to the edge of the village and had passed two houses when at last Tahu quieted. "I know who you are, Hema," she said in a soft voice. "I will struggle no longer, because I love you. Release me and I will walk beside you."

Completely disarmed by her gentleness, Hema acquiesced. He let go his hold upon her hair and put her down. The instant her feet touched the earth a wide fissure opened where she stepped, and Tahu disappeared within. The cleft shut behind her, and Hema was left alone.

"*Aue!*" he wailed aloud. "I have lost the breath of life, and beauty is gone from the world. It is better that I should die without delay." And he went home to Hina with tears streaming down his face.

"You are a good and dutiful son," his mother observed when he stood before her, "but perhaps you are not as clever as I had imagined. Go again to the river tomorrow, and this time do not let Tahu's feet touch the ground before you have passed four houses."

Hema went again the next day and seized Tahu as before. But despite her entreaties and despite her caresses he managed to keep his head till he had passed four houses. Only then did he set her down. Obviously Hina's words had been wise ones, because the earth did not open and Tahu did not run away. Instead, twining her hand in Hema's, she walked docilely beside him to his home and became his wife.

When it became apparent that Tahu was to have a child, there was much interested speculation in the village concerning what manner of offspring might result from the union of a man and a water nymph. That it would be an exceptional child no one doubted; and when at last a son was born they were not disappointed. The babe's color was unlike any ever seen before and was the reason for his full name— Tafai-of-the-Red-Skin. His hair was not like that of other Tahitians, being red-brown rather than black, and in his eyes there burned a brightness and intelligence which were directly traceable to Tahu. That he was also to inherit his mother's magical powers was demonstrated before he was nine.

54

At that time he played frequently with three cousins several years older than himself. These boys, whose names were Ta, Pua, and Temata, were considerably bigger than was Tafai in these early days of his life, but despite this advantage they always came out second best in whatever game or contest they undertook. All three were of a naturally jealous disposition, and the humiliation of constant defeat developed in them a lively hatred of the younger lad.

"This time," said Temata one day, "we shall get the better of him. Tafai knows nothing of boats. We shall build toy boats and sail them. Ours will go faster than his."

The cousins went to work and made their boats, whittling the hulls from small pieces of driftwood and making sails of thin strips of bamboo. Tafai, as usual, entered happily into the game, but instead of using heavy wood for his craft he climbed to the upper mountain slopes where grows the 'a'eho cane and there selected a reed of that feather-light material. Back in the village he carefully cut off a segment of the cane about a foot in length and to the stern attached a thin, yard-long strip peeled from the heart of a palm frond, to trail behind the craft and serve as the rudder. To either side of the central 'a'eho float, so that they branched out in a broad ∨, he attached two more of the delicate frond strips to serve as balancers. A final thread of the same material he inserted in the bow, then bent it back in a sweeping loop to meet the little hull amidships; this was a fragile mast which held up to the wind the large, spreading, heart-shaped *purau*-leaf sail.

It was late in the afternoon when the cousins went down to the beach with their new toys, and a light breeze ruffled the lagoon. Soon Tafai appeared bearing his handiwork, which, at a little distance, looked like a big leaf that had become entangled with some vines. The older boys stared in astonishment.

"What is that thing you hold?" Temata demanded.

"It is a *titiraina*," Tafai replied.

"Who says so?"

"I do," said Tafai. "I have made it and have called it a *titiraina*." (So, incidentally, it is still called by all the children who continue to this day to amuse themselves with Tafai's near-miraculous toy canoe.)

Temata laughed loudly. "Do you expect it to sail?" he asked contemptuously.

"It will sail," Tafai smiled with his customary good humor, "and it will also fly—on land as well as sea. Look." He placed the toy on the smooth sand, the wind caught at the dry leaf, lifting the cane float into the air, and the *titiraina* skittered away down the beach, trailing the steadying, spiderlike fronds behind it. Tafai ran and captured it and returned a little out of breath. "You see? Shall we try them in the water?"

Temata was now scowling darkly, and his two brothers also looked sullen and disgruntled. But they could think of no way to avoid the game they themselves had begun, and so they went to the edge of the lagoon and set their toys afloat. The three wooden boats lumbered out from shore, slapping clumsily against the wavelets, sometimes coming to a near stop, then tottering slowly on again.

"Blow, wind," shouted Ta, "and carry my boat to the foaming reef!"

"Blow, wind," shouted Pua, "and take my boat to the open sea!"

55

"Blow, wind," shouted Temata louder than his brothers, "and send my boat to the long horizon!"

Tafai said nothing but bent down and carefully launched the *titiraina* upon the dancing waters. Immediately it whisked away like some fantastic, winged water bug, skimmed over the lagoon past the lumpish, struggling crafts of his cousins, and continued merrily on and on, through the pass and out to sea, where it was soon quite lost to sight.

"*Aue!*" Tafai exclaimed, clapping his hands in delight. "Was it not a pretty thing to see?"

By way of answer Temata snatched up a big stick and in sudden rage brought it down with all his might on Tafai's head. Ta and Pua leaped upon the younger boy at the same time. Beneath their furious blows Tafai fell senseless to the ground and moved no more.

"Oh," breathed Ta fearfully as he looked down on the inert figure, "what have we done?"

"He is dead," Pua quavered, "and we shall be punished."

"We have killed him, and Tafai will not bother us again," said Temata, but, despite his attempt at bluster, his lips trembled slightly. "We must hide him before we are seen," he added, and immediately all three began hurriedly to dig a pit in the sand. When they had done they tossed Tafai in and covered him up. "His mother will ask if we have seen him. Say no," Temata instructed them. Then they went away from that place.

Tahu, however, asked the boys nothing. She knew instantly what had happened, and, going quickly to the beach where Tafai lay buried, she knelt and uncovered him and said: "Let my *mana*—my magic—flow into you. Let life course anew in your veins." Tafai opened his eyes and lived again. Then, still seated on the sand, Tahu said: "Stand beside me and open your mouth above my head. In that way you will take to yourself the powers which your mother brought from the nether world." Tafai did as he was told and so absorbed all of Tahu's marvelous abilities.

Men watched Tafai's development with increasing interest after these occurrences, and by the time he had reached manhood his stature was greater than that of any of the three youths who had treated him so badly. His curling auburn hair and his reddish skin set him apart from all others of his race, but so also did his skill in sports and war. He was not yet twenty when he became warrior-in-chief of Tahiti.

There have been few great Tahitians who have been content to spend all their lives on the island where they were born, and Tafai was no exception. The day came when the urge to explore new lands seized him, and to his parents he said: "My dear ones, Tahiti is not big enough to contain me. I must go."

Tahu made no objection, but Tafai's father, Hema, was now enfeebled by age. "Do not leave me, my son," he pleaded. "I am old, and you are my last support."

However, the wanderlust was strong within Tafai and he could not remain. "I shall return," he promised, "and if fortune favors I shall bring back high honors for our house."

So with priest and trusted crew he made sail on his double canoe and sped out the pass through which his *titiraina* had once flown to a childish victory. It was no toy that Tafai now rode, but a vessel of stout planking bound with tough sennit, a craft built to match the muscles of grown men and to pit its strength against the great ocean. And it was no childish enterprise upon which he now embarked but perilous adventure fit for boldest warriors.

"Bear north, Ahiri," Tafai instructed his friend and pilot. "We go on to great discovery, for I seek fresh islands that men have never seen and never trod. Keep the bows in the north through all the days, and if other lands exist we shall surely find them."

"And if there are none?" Ahiri inquired calmly.

"In that case we shall eventually come to the place where the oceans plunge downward to darkness and Te Po."

"We shall die."

"And be done with searching," Tafai agreed.

A great many suns passed over the seafarers. The men's skins turned slowly black and even Tafai's became a ruddy brown; but still no land was seen. Then, at dawn of the twentieth day, a lookout cried: "O Tafai! Spray from the falling ocean fills the sky and we near the entrance to Te Po!"

Tafai went forward and climbed the prow. He gazed ahead. "Not spray," he said after a moment. "We have come upon a wonder: it is smoke we see, and the ocean burns."

"Turn back, Tafai, turn back," the men exclaimed. "Bring us not into a sea of flame!"

"Would you have me turn away from such a marvel?" their leader demanded sternly. "Bear on, my pilot; come closer to the wind. Speed us forward, for now I see more than smoke and falling ash. I think we are about to raise the king of islands."

Tafai's vessel bounded over the waves, and soon an island greener than rain-drenched Moorea, vaster than spreading Hao, higher than Tahiti, grew up out of the sea. From its fiery mountains an enormous plume of smoke soared up to flatten against the clouds.

"Because of our voyage," Tafai exulted, "the world has grown. We have found a new land for our people where they may live and multiply. Let us give it a name, my fellow warriors, and let us call it Burning-Hawaii." *57*

They went on and ran their craft ashore. They explored the land and found it rich and good—so rich and so good that many months passed before the thought of return came to any one of them. At last, however, they set out from Burning-

Hawaii, which lies above, for Tahiti, which lies below, and made their way successfully to the old, familiar country. They were received with rejoicing, and feasts were spread, and all was excited talk about the new island where the mountains belched bright fire. Many began immediately to gather their families and to make preparations for the voyage which would bring them to a new home in Burning-Hawaii; and Tafai himself would have been tempted to go had not sorrow as well as gladness met him upon his return.

"I do not see my father," said he to Tahu when the press of welcoming friends had thinned. "Where is Hema?"

His mother's eyes were sad when she replied. "He waited long for you, Tafai, but at last, like many another, he became convinced that you were lost. He had then no desire to live, and so, of course, he died."

"Am I the cause of my father's death?" Tafai groaned. "Is it thus the gods reward me for finding magnificent Hawaii?"

"Do not rebuke the gods," Tahu reproved. "It was Hema's wish to die, and, as you know, for those of our race no more is necessary."

"But he thought to join me, and now he is alone!"

Tahu looked searchingly at her son and read plainly the depth of his sorrow. "I, too, grieve sorely for your father," she said. "If I should help you, would you dare attempt to bring him back?"

"Only show me the way," Tafai exclaimed. "I ask no more."

"And little more can I do. I have the power to open a path to the underworld, but once you are on the dismal road no one on earth can give further aid."

"Haste, then," Tafai urged impatiently. "I shall stop for neither feast nor celebration while Hema languishes in darkness. One friend I know who will not shun such danger: Ahiri, who piloted my canoe. Him alone I shall take with me."

As Tafai had guessed, Ahiri leaped at the chance to accompany his chief, and it was not long before the two men, accompanied by Tahu, left the village. Tahu led the way to the river Vai-po and stopped beside the pool in which Hema had first discovered her.

"I was once goddess of this stream," she said to them, "and there is no part of its riffled bed that is not known to me. At the bottom of this pool lies the entrance to Te Po. Swim down, Tafai; swim down, Ahiri. You will see a passage in the lower bank. Enter it and go on. You will rise to the surface of a lake of black water, and the roof above the lake is the ground on which we stand. I can tell you nothing more. So go, Tafai; and go, Ahiri."

"Stay, Tahu," they both replied, and plunged into the cool river. Straight to the bottom they swam, turned into the passage, and with quick strokes pushed on. A minute passed, two; then they burst upward to gain the dim, night-tinged air of the lake Tahu had described. The sound of their heavy breathing echoed across the black, still water, and immediately a voice called out.

"What do I hear, and whence comes the odor of mortal man?"

The two men turned and saw an old woman seated before a small hut on the far shore. Quickly Tafai put a finger to his lips, warning Ahiri to silence, and slowly they swam toward her. Uhi, as the ancient dame was called, raised her head in the attitude of the totally blind and sniffed the air. She mumbled to herself and then, evidently deciding that the splashing she had heard was only the long-eared eels which infested the lake, returned her attention to the meal she was assembling. With groping hands she arranged before her two halves of breadfruit, two roots of taro, two cups of coconut sauce, and two cups of water. While Tafai and Ahiri crept onto the shore she began to eat. Ahiri, as it happened, was very hungry, and, seeing clearly that Uhi was blind, he cautiously helped himself to one portion of everything she had. When Uhi felt for more she found nothing.

"What thief has come sneaking into the underworld?" she demanded angrily.

"It is I," said Tahu's son before Ahiri could reply.

"Who?"

"Tafai."

"Tafai, is it?" A crafty smile appeared on Uhi's seamed old face. "You must be a remarkable man to come into the land of the dead before you are summoned. Seat yourself comfortably."

Tafai made no move to comply, but Ahiri looked down before accepting the crone's invitation, and his eyes fell upon a most beautiful object. Lying upon the ground temptingly close to his feet was a headdress of brilliant red feathers worthy of a king. Impulsively, and before his companion could prevent it, he reached down and snatched up the gaudy ornament. Immediately he cried in anguish, "Tafai, I am caught!" Hidden in the feathery lure was a cruel, long-barbed hook which bit deep into Ahiri's palm.

"A fish! A big fish!" the witch shouted triumphantly, and she jerked taut the cord which was attached to her wrist and drew it in swiftly, hand over hand, till Ahiri was in her grasp. In a trice she had wrapped the line about him so that he lay bound and helpless at her side. "Well, well," she cackled, "here is something better than breadfruit, better than taro or coconut sauce."

So quickly had this happened that Tafai had no chance to move. And even now he maintained a respectful distance. Uhi was only a woman, and an old one, but she was a denizen of Te Po and a sorceress as well. Brute strength, he knew, would get him nowhere in the underworld. Nevertheless he said boldly, "Release your fish, Uhi, or I shall call upon my friend the shark who swims the Milky Way."

The old woman laughed derisively. "And does the Milky Way flow into the black waters of my lake of darkness? No, Tafai, the shark cannot help you here. But I will throw back the fish I have caught if you will do me one small favor." Here Uhi paused to chuckle again, secure in the belief that Tafai could not possibly perform the task she was about to set him. She pointed to her empty eye sockets. "Restore my sight to me and you shall have your wish."

Tafai looked up at the top of a coconut tree which stood by the shore and saw there two very small, newly sprouted nuts. "You shall see again," he pronounced and began to climb the tree. He wrapped his long arms about the rough bole, raised his legs till they were bent beneath him in a squatting position with the soles of his bare feet firmly wedged against the trunk; then he straightened to his full height and reached above for a fresh hold with his arms. In this manner he ascended swiftly in a series of leaps. But it was no ordinary tree that Tafai climbed, for as he went upward, so did the tree. He climbed faster and the tree grew faster, and always the two small nuts dangled just beyond his reach. Finally he paused for breath and, looking down, discovered that he had come a truly astonishing distance above the lake and that Uhi and the prostrate Ahiri were almost lost to sight. "This cannot go on forever," he thought, and started up again. Tafai was right. The treetop at last collided with the ground that formed the ceiling of Te Po; it pushed up a considerable mound on the outside earth close beside the river Vai-po—a mound visible to this day—and then came to a stop. Tafai plucked the two young coconuts and descended. One after the other he popped them into the sockets where Uhi's eyes once had been.

With a cry of pain the old woman clapped her hands over her face. Then, slowly, she removed them. "Why," she exclaimed, "I behold a handsome man with a skin of glowing red. I can see, I can see!"

"Do not forget your part of the bargain," Tafai cautioned. "Release my friend."

"That is little enough," she replied and cut Ahiri's bonds. "Is that your only desire?"

"No. There is another thing."

"Whatever it is, you shall have it."

"Tell me, Uhi, where in the underworld must I look to find my father?"

"Your father?"

"When he lived in Tahiti he was called Hema."

"Ah, yes," the ancient one nodded, "and so he is called here."

"Then you know where he is?"

"That I do. Although I have been blind for many years my hearing is keen. No bit of gossip fails to reach me. Nothing happens in Te Po but that I know of it."

Tafai smiled. "In some ways this region is little different from the earth above. There also old women know everything that takes place, however trifling."

"Perhaps it is so," Uhi admitted. "But there are dangers here unlike any you have ever encountered, and to find your father you must meet them. Hema came here, not in the usual manner, but of his own free will. If I remember rightly it was from grieving for you, his son, that he chose to die. The gods did not approve, and in punishment he was delivered to the goblin hordes of Uru. Uru is ruler of a large portion of this realm, and he is without a heart. Still more cruel are the terrible creatures who serve him, and who now hold Hema prisoner. I have never seen the myriad monsters of Uru, but from all I have been told a man might, when first he lays eyes upon them, think to be in the throes of a frightful nightmare, and perhaps the gods themselves dreamed feverishly when they created them. How else can I explain the horrible mixture of beast and fish and man which they embody? Human heads set within the writhing tentacles of octopuses, upon the shoulders of wild boars, on the necks of eels, scavenging birds, lizards, and snapping turtles; sea slugs with arms and legs, centipedes that stand erect, great crabs and lobsters with leering faces, deadly tridacna clams that walk and speak—such are the goblins of Uru."

Even Tafai blanched a little at the picture of madness which Uhi painted, but he said sternly, "Where shall I find them, and where shall I find my father?"

"Follow the shores of this lake of sooty waters," Uhi directed. "At its end you will see a grotto studded with conch shells. In the heart of the grotto you will see a passage leading steeply down. Enter it, brush aside the cobwebs, strike down the bats that fly against your face, and keep on till you come out upon a forest. Enter it also. It is the forest of Uru. There you will find your father bound to a dying tree; there you will find Uru's people; and there, bold youth that you are, you will probably forever remain, an additional source of amusement for goblin torment."

Tafai thanked the old woman, and he and Ahiri had started on their way along the shore when she called after them. "One secret I will tell you because of what you have done for me. If you are intelligent, it may be that you will use the knowledge to your advantage. At first cockcrow Hema's guardians rush to their dwelling and fall immediately into deep slumber. That is all; now be gone."

The two men went on. They found the cave studded with trumpet shells and entered it. They found the bat-filled passage and entered there. Down, down toward the center of the earth they went and at last stepped out of the grotto and into the borders of a dense forest. A thick carpet of moss lay underfoot, and the two men moved on noiselessly; but they had penetrated the woods to no great distance when a sound met their ears and brought them both to a stop.

Ahiri looked about apprehensively at the heavy blanket of leaves that surrounded them on all sides. "I do not like this place, Tafai," he said in a hoarse whisper. "A thousand pairs of eyes might watch us and we would be no wiser. And what is that clamor which sends cold fingers running up along my spine?"

"It is goblin laughter that you hear," Tafai answered. "And that wail which rises and falls like chill night wind by the seacoast caves is my father's cry of agony.

Follow me quickly, Ahiri, for we shall either rescue him or join him in his endless suffering."

Recklessly, now, they both plunged ahead, hurrying between the trunks of hoary trees that had been growing in the sunless grove since ever Te Po was first imagined. They ran on till the fiendish uproar was loud in their ears. Then abruptly the forest thinned, and Tafai, stretching a hand behind him, brought his companion to a halt. The next instant he drew him behind a giant tree, and from the concealment of its massive trunk they stared out upon a scene which had never before met the eyes of mortal man. The words of Uhi now echoed in Tafai's thoughts: "Nightmare, Uhi said? Ah, Uhi, you were blind, and what you spoke was only hearsay, but in it was much truth. What words can have conveyed it to you? What words, and whose, showed to you the hordes of Uru in their hideous reality? Someone more skilled in our rich tongue than I must have whispered in your eager and receptive ear."

Hema strained at the bonds which held him erect and helpless against a gaunt old tree whose branches reached crookedly above him in wordless anguish. In a wide circle on the ground about him, in the limbs of the near-dead tree, in the air about his head, swarmed the grotesque army of Uru. Everywhere the two men looked they saw the insane figures. There were those that flew and those that crawled, those that leaped and those that danced, those that slithered on the mossy ground, those that clawed their way upon the bleak, grey tree. With gaping pincers, with curving talons, with sting-barbed tails and cruel tusks and clutching tentacles, they tore and ripped, prodded and lashed at their hapless prisoner, while from the throat of every one there poured the screeching, demoniac laughter which the travelers from above had heard. It was sheer delirium upon which Tafai gazed, and he wondered, his senses momentarily numbed with horror, which was real and which was false: this world of frenzied noise and senseless, whirling movement, or the fair and ordered one from whence he came? Which was the dream, Tahiti or Te Po? Could the same hands have fashioned both? Could the same gods have made Tahiti of the white sands and the black, of the green mountains and the blue— Tahiti, where man was man, beast was beast, and fish was fish, each being complete and good and noble in its own perfection—only to turn to Te Po and there jumble all together in a frightful mixture in which all creation was ridiculed?

An imploring cry cut short his thoughts. "Tafai!" came his father's call. "O Tafai, my son. If you still walk upon the earth, hear my voice and come to me. Let your love lead you over the lake and down the sloping corridors of Te Po. Deliver me from torment and bring me again to the light of day!"

Tafai-of-the-Red-Skin took a deep breath, and then from his mouth came the piercing crow of a cock. "To-tera-te-oo!" he shouted. "To-tera-te-oo!" Again and again the high-pitched crow sounded above the din of the forest. Then silence fell.

"Dawn!" exclaimed one of the goblins. "Dawn is here. Away, away!" And the awful tribe rushed from the scene of its grim sport and disappeared among the trees.

Tafai took note of the direction they had gone and then ran to his father. Ahiri was close behind him, and together they unbound the fainting man and laid him upon the ground. From a spring Tafai brought water and carefully washed his wounds, covering them with healing leaves.

Hema's eyes opened and a long sigh escaped him. "Your hands are strong, Tafai, but they are gentle, too. Come closer, son, and receive a father's gratitude." Tafai put his face beside Hema's and they touched cheeks in the manner of those days. Then he straightened.

"Can you lead me to the home of Uru's goblins?" he demanded.

"Yes," Hema replied, "I know it well. They live in a long, narrow house made of palm thatch to which there is a single entrance. They will be sleeping now with their deformed bodies piled together in a great heap covering the entire length of the earth floor. But though their slumber is sound it is of short duration. We must hurry if we are to make our way above before we are pursued."

"I have a task to perform before I can leave this place," Tafai announced. He lifted his father to his feet. "Are you strong enough to walk?" he inquired. "If not, Ahiri and I shall carry you."

"I can walk," Hema replied.

"Then take us to the goblins' lair."

From his son's determined expression Hema saw that it was of no use to demur, and so he led the way. As they went Tafai stopped twice—once to pick up a heavy, knotted branch which he swung in his hand like a club, and once to gather two small pieces of *purau* wood. In a part of the forest where the trees grew most densely they came upon the house Hema had described. Tafai glanced through the open door and listened for a brief moment to the sounds of stertorous breathing which came from the rank darkness within. Then he seated himself on the ground a short distance away and took up the two *purau* sticks. One of them was roughly pointed, and this he applied to the other, rubbing it back and forth vigorously, rapidly.

"Why do you make fire?" Ahiri asked in a whisper.

"Do you think to cook food," his father demanded, "at a time when our lives hang forfeit? We must hasten upward, along the passage, across the lake, through the river Vai-po to reach the sun."

"I am not thinking of food," said Tafai. "I shall burn them out and kill each one." He blew on the dry dust which had formed upon the lower stick and smoke appeared. He laid a bit of dried frond on the smoldering wood, and flame sprang up. He lighted a larger frond and ran with it flaming in his hands to the rear of the house. There he touched it to the brittle thatch in a dozen places, then raced back to the door. With his heavy club raised, he waited.

63

Black smoke soon billowed up through the ghostly trees, and a moment later Te Po was illumined with dull red flame. Roaring and crackling, the conflagration spread over the tinderlike coconut leaves.

"*Te auahi!* Fire, fire!" rose the goblin screams, and tumbling madly over one another they fought to reach the door. As they burst out, running, crawling, sidling, flying, Tafai struck them down with his mighty club and kicked aside their dead and mangled bodies.

"Out, fiends of Te Po!" he shouted. "Out, and die beneath Tafai's avenging blows!" Faster and faster the club whirled, and each time it descended life was crushed from another of Uru's misbegotten tribe. Finally the last of the goblins scuttled forth and Tafai pinned it to the earth.

He cast away his bloody weapon and looked down at the tangled bodies that surrounded him. "The underworld," he observed, "will never be a pleasant place, but at least the hellish laughter of these distorted creatures will never sound again."

Tafai and his father and Ahiri then made their way upward. At Uhi's hut they stopped long enough to eat some long-eared eel which the old woman served them. Thus refreshed, they swam the black-shadowed lake and came up at last through the clear waters of the hollow river.

Hema climbed out upon the bank. He felt the green grass beside him, he looked up at the cloud-capped mountains, and he breathed the salt wind from the sea. "Land of beauty," he said fervently, "never willingly shall I leave you again."

Tetua ceased speaking, and for some moments we smoked silently in the dark.

"That was a fine story," I said. "But is it all? We were speaking, if you remember, of the movement of islands. Did you not say that Tafai once . . . ?"

"Yes, yes," he interrupted. "I do not forget, and you have heard only the beginning. But it is late, Viriamu. It is time we took to our sleeping mats. There will be another day."

The Demon Tree of Burning-Hawaii

THERE had been showers in the night, both in the mountains and along the coastal plain; and the morning which followed was of the sort which comes as a surprise to the newcomer in Tahiti who had thought to find himself in steaming tropics where heat is heavy throughout the year. The day to which we wakened was bracingly cool, of a crispness that reminded me of fall in New England. And to make the impression quite complete, drifting smoke from somewhere in the district brought the pungent smell of burning leaves.

It must have been on just such an early dawn that Tafai set forth on his second famous voyage. We decided, Tetua and I, to tramp as far as the long promontory of Haapape, or Point Venus—the same on which Captain Cook and his company of scientists stood almost two centuries ago to observe the transit of the planet Venus. Our feet had scarcely touched the firm wet sands by the water's edge when Tetua launched into his tale:

A number of years had passed since Tafai's discovery of the burning islands to the north, and in that time many canoes had crossed the ocean between Tahiti and the new land. Each one had borne a load of settlers who crowded the twin hulls with their livestock, their weapons, and the sacred relics of their family temples. Of all those who left, none returned. But rumors came drifting back along the lonely sea-trail telling of a people grown proud and independent in their adopted country. The departed ones, it was said, now had their own kings and chiefs and priests, and they no longer called themselves Tahitians. Hawaiians they claimed to be, and such, of course, they were. The songs of the homeland became altered and, gradually, the language, too. Even their gods were new, and among the greatest was she who dwelt within the volcano's rim—Pele, goddess of fire, goddess of Burning-Hawaii. But of the many stories which the winds carried southward to old Tahiti not all were of changing custom or religion, and perhaps the most repeated was that which told of the wondrous beauty of a girl. Te-rai, some said her name to be, while others insisted she was called Te-ura; but all agreed that in her, Hawaii had given birth to a flower of unmatched loveliness.

Tafai's cousins—the same three youths who, in their jealousy of his accomplishments, had once made a vain attempt to take his life—were now grown men, warriors of no mean ability. For long they had avoided open hostility with their younger relative, but the old rancor still gnawed at their vitals and there was not one of them who did not dream of somehow, someday, sending red-skinned Tafai into complete eclipse by a great deed of his own. Temata, the oldest and most aggressive of the cousins, had long mulled over the accounts of the far-off Hawaiian beauty before he came to a decision and addressed his brothers.

"Listen to me, Ta and Pua," he said. "Since the day Tafai made fools of us in our games with toy boats, since the day we killed him and buried him in the sand, only to see him brought back to life unharmed, we have waited for our chance to outstrip and humble him. That chance has come. We shall sail to Hawaii where lives a woman more beautiful and wise than any other. We shall woo her, and the one she chooses shall marry her and bring her back to this island. Never will Tafai find a wife to equal her. He will burn with the same jealousy that has tormented us these many years, and the lucky man will be the envy of all others."

Ta and Pua readily agreed to this proposal, and they went down to the shore, where they bailed out their double canoe and began to equip it for the voyage. They fitted sails of freshly woven matting, and they laid aboard vegetables, live fowls, and gourds filled with spring water. A small crowd soon gathered to watch these preparations, and idle questions rose on all sides. Where were they bound? What was the reason for their going, and when would they return?

It would have been better for them if they had kept silent in regard to these matters, but, being natural braggarts, they found this quite impossible. "We are off to Burning-Hawaii," they replied, "and when we return you will see Te-ura of the carmine lips and night-black hair riding with us in our big canoe."

No one had ever before thought to carry off a woman from the warlike Hawaiians, and the news passed from mouth to mouth with more than usual rapidity, till it came at last to Tafai himself. He received the information quietly and made no comment at the time, but his mother noticed that, in the days following, her son appeared strangely preoccupied.

The morning arrived when the three brothers put to sea with a large crew of trained oarsmen, and Tafai watched them go out the pass, lustily chanting songs of their own prowess and of the great things they were about to do. Then he returned to his mother's house, where he seated himself silently beside her.

"You are moody, my son," she remarked. "Does something trouble you?"

"No," he replied, "there is no trouble. But years have passed since I returned from my last voyage. Years have passed since I penetrated Te Po, and once again a restlessness grows upon me."

"You should have a wife, Tafai," said Tahu soberly. "Then perhaps you would be content to stay at home."

"Would a wife still my longing to roam the far-flung oceans?"

Tahu smiled. "Probably nothing could do that, for the longing sings within your blood. Nor could it be otherwise since you are my son. I do not forget that the river, of which I once was goddess, flowed to mingle with the salty deep, and that it is only natural your first love should be the sea. Always, I think, Tafai, you will be a wanderer; but a woman in your house might make more happy the days you spend with us. I see your eyes bent upon the dwindling sail of the canoe in which your cousins ride. Do your thoughts, too, fly toward this girl whom they call Te-ura?"

Tafai tried to hide his confusion with a laugh, but he said truthfully, "Yes, I have thought of her."

"Then go to her," his mother advised. "I could wish your fancy had fallen upon one of our own people, for a girl of Tahiti will always prefer this to any other country, while Te-ura might, in time, yearn for the fiery land from which she came. But if the stories men tell of her are whirling in your mind, you will never be satisfied till you have seen her. So I say to you, go."

Tafai rose and took up the long shaft of his shoulder spear. "Very well," he replied, "I shall go."

"And how do you intend to voyage?"

"Why," said he, surprised by his mother's question, "I shall assemble a crew and fit out my canoe."

"Before you have done that," Tahu pointed out, "Ta, Pua, and Temata will have reached Hawaii."

"That is true. But how else can I do?"

"Take this," she instructed, handing him a small coconut shell. "Place it on the water and it shall be your canoe."

Tafai knew better than to question his mother's words. Carrying spear and oar he went down to the shore and placed the little shell on the surface of the quiet lagoon. Immediately the shell began to grow, and, as its curving sides expanded, a mast, complete with shrouds and tightly plaited sail of frond, sprouted up from the center. When it was large enough to accommodate his tall, muscular frame, Tafai stepped aboard. Holding the tiller in one hand and the sheet in the other he drew away from the beach and skimmed out over the shimmering shallows with a speed nearly equaling that of the feather-light toy which, as a boy, he had set afloat on the same waters. As he swept through the pass, where the transparent green of the lagoon gave way to the blue of the deep, he recited a prayer to his ancestors and then settled back for the long voyage ahead.

At nightfall he made out the tips of the spars on the high-masted vessel that he pursued, but it was still many miles away. The three conceited brothers little suspected the presence of the coconut shell which hurried along, bouncing from wave to wave in their wake.

67

The next morning, however, Temata chanced to look astern. "Ho!" he exclaimed in alarm. "What is this thing like an inverted, winged turtle which follows us?"

"Turtle?" said Pua. "No. It is an *'umete*—a wooden bowl for mixing poi—that has become bewitched."

"*'Umete?*" said Ta, whose eyes were keenest. "No. It is the half of a coconut, and it holds a man with red skin."

"Tafai!" Temata bellowed. "That trickster again! Trim sail; come closer to the wind, and he shall sink once more beyond the broad horizon."

Men scurried over the decks, and the heavy matting of the sail was hoisted to the very peak so that its last square foot might draw wind. The big canoe gained way and charged over the oncoming waves, ploughing its bows through their massed weight and bringing green water aboard at each impact.

"Lighten ship!" Temata shouted. "Take hollowed gourds, and bail; fling out the sea!"

A dozen of the crew grasped bailers and began frantically to toss overboard the brine which raced into the bilges, but when the three brothers looked behind, they saw that Tafai's strange craft continued to gain. Instead of battering and fighting the seas, the incredible coconut appeared to ignore them completely; and the manner in which it skipped lightly from crest to crest could hardly have failed to strike a disinterested spectator as laughable. But to Ta, Pua, and Temata there was nothing amusing in its swift approach.

"Paddles!" Temata screamed. "Out with the paddles!" Two-score blades went over the side and stroked together. But though the men strained their backs and arms and churned the sea right willingly, the distance between the two vessels steadily lessened.

"It is the same accursed story," Temata fumed. "When we were children we fashioned clumsy boats of driftwood while Tafai made his victorious *titiraina* of cane and leaves. And now as men we stand on this bucking, lumbering thing of hollowed logs while that off-color rogue lolls at ease in his absurd saucer." Beside himself with rage, Temata ran down the length of his ship shouting at the fast-tiring paddlers on either side. "Faster," he cried, "faster! Will you let a single man fill us with hot shame? Are you warriors or are your muscles those of babes and women? Faster, I say!" But the crew could do no more, and instead of cutting with swifter blades their strokes became increasingly ragged. At last, when the coconut shell was close abeam, they ceased their efforts entirely and lay upon their paddles exhausted.

68   Tafai waved a hand. "Ahoy, Temata-*ma!*" he called. "*Ia ora na*, clan of Temata, may you live!"

"And may you founder and pass forever from sight," Temata roared, his face black with anger.

Tafai smiled and again waved his hand. The fantastic shell planed on with the wave tips spanking merrily on its rounded bottom, and at last it disappeared beyond the horizon.

When, a number of days later, the disgruntled brothers disembarked on the Hawaiian coast they discovered Tafai's fantastic craft beached nearby. They had barely put foot ashore when they saw its skipper coming to meet them.

"You have been a long time on the way," Tafai observed when he stood beside them with his big spear balanced on his shoulder. "But I would not take advantage of you; I have waited. Now, if you are ready, we will go in search of the young woman who has brought us so many thousand miles from home."

Tafai's cousins were at no pains to disguise their displeasure at his presence, but they fell sullenly into step with him, and together the four men set off for the largest of the Hawaiian villages, where the fabled Te-ura was known to live. Evidently a lookout had detected the arrival of the Tahitians, because when they entered the settlement the streets already were lined with people. Several tattooed warriors stepped forward and promptly led the newcomers into the council house of the chief.

Tafai regarded the island ruler appraisingly. "It is clear," he thought, "that food is plentiful here. How otherwise could this man's girth so nearly approximate his height?"

The corpulent chief was seated cross-legged on the floor, and he looked up at Tafai from beneath bushy brows with an unfriendly expression. "Do you come to settle?" he demanded.

"No," Tafai answered frankly, "we would exchange Tahiti for no other island."

"Then why are you here?"

It had been Tafai's intention to await a more favorable opportunity before broaching the reason of the visit, but before he could stop him Temata blurted, "We have come so that Te-ura may look upon us and choose the one she would prefer for a husband."

A frown creased the chief's brow. "Te-ura is my daughter," he said slowly, "and I think she has no need of a foreigner for a mate. Has it not occurred to you that we Hawaiians have young men aplenty, all of them suitable husbands for our women?"

"If Te-ura is all she is reported to be," Temata continued rashly, "she should marry a man of prowess."

The chief laughed briefly, and it was not a pleasant laugh. "I see you hold a high opinion of yourself. Am I to accept your word for your rare abilities?"

"My brothers will confirm what I say. In Tahiti I am thought a great warrior."   *69*

"And what of this man who says so little? What do you call yourself?"

"Tafai is my name."

"Well, Tafai, are you also a great warrior?"

"That," he replied simply, "I will leave for you to judge if you care to put me to the test."

The chief nodded ponderously. "Your words have a sound I like better than your friend's. Never fear, we shall give you four a chance to prove what sort of men you are." He glanced at one of his guards who stood nearby—a big, barrel-chested man whose dark face bore a bright, deeply slashed battle scar. "What do you say, Keolo? Shall we let them pit their strength against the 'Ava?"

Keolo bared strong teeth in a wide grin. "There will be sport for the people," he said with relish. "Let all assemble to watch them die."

Temata paled. "What is this 'Ava of which you speak?"

"You will see in due time," the chief replied. "However, if it will put you more at ease, I shall tell you that no man has survived who dared to challenge it."

The three brothers looked at each other uncertainly, but Tafai said calmly: "If we are to risk our lives, grant us to see first the one for whom we do it. Perhaps the tales which reach Tahiti have, in their passage, grown out of all proportion to the truth."

"That is a reasonable request," Te-ura's father agreed. "Lead my daughter here, Keolo, and let these gallant suitors judge for themselves."

The warrior left and soon returned, preceded by a tall young maiden of fifteen or sixteen years of age. Looking neither to right nor left, and walking with the assured, easy grace of those born to high position, she went straight to her father.

"You have sent for me?" she asked with a trace of annoyance, as if she had been interrupted in some pleasant pastime.

"Here are four lusty fellows who have come all the way from Tahiti for imagined love of you," said the chief.

Now Te-ura took notice of the strangers. Clearly, her beauty was such that she must have had many suitors since first she reached maturity. But probably the woman never lived who would not feel a stir of interest at sight of a man who had crossed an ocean on her account. The girl's eyes passed over Ta and Pua and Temata, then came to rest on Tafai. She smiled in ingenuous delight. "This one is handsome. And see the color of his skin! I think he takes it from the sky at sunset."

"You are not here for your own entertainment, daughter," the chief reproved, "but only that these men may see for what reason they go to meet the 'Ava."

"The 'Ava!" she exclaimed. "Are they so soon tired of life?"

"No," her father answered grimly, "but they have come hoping to take our greatest treasure back to their little island. This they would not do if they did not think themselves superior to those who live beneath the burning mountain. So we shall see." He turned to the four voyagers. "What is your decision, Tahitians? Do you still persist, or will you now sail back the way you came?"

All this while Tafai had not removed his eyes from Te-ura. The tales which were told, he concluded, were the truth. Never before had he seen such slender loveliness. And if the tilt of her chin or the bold glance of her dark eyes betrayed an overly proud and willful temperament, those were characteristics which would soften once she had found the man who was her equal. Tafai felt himself to be that man, and so he said, "The tales are true; I am ready to fight for her."

"What about your companions?"

"They will have to speak for themselves."

Although Temata and his brothers had been no less impressed by Te-ura than was Tafai, their longing to possess her was much diluted by the peril into which they had stumbled. But to leave the field to their detested rival was unthinkable, and one after the other they muttered their willingness to continue.

The chief heaved himself to his feet. "This," he remarked, smacking his thick lips in anticipation, "will be a day which we Hawaiians shall long remember. Have the conch shells sounded, Keolo. Summon the people to assemble on the borders of the plain where Te 'Ava stands, deep rooted and unbending in the dark, volcanic soil."

Within a few minutes the exodus from the village began. The trumpeting of conchs and the shouts of criers announcing the coming contests rang in the streets. "Leave your homes, Hawaiians," they called. "Leave your tapa-beating, your poi-making, your thatch-weaving, your talking and singing. Come out from beneath your roofs; come out to witness the sport which our great chief will provide. Take the paths to the broad, bare field that is swept by the revolving shadow of the demon tree! Four men from the distant south will do battle there today. Come, and you shall see their struggles with Hawaii's tree possessed. It is Te 'Ava! Te 'Ava, whose eight radiating roots writhe upon the bone-strewn ground; whose ninth root draws blind strength from the darkness at earth's center; whose black spirit gropes unceasingly for the flesh of man. Te 'Ava is the tree; Tahitians are the victims; Burning-Hawaii is the place!"

Such were the words of the criers, and the people streamed out of the village, crowding the trail, pressing on to the desert field while dogs and children, catching the general excitement, raced barking and shouting back and forth along the line. Not a soul was left behind. Those who were too old or infirm to walk were carried on the shoulders of the young; tots who had not yet learned to walk rode upon the broad hips of their mothers. Te-ura had gone to wrap her finest cloth about her body in honor of the occasion. Her father had donned his feathered helmet, and a long necklace of shark's teeth hung down to his expansive stomach. When all the populace stood crowding about the field, drums sounded. The chieftain and his party had arrived and now crossed the open space and made their way to their mats. Following them, and accompanied by the stern-visaged Keolo, came the four Tahitians.

"Is that the tree?" Tafai demanded, when his eyes fell upon the solitary tree standing on the plain.

"It is Te 'Ava," Keolo replied.

"I have seen many a larger one in Tahiti."

"Te 'Ava does not waste its strength in reaching for the sun," the Hawaiian explained. "It hugs the ground, it grips the dense, impacted earth with an embrace none has ever loosened, and its anchor is Te Po. Here, stranger, in its enfolding roots, your travels will end as have those of many another man."

Tafai came near the place where Te-ura had seated herself beside her father. She was in the act of arranging a large red blossom in her hair, but when his shadow passed over her she looked up, and for the second time she smiled. "You must succeed, Red-Skin," she whispered. "You must win if you would have me come to you."

The Tahitians took their place, a little apart, as Keolo indicated. Tafai lowered his spear till the point rested at his feet, and he leaned upon it with both hands clasped about the thick, tough shaft. An end to his travels? "No," he thought, as he gazed at Te-ura of the glowing eyes and vibrant youth, "that surely cannot be. I see before me a journey more fascinating than any I have made, one leading as far as ripe old age, a long voyage, rich in companionship, on which this girl and I shall embark together. I think not the end, but the beginning, lies at the foot of this demon tree."

At a signal from the chief the conchs were blown again, and the chatter of the crowd was stilled. "Are you ready, Tahitians?" he demanded of Tafai.

"We are ready."

"Then we shall begin. I am a fair man, otherwise I should not be chief of a great nation. For that reason it is my command that the eldest among you shall attack first, and the youngest last. In that manner he who has had the least experience of life shall draw a few additional breaths while awaiting his turn, and I consider that to be just and fitting."

This display of the chief's wisdom was met with a murmur of approval, but Temata, to whose lot thus fell the opening contest, seemed unappreciative. He remained silent and made no move to advance.

"Come now," said Tafai after a moment. "Take your spear and strike lustily, as befits a warrior of Tahiti."

Only then did Temata take a step forward. He took another and another but they were cautious steps, hesitant and reluctant, and they clearly betrayed his fear.

Cries of derision soon broke from the spectators. "Is this the one who calls himself great in battle? Are no warriors left in old Tahiti since we Hawaiians came away? Attack, or lay down your spear and run to your ship and to safety."

This last Temata would have been pleased to do, but even stronger than his fear of death was his fear of ridicule. He advanced toward the unnatural monster which confronted him, but he was still a hundred yards away when suddenly he stopped, and his eyes widened in nameless dread. The 'Ava moved. The upper branches swayed as if shaken by a human hand or by a quick gust of wind; but no man was nearer than Temata, and there was no breeze. The trembling of the leaves increased, the sibilant sound of their rustling filling Temata's ears, whispering to him of doom; and in the next instant he saw the ground all about the squat, thick trunk stir with sinuous movement. Sensing, with some unknown faculty, the approach of a victim, the eight reaching arms of the 'Ava came to snakelike life. They spread, coiling and twisting, over the barren earth; they raised tentacle tips in the air to sway from side to side, feeling blindly for a form about which to twine, for a body to crush, a life to extinguish. With a gasp of horror Temata fell back.

The chief turned angrily to Keolo. "Drag him from the field," he commanded. "We have come to watch deeds of valor, not an exhibition of cowardice. Enough of these Tahitians with hearts of timid fowls!"

Keolo started to do as he was bidden when Tafai stopped him with a word. "Do not interfere," said he. "Temata will attack; he only awaits a sign from me."

Tafai had little reason to hold any affection for his cousin. At that moment he was thinking of him, however, neither as a relative nor as a rival, but simply as a Tahitian who was in danger of disgracing his homeland. On that account he chose words carefully calculated to serve the purpose and, cupping his hands to his mouth, shouted: "Temata! Remember the contests of our youth. Who was it that took from you the prizes for the shooting of arrows, the running of races, the swimming, the diving? It was Tafai. Now, throw down your spear; leave the 'Ava to me. 'Who killed the 'Ava?' people will ask; and others will answer, always the same, 'It was Tafai!' "

Tafai was far from feeling the confidence which these words would indicate, but when they reached Temata they had the effect he intended. The lifelong jealousy he had harbored against his younger cousin flared up, and the black rage that followed it drove every other thought from his head. "It shall be Temata who conquers," he growled, "and may that red-skinned devil pass into final oblivion!" He rushed forward and had come to the distance of a spear's cast from the trunk when a great root shot out and clasped him about his middle. Temata was lifted, struggling helplessly, high into the air, high above the top of the rocking tree, then whipped down with terrific force and dashed against the hard ground below. In less than a minute Temata himself had attained a very permanent sort of oblivion.

"One is gone and three remain," cried the onlookers. "Who goes next to feel the power which the 'Ava sucks from the underworld?"

73

The chief peered up through his shaggy brows at Tafai, who leaned upon his spear with expression unchanged. "Tell me, captain of the coco-shell canoe, do you continue to desire my daughter for a wife?"

"She appears no less fair to me," Tafai answered stoutly.

"Perhaps," said the beplumed ruler, "you will be of another mind before your turn arrives. The 'Ava thrives upon those it destroys; its fury mounts with each one crushed. Let us hope there is a better man among you than he who called himself Temata. Who then, of those still living is the oldest? Step forth."

Pua went against the tree bravely, but, although like his brother he advanced slowly, the end of his journey to extinction came with a speed that was breathtaking and horrible. The moment he had come within reach he was seized by an encircling root and drawn with a rush against the trunk, where the other tentacles folded about him, snuffing out his life.

The people shouted, but the chief grew impatient and scornful. "So far," he grumbled, "you provide us with little entertainment. Many Hawaiians have done better. Cannot one of you land a blow?"

Ta was as swift of foot as he was keen of eye, and, without waiting for the command, he darted off across the field, dodging, twisting, and turning so nimbly that the 'Ava at first sought for him in vain, and a spontaneous cry of applause broke from the people. He gained the trunk and struck it with his spear, but as well might he have struck the foundations of Hawaii's burning mountain. Goaded by the pinprick of Ta's weapon, the 'Ava plucked the unfortunate Tahitian from its base as if it removed some plaguing insect, whirled him round and round above the highest shuddering branches, then suddenly released him, and he hurtled through the air to fall with a sickening thud directly at Tafai's feet.

Tafai looked down at the sprawled, inert body. "You fought with spirit, Ta," he murmured, "but the heart of the 'Ava lies not within its trunk." Then to the chief he said: "These men were not my friends, yet they were of my blood. You have set each one of them an impossible task and now all are dead. In my country, when strangers arrive from across the seas, we heat the ovens and prepare feasts. We make music and contrive dances in their honor, that the days they spend with us may be happy ones. I see that you in the north now have other customs, harsh customs, and that you yourselves have grown hard."

"We are warriors," the chief corrected, "and hold pity to be a weakness. Does your courage flag?"

"It does not," Tafai replied. "But when I have won Te-ura for myself I shall take her speedily from so inhospitable a land."

74

"Te-ura is sprung from this soil. She is of Hawaii and will never consent to leave it," said the older man confidently.

"A woman should put her husband first and follow him wherever he may go."

The chief dropped the shark-tooth ornament with which he had been toying and waved his hand impatiently. "There will be time enough for such discussion when you stand before us victorious. The 'Ava waits. Have done with talk."

In answer Tafai lifted up his mighty spear and faced the demon-tree.

"No," Te-ura exclaimed suddenly, and then, heedless of her father's frown, the words came quickly from her lips. "Go no nearer to the 'Ava or your fate will be the same as that of the many who have preceded you. You are too handsome to die, Tafai. You have shown your willingness to fight for me; be content to live forever in Hawaii, and I shall gladly be your wife." She sprang up and came close to him. "Stay with me, Tafai," she pleaded, "and I shall cause you to forget Tahiti and all that you have ever known."

Tafai put her gently aside.

"You will die!" she cried. "Turn back, turn back!"

But Tafai was already on his way across the bleak field whose soil had drunk so much of blood and seen so much of tragedy. With steady and determined gait he marched, his four-inch-thick shaft of ironwood gripped solidly, its point aimed low and his eyes fixed unswervingly upon the deadly foe. At sight of the great red-skinned warrior who walked so boldly, so confidently past the bodies of his slain comrades, toward the same enemy that had struck them down, a tremendous cheer rose from the watching throng. Here at last, they sensed, was one who would not easily succumb, one who would fight to the last breath, giving Hawaiians a subject for song and talk for many a year. And as Tafai approached, the 'Ava also seemed to feel, in some dark, mysterious way, the nearing of real challenge. A tremor ran through it, and it shook as if seized by a paroxysm of rage. Dust rose in a cloud from the ground where lashed the outspread roots, obscuring the wildly tossing upper branches which clashed together with the clanging rattle of dry bones. Never had such fury, such lust to kill, been seen in Hawaii, and with the earth trembling beneath their feet the crowd looked on in silent awe.

"Tree of demons," came Tafai's deep-throated shout, "tree bewitched by the fiends of night, tree called Te 'Ava, it is I—it is Tafai! Tafai, who purged the hordes of Uru from the world below. Beat your grasping arms, whip your heavy boughs, fill the air with screaming winds. Not so will you avoid defeat by Tafai!"

The last of the Tahitians charged into the maze of writhing roots, driving straight for the base of the trunk. On he dashed, past the frantically searching tentacles, his spear held tight against his body. Racing at full speed, with all the weight and momentum of his rugged frame behind the blow, he plunged the sharp-pointed shaft deep into the black earth, deep into the downward-sinking, downward-clutching taproot of the 'Ava. Quickly the constricting arms wound about him. The dust settled, and the people watched in wide-eyed amazement. Where before was frenzied motion, now they beheld two antagonists who, save for the quivering

75

which betrayed titanic effort, stood stock still. Where before was awful clamor, now there was silence broken only by a faint snapping in the tree's taut limbs. The tentacles strained upward seeking to snatch Tafai aloft as they had all others, but Tafai clung to his spear, to the spear of iron-like wood, buried now in the very heart of Te 'Ava. The harder the encircling bands about him pulled and wrenched, the more tenaciously he gripped his weapon, prying, always prying at the monster's vitals. So for long moments while all Hawaii held its breath, the man and the living tree remained in deadly struggle, swaying almost imperceptibly back and forth. First the 'Ava, gaining slight advantage, lifted the Tahitian's heels from the ground, and then Tafai, taking new hold upon his mighty lever, brought himself back to earth.

Long since, the ponderous chief had risen to his feet to stand spellbound like his subjects. Now he raised a fist in the air, and a roar of admiration and encouragement burst from his throat, shaking the strings of shark's teeth upon his chest. "Hold fast!" he bellowed. "Hold fast, champion of fire-glowing skin, and men of all the islands will do you honor!"

"Hold!" shouted the people, taking up the cry. "Hold, hold!" they chorused all together.

If Tafai heard he could give no sign. Tighter, ever tighter, the bonds clamped about his sweating body; more, ever more, they lifted him from his stance, and always with greater difficulty he regained unstable footing. Only by a last mighty effort could he win the victory. It must be quick; it must be now.

"Up," he groaned aloud. "Up, accursed taproot, long eel which twines craven in the dark below. Up into the light and die!"

With legs widespread, with knees half bent, with arching back and straining arms, Tafai heaved himself on his spear. He flexed the sturdy shaft till it curved like a well-drawn bow, till it trembled like a thing alive, till there came a rumbling and crackling from far down in the earth. Again the topmost branches of the 'Ava shook, but this time it was not a dance of vengeful fury, but the agonized shudder of a creature which feels the mortal wound. Up came the trunk, up came the torn, bleeding roots, up came the entire fiend-ridden tree, ripped from its anchorage by the terrific thrust of Tafai's shaft. Lifted into the air, it hung momentarily with arms sprawled like a huge spider flung against the sun—then crashed, a writhing, shapeless mass. Immediately Tafai was upon it, beating down the roots and branches which still moved, slashing the sinister 'Ava till every part was still. Only then did he lower his spear. Only then did the ring of spectators, who had watched the final overthrow of Hawaii's terror, break into mad acclaim and rush out onto the field to surround the hero who had vanquished it.

No man expected to see another miracle on that day. But it will be recalled that in his youth Tafai had, at his mother's direction, opened his mouth above her head and so absorbed the water nymph's magical powers. Now, with as little trouble as his mother had then experienced in restoring him to life, Tafai stepped to the side of his kinsmen and one after another, in the order in which they had left it, brought back to the living world Temata, Pua, and Ta. Great was the amazement of the Hawaiians, and to Te-ura and her father it was clear that in Tafai she had a suitor who, besides being a hero, possessed unusual abilities.

Tafai presented himself before the chief. "With your permission I will take the wife I have won and return to my own country. Before leaving I will tell you a secret which may serve to lessen your sorrow in losing your daughter: sever the roots of this defeated tree; let all the maidens of your island be given the task of chewing them; add water to the well-chewed pulp and then strain the whole. You will have a drink which will gladden all Hawaii. One thing more I will tell you: use it sparingly lest the demons that I have stamped out come to life again in the bodies of those who imbibe."

Tafai then went to Te-ura and took her hand. "I have walked in great danger to possess this small hand," said he, "but I am well pleased; your beauty will adorn my homeland. Come, we shall go to my ship." To his astonishment the girl drew away. "How is this?" he demanded. "Is my color less pleasing when it is dimmed by the dust of battle?"

"No, Tafai I love you more than I did before."

"Then gather your belongings and chose those attendants you would have to serve you."

But Te-ura shook her head. "I cannot leave Hawaii."

" 'Cannot'? What is the meaning of that? If your legs refuse to walk I shall carry you!" And before she could protest, Tafai gathered her up in his arms.

The chief placed a detaining hand on his shoulder. "Force will avail you nothing," he said quietly. "If you take her unwillingly she may never live to see the shore for which you sail."

Slowly Tafai lowered the girl to the ground, and for a long moment he remained gazing at her thoughtfully. "I begin to think," he observed at last, "that perhaps I had done better to listen more carefully to my mother's words. 'I could wish,' she said to me, 'that you had chosen one of us, for a girl of Tahiti will prefer it always to any other land.' But my brain was filled with visions of Te-ura; I was headstrong. And so also," he exclaimed suddenly, "is your daughter. Does she not realize that Tahiti is first of all the islands, that its brooding temples are the largest, its mountains highest, its lagoons broadest, its flowers brightest?"

"All that you say may be true," the chief replied, "but Te-ura's home is here."   *77*

"And have I beaten my way across the seas to this place of soot and ashes and feeble friendship all for nothing? Have I torn up and destroyed the 'Ava only to return with empty hands? No, I do not so easily release that which I have won."

The chief and those others who had gathered near fell back at the violence of his outburst, but Tafai's fury mounted. "Temata!" he shouted. "Ta, Pua, and Temata! Listen to me. Another task is here to confront us, and these are my commands. Take the husks of a thousand coconuts, take the bark of scores of *purau*, weave strands, weave cords, weave ropes longer, tougher, stronger than man has ever done before. Make hawsers the girth of my own thigh, and drag them to the sea. I am Tafai—and Tafai does not return alone. I shall go, and I shall take Hawaii with me!"

Whether the brief visit the three brothers had made to the beyond had caused a change in their characters, or whether their gratitude at being brought back to life overshadowed the jealousy that had so long rankled within them, is hard to say. Possibly only the fact is important and not the reason for it. They went to work with a will, with such fervor and enthusiasm for Tafai's stupendous scheme that the by-standers, at first merely curious, were seized by the same contagious energy. Soon great numbers, as if working under a spell, were busily plaiting and weaving, binding and splicing the native barks and fibers. Before a day had passed huge piles of rope lay heaped by the shore.

Then, at Tafai's curt command, the double canoe of his cousins was set afloat upon the bay. Lines were made fast astern and run to the boles of coconut palms at the beach's edge and to other trees farther inland. Stout cords were bound about great boulders, about the jutting pinnacles of cliffs, and about the crest of hills. The largest hawser of all, fashioned by Tafai's own hand, stretched up to the nearest mountain peak.

When all was in readiness Tafai-of-the-Red-Skin stepped into his coconut shell, and, attaching to his craft a single great rope from the bow of the double canoe, he pushed out ahead. Standing tall and straight beside the mast, he called to the thousands who crowded the sandy shore. "People of Hawaii! Stand quietly, and by neither word nor deed distract us from our earnest purpose." His eyes turned to his cousins and to the alert crew manning the big canoe. "Tahitians! At my signal, hoist your sail and dip your paddle blades. We shall move, and with us shall go all this great northern land with its plains and valleys, its rivers and forests, its men and women. From my mother, Tahu of Tahiti, will come magic power. But heed my warning: keep eyes to the south and do not turn back or the invisible thread will snap and her *mana* cease to flow."

Tafai stooped, grasped the sheet, and for a minute stood unmoving as though listening to the all-pervading, expectant hush which hovered over the bay. "Up sails," he cried, "and brush the scudding clouds. Down paddles and scrape coral from the ocean's bed. Leap forward, my flying shell; leap forward, canoe of Temata. Draw, ropes of sennit, come taut and hard and straight; you are the tendons, you are the sinews that shall bind Tahiti and Hawaii and make them one!"

Strong hands pulled on the lines, and the spreading mats rose up and caught the breeze. Strong arms swung the paddles and took hold upon the sea. The tow cords lifted dripping lengths from the bay, stretched tensely and arrow-straight to tree and stone and crag and hill. Tafai's ship of coco shell surged over the water; the double canoe charged into the blue-green waves, and, while the throng upon the strand stared, their smoke-plumed island stirred, shuddered, and started ahead, parting the ocean deep. Jutting headlands cut through the onrushing billows, bald-faced cliffs battered aside the rolling swells, and spume soared skyward to drench the shores, the plateaus, and even the central forests, with cool, salty rain.

"O my mother," Tafai exulted as, with never a backward glance, he clasped the sheet and tiller, "your magic is a power which draws me ever home. It enabled me to part the 'Ava from its clutch within Te Po, and now Hawaii has let go its hold upon the bottom of the sea!"

From every side cries soon arose upon the land and although some were joyful, many more were sad or rang with stark dismay.

"We are lost, lost!" an old woman wailed. "The ground moves beneath us, and gone is all stability!"

"She is right," Keolo of the lurid battle scar growled angrily. "We are led on a leash like a pig drawn to slaughter."

The chief nodded solemnly. "Sovereign Hawaii is no longer its own master but moves tamely in the wake of this man of wizardry. It is an evil day, my people, and when I gaze into the future I see our life and customs fading, our very name forgotten, all swallowed by the mother country from which we broke away."

Bitter tears started down Te-ura's brown cheeks. "What woe," she sobbed. "What sorrow, what weight of grief! Shall my native soil melt away in the embracing ocean? Shall it drift on to form a humble appendage, a mere footstool for the grasping southern woman called Tahiti? I would rather die if by so doing I might prevent so terrible a tragedy!" Despondently the girl flung herself into her father's arms, pressing her face against his broad chest till the shark teeth bit into her flesh.

Abstractedly, the chief stroked her hair while he murmured his compassion. Then, suddenly, he put her from him. Holding her at arm's length he looked deeply into her brimming eyes. "Your death would accomplish nothing, Te-ura," said he speaking slowly and distinctly. "Living you may wield a magic more powerful than that of the man with reddish skin."

"How?" she demanded, quickly brushing away the tears. "Only tell me how!"

A faint smile touched her father's lips. "You are young, my child, but do you not yet realize the strength you hold? What, think you, brought so great a warrior as Tafai to our shores? Will you say, 'the wind, the unseen current, the restless tide, the draw of sail or stroke of paddle'? No, none of these. A tale of beauty sent him forth, a rumor of loveliness carried him on, a vision of delight winged him over the swirling waters. You were the vision, yours the beauty. Te-ura was the lure, Tafai was the fish."

"And instead of catching we are caught."

"You heard Tafai's words to his men: 'Do not look back lest our *mana* leave us'. Does it tell you nothing? Does it not tell you how you, though a girl of tender years, may break the charm and plant Hawaii firmly once more on the ocean floor? In your body you hold all the enchanting mystery of our great island. It is a wonder from which no man can turn away. Make use of it and snap the bonds which drag us southward to the sluggish seas of Tafai's homeland; make use of it and break the ties which draw us toward the dominating parent of our race. Dance, Te-ura. Dance the hula of Hawaii!"

Always the hula has been a dance of love, but never has it spoken of a love so deep as it did upon that day. It told not of Te-ura's affection for a single man, but of her passion for a land and people. A dozen youths snatched up as many cloven coco shells, others seized dried sticks, a broken gourd, a seed-filled calabash. In a circle by the shore they flung themselves down and began to beat quick rhythm. With a clap of hands Te-ura leaped in before them. Facing the sea, facing Tafai's steadily advancing ships, standing where cool wavelets washed her nimbly moving feet, she swung into the dance. Salt wind ran rippling through her hair; salt spray fell upon her parted lips, upon her supple, undulating arms, and upon the fine, swaying fringes of her skirt. There, at the brink of the sea, she wove a pattern of fantasy, a design which reflected all the haunting beauty of the land where she was born. Te-ura's hula echoed the movement of bird and cloud and fish, the gay nodding of wind-brushed leaves and flowers, the burst of volcanic flame, the cascading turbulence of mountain streams, the gentle fall of rain. Words of an ancient chant she fitted to her dance—a siren song well calculated to turn the most determined mariner from his intended course. Down to leeward it drifted and reached the ears of Tafai and all who went with him. Only see, it said to them, the pleasures which lie so close behind. You have but to pause, to stop, to turn about, to find the potent, heady magic which is all Hawaii.

Not by so much as the twitch of a facial muscle did Tafai betray the great desire he felt to wheel, to rush back and accept gladly all that Te-ura offered. He gripped fast the tiller, his eyes fixed straight ahead. In the double canoe of Temata also there was no man who had not the feeling that in Te-ura's seductive song all nature cried out to him to abandon every other thing and look behind. But the crew, mindful of Tafai's last command, held to their paddles and kept on.

There are some who will say that Tafai would have done better never to have brought back to life the three cousins who had already caused him so much trouble. It is likely, however, that many more will agree that in the stupendous enterprise in which he was now engaged Tafai was moved by a mistaken zeal and that, all in all, it is a more attractive world with Hawaii still remaining in one place and Tahiti in another. In any case, so it was to be. The brothers stood in the stern of their vessel, and in this fact some slight excuse for their conduct may be found. They were nearest to the tantalizing music and to the lodestone that was Te-ura. For a moment, as they looked uncertainly into each other's faces, the disposition of the Pacific islands hung in the balance. Then, in a common impulse, the brothers whirled about.

Even as the wills of Ta, Pua, and Temata had snapped, the great cables which bound them to the land now burst asunder with loud report. Hawaii came to a rigid halt and, as is commonly known, never moved again.

Tafai stood up in his ship, and for a moment his great body shook with rage. But just as quickly his anger left him. On the shore he saw the gathered people, in an excess of joy at their liberation, throw themselves into the fervid dance, and in the center of them all, with head flung back and inexpressible gladness shining on her lovely face, was Te-ura. Tafai shrugged his red-bronzed shoulders. "Well," he thought, "I have had successes and today very nearly garnered still another. But the gods have decreed it is not to be." He waved the abject brothers forward, then seated himself and took new hold upon the helm.

Again the coconut shell skimmed lightly over the waves, bringing Tahiti nearer with each slapping impact, and as he went Tafai discovered with some surprise that his heart was very light. He had gone no more than a few leagues when suddenly he nodded his head with vigor. "You were right, my mother," he said aloud, "and I have made a long voyage only to discover what now I feel with surety: my wife waits for me at this moment on Tahiti's priceless soil."

Queen Putu and
the Whales of Nuku Hiva

TETUA and I had walked briskly, but the day was well advanced before we reached the goal we had set for ourselves—Point Venus. The air had lost its early freshness, and during the last mile I was beginning to feel the sands pushing retardingly against my feet. Though Tetua had been speaking all the while, giving full value to every dramatic incident of the tale of Tafai, his stride had lost none of its strong, free rhythm. Perhaps he found tonic in the sound of his own richly vibrant voice, drawing even more pleasure from the telling than I did from the listening.

Always I marveled that his strenuous activities took so little toll of his resources; and when we came to the point of land where the lighthouse stands, he appeared as fresh as he had at dawn. When I sank down gratefully in the shade of the tower with my back to the cool masonry, he joined me, however, without complaint. We made cigarettes and lighted them, and for some while I had been lost in the sort of waking doze which so often accompanies complete physical comfort in tropical countries. My eyes, although they rested on the succession of marching waves which stretched away before us in the direction of Bora Bora, at first perceived nothing. Then, quite suddenly, I saw it. In the near distance a column of spray shot into the air.

"Look," I exclaimed, sitting bolt upright. "Look there, Tetua!"

He smiled and nodded. "Yes, Viriamu. A whale. Have you never seen one before?"

By that time I was on my feet, gazing out to sea in the hope of catching a glimpse of the big mammal rolling its ponderous length through the waves. But there was no sign of it, nor did the spout show again.

"He must have sounded," I said seating myself once more beside my friend. Then, tardily, I answered his question. "In all these years it is the first I have seen blow."

"That is not surprising," Tetua observed a little sadly. "Like much else I would gladly see restored, they are nearly vanished from this part of the Pacific. Once they were many. So also were the vessels that came hunting and destroying them.

Whaling ships still touched here in my own boyhood, and from my father I have heard how their masts used to make a forest in the harbor of Papeete. A brave sight it must have been, yet I do not regret having been born too late to witness it, any more than I grieve not to have seen the lusty tars who then overran our island. Hardly a day is said to have passed when the cries of '*Tero, tero!*' did not echo down from lookouts posted in the trees hailing a new arrival."

"*Tero?*"

Again Tetua smiled. "You do not know that word? It was what we Tahitians made of the whalers' shout, 'Sail ho'. But," he continued, "the invaders did far more than add new words to our speech, and the evidence of it is still with us in impoverished blood, sickness, abandoned *tapu*, and forgotten ways of life." Suddenly he gave a vigorous slap to his bare knee. "Let us talk of other matters. There is no reason why our minds should dwell on things that are beyond repair and far from giving pleasure. We can, instead, look back on happier times. If you are in the mood, I could tell you a story of whales in the days when they served our people well and when, far from putting a bounty on their dead bodies, we justly punished those who killed them."

I crossed my legs comfortably before me. "Do so, Tetua."

"Very well," he replied, "I will."

In the Marquesas Islands, some eight to nine hundred miles to the north of us, there lived long ago upon the island called Nuku Hiva a woman by the name of Putu. Putu had the appearance of a queen—and such she was. Polynesian women are by nature stately, and even in those of humble birth one often sees a bearing little short of regal. In Putu this racial trait appeared at its finest. Her walk, her expression, her every gesture spoke of authority and the habit of command. She had beauty, too, although it was of a coolly austere sort, aloof and proud. Ten years and more she had been widowed, yet in all that while, so detached was she, so unapproachable, so bound by exacting *tapu*, that no man of Nuku Hiva ever dared to speak to her of love. Putu was, however, a woman of great contrasts, and there were times when she dropped the unbending dignity of a ruler as she might have let fall the gauze-fine tapa which wrapped her graceful body. At such times she would unbind the circling coronet of her hair, letting it stream out upon the wind, and, casting aside all restraint, she would revel gloriously in complete freedom. Yet she was then even less accessible than when cloaked in her more customary reserve, for she would forsake the confining land for the playground of the far seas. Not by canoe did she go, not by boat or raft or ship. How, you ask? Astride the huge bull whale, Tokama! At such times Putu forgot all the cares of state, forgot even that she was queen, and if she had any lover in the world it was the great sperm whale, or else the sea itself.

83

To this day there is dispute among those who still speak of her as to just what urge sent Putu forth so frequently from the confines of her kingdom. Some say it was restlessness and an innate impatience of the rigid laws, the many *tapu* and injunctions which then governed island life. Others claim it was a desire to explore the seas and have knowledge of other islands. More likely than either of these, it was simply joy in exuberant, untrammeled movement, joy in being near, in being a part of, the dark-blue living ocean, the clouds and rains and broadly sweeping winds. Despite Tokama's high-spirited, lunging progress, it was rest and refreshment which Putu found upon the whale's gigantic, friendly back. There no other duty called than to thrill to the next oncoming wave, the next school of flying fish or leaping dolphin, the next view of strange, distant land and waving palms.

However far behind Putu might leave her people, she was not alone on her exciting voyages. She shared them with the two beings who were closest and dearest to her—her daughters. And as Putu had twin daughters, so had Tokama twin sons. Flanking the queen on either side, flushed with the wild radiance of early youth, each girl rode her own sportive, not yet full-grown whale. What a sight they made—the three royal women of Nuku Hiva, the three warm-blooded chargers of the deep. Little wonder that the memory of them still haunts the minds of men. Often they were glimpsed by dwellers on lonely atolls, by fishermen of Vavau Island, by posted lookouts in Tahiti, but never fully, never clearly. Passing the shores, they kept well to sea, usually traveling in the midst of small storms where cold air swirls and all is brief and furious energy. There, in the center of hurrying squalls, they might be seen, though only fleetingly, tantalizingly. A man would catch the reflection of wet, brown limbs, the shadow of wind-tossed manes of hair, the glistening of sleek-backed whales or the hazy plumes of their vapory breath. Seeing no more, he would stand entranced till the merrily blustering cloud had passed from sight bearing its glad company below the horizon and then, one supects, might plod dejectedly back to his house, there to stare with momentary impatience into the face of a faithful but perhaps heavy-footed wife.

Yes, Putu and her roving daughters were enough to make the fairest of ordinary stay-at-home women look very tame in comparison, albeit such was far from the queen's intention. They realized as well as you and I that few but queens and princesses are free to roam the earth at will, and it is fortunately so. For who, otherwise, would nurse the babes; who would plait the roofing thatch, light the candlenuts, and feed the evening fires? Most people are born to fulfill similar honest, humble tasks, but there are others who seem as clearly destined to decorate the world, to leave forever in their paths happy memories of elusive beauty, echoes of joyous laughter, and the taste of boundless zest for life. Such, certainly, were Queen Putu and the princesses Rua and Tahine, and it is cause for pity that they no longer live to brighten the ocean with their gay, tempestuous passage. A pity, too, that ever since the days of which I speak the descendants of the faithful Tokama and his sons have moved to the loneliest of the deep sea trails and now completely dissociate themselves from men.

This is the story of how the glad wanderings of Putu, her daughters, and the three whales came to an end. It is in part sad, in part grim, but so it is told.

It was evening of the third day following Queen Putu's departure on one of her periodic voyages. The sun had barely set when a lookout, no longer blinded by the reddish glare, called down from his perch among the uppermost fronds of a tall coconut tree which stood hard by the royal village.

"They blow," he cried. "In the west, they blow!"

Hurriedly the people gathered on the shore to watch, fascinated, as with powerful driving strokes of their enormous flukes the whales raced into the mountain-rimmed harbor, then slowed to glide serenely through the open gates of the great coral basin which was their home. The two girls and their mother slipped from their mounts and swam the short distance to shore, where loving hands waited to draw them up onto firm ground, to wrap dry, sweetly scented cloth about their bodies, and to wreathe their heads with flowers. This done, the three women walked to the royal dwelling, followed closely by the priests and chiefs and, at a greater distance, by all the villagers. Inside the spacious pandanus-roofed house, lights already glowed and food was spread upon green banana fronds. Because Putu, Rua, and Tahine never paused to eat during their extensive travels they were very hungry and promptly gathered about the waiting feast. Like all Polynesians, the queen and princesses ate with their fingers, and so it was that the rulers of Nuku Hiva helped themselves to the raw fish steeped in lime juice, the roasted pork, the baked octopus, the steaming breadfruit and taro. First dipping each morsel in coconut sauce, the royal women voiced their approval with loud smacking and sucking as they ate. This manner of dining sometimes appears strange to those who have known no other people and no other land than their own, but it must be remembered that several thousand miles stretch between the eastern borders of the Pacific and the islands of Nuku Hiva and Tahiti, and that at such a distance customs and manners may be vastly different. Certain it is that if ever Queen Putu had witnessed a man spearing and shoveling his food with the various implements used elsewhere, she would have considered the performance awkward and undignified.

While the meal was in progress within, there was preparatory bustle going on without. So when a half hour later the queen and her daughters reappeared, now much refreshed, they found the representative men of the kingdom waiting to seat themselves upon newly cut fronds arranged in a large semicircle about the palace. *85* Many long tapers of tightly strung candlenuts, flaring and sputtering where they stood implanted in the ground, illumined the faces of the nearer chiefs and sent a vague diffused light as far as the massed men, women, and children beyond. Several thicknesses of *fara* matting lay near the wide doorway, and upon them Putu and the princesses took their places. When all were seated, there was an interval of silence during which nothing stirred save the fantastically enlarged shadows of the people. Then an elderly, bearded chief rose and came forward.

"Speak, Hau," said the queen. "Have there been happenings of importance since our departure?"

"Each day which passes on Nuku Hiva," he replied gravely, "is of importance. So also is our most trivial act, since our time on earth is not unlimited."

"You are quite right, old friend. Tell me the things that I should know."

"I shall do so. First, we are more numerous by two than when you left. A son was born to Rai, another to Ru, and a girl child to Temea."

"That makes three," the queen observed.

"It does. But death has also been here, and Hiti has left us. The manner of his going was this: a brown rat, the shadow of a voracious ghost, was heard to gnaw the rafters of his house during the night; in the morning Hiti was dead."

"Here is cause for sorrow," Putu murmured, her eyes downcast. "As both fisherman and warrior he served me well." She raised her head. "But my heart is gladdened that we count two more than we did before. What else, venerable man?"

"There has been an irregularity."

"Yes?"

"The sow which is the property of Vehetua plundered his neighbor's taro patch, sinking its snout into the soft mud, tossing up the good roots and devouring them every one."

"How did this come about?" asked the queen.

"Through the failure of Vehetua to lash a cord about the sow's leg and attach it to a suitable tree."

"Then," said Putu, "let the sow be given to the neighbor and let Vehetua plant a new patch of taro which also shall be the neighbor's. Is that all you have to say?"

"No, I have not done." The aged chief paused impressively. "The thing of greatest importance I have saved for last. Now you shall hear it. Yesterday, in the hour of greyness before dawn, a stranger was seized as he attempted to enter the house before which we are now gathered—the house which is sacred to yourself and the princesses, and forbidden to all others. He was seized and held, pending your arrival."

"Who is this man who holds *tapu* so lightly?" Putu demanded, frowning. "And what has brought him here?"

86 "Kae is the name he goes by," Hau made answer, "but as for the manner of his coming you had best listen to his own story. For my own part I like neither his appearance nor the sound of his tale."

At a clap of the chief's hands two warriors came forward with a captive between them. Both of the Nuku Hivan braves were tall, but the foreigner was taller. He walked with an arrogant swagger and showed plainly his annoyance at being held as a prisoner. Arrived before the queen, the two guards released the prisoner and stepped back a few paces.

Putu fixed the newcomer with her level gaze, and, although at first he bore it well, his eyes soon turned away, and as time passed without a word from the queen he shifted uneasily from one foot to the other.

"What are you doing here, Kae?" she demanded suddenly.

"Doing?" he replied, taken aback by the abruptness of her question. "Is it a crime to set foot on Nuku Hiva?"

"Answer!" old Hau snapped.

Kae appeared to pull himself together. He took a long breath. "Very well," he began, "this was the way of it. Ten days ago my ship foundered in a gale. My crew was lost. I clung to a bit of wreckage and drifted to this shore. That is all."

"So," said Putu slowly, "for ten days you have been without food or drink; for ten days your body has been washed by the ocean brine."

"For ten days," he repeated.

"Well," she remarked calmly to Hau, "he lies. Anyone can see that he has not suffered for lack of food, and his skin is as smooth as mine. Before turning him over to the priests for sacrifice I should like to know what he seeks with us."

Kae was not unhandsome, but now the features, in which Queen Putu had quickly read both selfishness and ill temper, became weak with fear. "No," he cried. "Not the priests with their stone and bamboo knives, not the cold altar slabs with their spreading brown stains! Give me the means to leave and I will go back to my own country and never return again!"

"From what land are you?" Putu asked.

"From Upolu."

"Upolu?"

"It is south and west a thousand miles and then half a thousand miles again."

"Ah," said the queen, her interest in distant lands causing her to relax somewhat the severity of her tone, "I know it not by name. What shape does it have?"

"Like this," Kae replied, and he drew on the ground with a bare toe. "The shape is a slug, the color is green. The harbors are here, here, and here; the mountains there, there, and there."

The queen was nodding before he had finished. "We have been there. We have skirted and seen it, and if I am not mistaken you have seen us as well. You have seen my daughters upon their whales. It is to steal a wife that you are here."

Kae burst into loud protestations of innocence but although they rang false in Putu's ears she could not be sure. If she had known the depth of his duplicity, if she had known how he had boasted to his countrymen that by slyness and treachery

87

he would return, not with one woman for wife, but with twin princesses, then surely the evil man would have been dispatched upon the spot. Putu, however, had no means of knowing, and her rigorous sense of justice caused her to hesitate. And as she hesitated a further complication arose which not even the queen of Nuku Hiva could have foreseen. It came from her own daughters, and it served to tip the balance in Kae's favor so that he was spared to continue his devious schemes.

"Oh, Mother," said Tahine, and she was very near to tears, "perhaps he speaks the truth. He is not ill favored, and if it is for love of Rua or of me that he has come, have pity."

"Oh, Mother," said Rua, with her large eyes round and sad, "perhaps these are not falsehoods that we hear. But if they are, and it is because of my sister or myself that he is here, be lenient."

In all affairs touching her island kingdom Putu had always tried to let reason alone guide her judgment. Where the two beautiful girls who were so dear to her were concerned, she was, however, less successful. Here emotion took the upper hand and Putu behaved much as would any other woman in like circumstances.

Never had she been able to deny their slightest wish. Nor was it different now.

"Am I," she protested, "to send a ship full of men on a dangerous voyage all because of this man with his preposterous story?" Yet, even as she spoke, Putu knew that she would yield.

"There is no need of a ship," Rua suggested.

"There is another way," Tahine agreed.

"Another way?"

"Tokama!" they both exclaimed.

The quickly intaken breaths of many hundred bystanders sounded in the night, followed by a silence broken only by the faint sputter of wicks drifting in their shell-cupped pools of oil. Was it possible, the people wondered, that Queen Putu would permit such a thing? Tokama, the sacred whale of the royal family, Tokama, who had never felt the touch of human hand other than Putu's own, to be the beast of burden of this scoundrel from an unknown island?

For long Putu stared into the row of lamps at her feet, and for long she failed to speak. When at last she looked up, the smile which had played briefly over Kae's face was gone.

"Man of Upolu, a more difficult thing has never been asked of me, but since it is my daughters' wish, you shall ride upon the noblest mount that was ever granted humankind. You will cover a month-long voyage in short days on the back of the whale which, hitherto, has borne myself alone. This I make possible for a second reason also: thus shall I most quickly be rid of your presence and the sound of your lying voice. Be gone, then, at break of day. My trusted Hau will have opened the gates of the whales' enclosure and let you out to the open sea." The queen rose, signifying that the audience was at an end, and the circle of her chiefs and priests did likewise. "A final warning, Kae," Putu pronounced in a voice that cut sharply through the night. "Keep to the deep waters, for there lies Tokama's safety. Should harm come to him be sure my vengeance will follow you."

Putu and the young princesses went to their mats within the house; the people dispersed, and soon the place where so many had stood to hear the fate of the foreigner was deserted except for a single attendant who gathered the burning flares. One after another he picked up the beaded stems of candlenut and rubbed them out upon the earth. Increasing dimness followed in his steps, and by the time the last flame was extinguished, leaving only the soft tropic darkness in Nuku Hiva, the village slept.

But not Kae. In a closely guarded house he lay with eyes still wide, and a faint smile again curled the corners of his mouth. "She shall be humbled," he whispered, hardly able to contain his evil sense of triumph. "The haughty queen shall be brought low, and her daughters shall come to me!"

Two days passed after Tokama, with his riderless sons at either side, bore Kae away, and not once in that time had Queen Putu left her house. She refused to eat, refused to speak, and despite the attempts of her daughters to cheer her, the heavy feeling of dejection which had assailed her from the first grew hourly more deep. What could be the meaning, she asked herself, of this sense of gloom and of impending disaster? Surely, in another day, or two at most, the glad cry of the lookouts would reach her ears and she would rush out like every other inhabitant of Nuku Hiva to scan the horizon and there discover the gushing, steaming spouts of her beloved whales. Surely her depression was unreasonable, but it remained and it intensified. Finally she could bear the waiting and suspense no more.

"Rua," said she, breaking at last her long silence, "go to the temple and ask the high priest to come to me."

The girl went close to the older woman, who sat with head bowed, hands folded in her lap. Lovingly she touched the firmly bound tresses of her mother's hair, the hair which had often flown so wildly beautiful upon the wind when Tokama lunged beneath her. "What is it you fear?" Rua asked sorrowfully.

"I do not know, I do not know," Putu replied. "But fear I do, and I would hear what the gods are saying."

Rua left the house and soon returned with an elderly man about whose gaunt frame hung the long, dangling fringes of a priestly cape. His deep-set, burning eyes rested on the queen. "You have sent for me," he stated quietly.

"I have," she answered. "My thoughts are greatly troubled. You have read the signs?"

"A priest has no more important duty."

"Then tell me. What have you done, what seen?" she demanded anxiously.

89

"I have slaughtered a first pig and a second; I have buried sacred sennit and then unearthed it; I have listened to the voices of birds and insects, to the murmuring of leaves in the temple trees, to the hollow whispering of wind in the feathered gourd of Ku."

"And what do you learn?"

"That blood will flow," said the priest impressively.

"Blood!"

"Yes, my queen. Enough to fill the veins of a thousand men."

"Can it be war?" she asked frowning. "Are we again to struggle with the raiders of Taipi?"

The faithful servant of the gods stood rigid and unbending before her, his eyes seeming to pierce the latticed bamboo which surrounded them as if he might be seeking further enlightenment in some distant place. At length he gave a slight shake to his head. "Like the streams of Havaiki which, after mountain storms, stain crimson all the sea, so now my mind beholds a river of warm blood. That is all that I can say."

"Very well," said Putu wearily. "Far from easing my apprehensions you fill my thoughts with fresh horror. But it was truth I sought from you, not soothing lies. Take my thanks, priest of Nuku Hiva, and go."

Even as the queen pronounced these words the crafty Kae, far to the south and west, approached his native land. First appeared the tips of the highest mountains; then quickly, for great was Tokama's speed, the steep and lofty slopes, the lower foothills and plateaus, and finally the level beaches came into view. The three whales with their single rider were sighted while still far off, and before they had reached the narrow channel to the harbor, every living soul upon the island had rushed down to the shore.

"It is Kae," they cried. "Kae has captured the great whales of Putu!"

The sound of their acclaim reached the unscrupulous man on Tokama's back. "Wait," he called to their too distant ears. "Wait, people of Upolu, and you shall see that Kae is mightier than this ocean king he rides!"

The two sons of Tokama lingered behind in the open sea, but Kae and his mount sped on into the constricted passage to the harbor. Had Queen Putu warned that in deep water lay Tokama's safety? Yes, that, assuredly, she had done, and as Kae recalled the regal woman's scorn of him he ground his teeth in anger. Carefully, deliberately, he guided the whale directly for a massive coral head which rose to within a few inches of the surface in the otherwise unobstructed channel. Tokama swam on, glad to be near the journey's end, glad to be so nearly rid of his unwanted rider; anxious for the moment when he might wheel and start back, at redoubled speed, toward his beloved mistress. At one instant he was free in his natural element, blue water beneath him, blue water to either side. In the next he smashed with terrific impact against the cruel, tearing coral shoals. Up he rose as if lifted by a tremendous submarine eruption and, impelled by his own huge momentum, plunged on over the sharp, stony blades of the sunken reef, to rest at last, high above the bay, in the unfriendly air of Upolu, with only his broad, fluked tail lashing futilely in the sea.

Kae leaped clear and standing knee deep in water wildly waved his arms to those ashore. "Bring hatchets," he shouted. "Bring axes, bring every cutting tool, and we shall saw and cut and slash till nothing is left of this servant of a hated queen but a mountain of dry bones!"

Canoes by the score launched out and came bobbing over the waters now churning under Tokama's struggles. In each canoe rode four or six or ten of Kae's people, and soon, pygmy-like, they swarmed about the body of the stranded whale. Tokama fought as long as life was left to him. More than once, with sudden convulsive movement, he sent sprawling, as if they had been so many stinging ants, those who crawled upon his back. But however hard he tried to grip the sea, however hard he tried to slide back to its cool embrace, it was in vain. Tokama's last voyage was done, and this he must have realized. With a monumental effort he flexed his giant frame, swinging his head about so that with a fast-dimming eye he might look off in the direction of Nuku Hiva. There to the north, beyond many horizons, rose the island where he had known life and human friendship. Now he lay dying, the first of his species to fall prey to what is most barbarous and ruthless in mankind.

In long ribbons the Upoluans ripped off the sleek, black skin; by great strips they tore away the thick, protective blubber. In an ever-growing fury their fevered energy mounted, as with crazed whoops and yells they swung the murderous implements of stone, of wood, of shell; and if a single man, witnessing the frightful scene, retained his sanity, he must have testified that the willful slaughter and the sight of the carnage which soon littered all the harbor served but to feed and fan the fires of their savagery. How well had Nuku Hiva's high priest interpreted the cricket-whirrings, the leaf-murmurs, the birdcalls and wind-sighs. Blood—blood was everywhere. From a hundred, from a thousand of Tokama's wounds it poured. Out upon the bay it spread in a rapidly widening circle to reach the white sand shores and stain them vivid red. Where Tokama's tail still flailed the sea, there rose geysers of pink foam; and many were those who, in their recklessness or through accident, fell beneath the heavy flukes to be battered instantly to pulp. At last a man found foothold on Tokama's head. That man was Kae, and in his hands he held a long-shafted spear. He raised it high, then brought it down, sinking it deep, deep into the helpless mammal's skull. A shudder passed through the length of Tokama's body; the enormous tail lifted once more and fell slowly back, to rest unmoving on the darkened waters.

A roar of triumph rose above Upolu, and Kae, drunk with his imagined power, beat with both fists upon his chest. "I am the greater," he raved, "Tokama is the lesser. I am the stronger; Tokama the weaker. I have conquered; he has succumbed. Come, princesses of Nuku Hiva, and seek your mother's whale, for thus you shall discover that neither beast nor man nor even the fairest of young women may thwart the wish of Kae!"

Drawn by a receding tide, the crimson river of Tokama's lifeblood flowed seaward and there fanned out to envelop his waiting sons and tell them with cruel certainty that he would never again rejoin them. Bits of flesh floated upon the grisly flood, and when the severed flippers drifted out the twin sons took them in their mouths and, bearing these tokens of disaster, set off for the unsullied seas of Nuku Hiva.

Three days later and thousands of miles away, an excited cry from the lookout broke the silence of early morning. "Whales! The sacred whales of Queen Putu!" A tall jet of spray shot up above the level sea. "The first one blows," he called down. Another plume of white mist burst upward. "The second blows!" Then there came a pause, a pause which lengthened minute by minute till the queen, standing with her daughters at the foot of the towering palm from which the sentinel kept watch, could bear no more.

"The third," she demanded breathlessly. "What of the third, warrior of keen eyes?" There was no reply, and, looking up, she saw that the man was slowly descending the greyish bole of the tree. "Speak!" she commanded when he stood before her.

"There are but two," he replied haltingly, unable to meet her glance.

"Two?" she repeated slowly, as if unwilling to believe. "Only two?"

Miserably he nodded. "Twin whales I saw approaching, twin whales of equal size."

A cry came from Putu's parted lips, a cry of such anguish that it wrenched the heart of everyone who heard and brought quick tears to the eyes of the princesses. "*Aue, aue,*" she wailed. "It is Tokama, whom I loved, whom I fed with my own hand; who bore me to the near seas and the far, through the short waves and the long; who breathed the cool trade winds and warmed them with his courageous body. Tokama is gone, is lost, and we are left to mourn."

The two surviving whales entered the pass, then glided through the gates of the coral basin which was their home. Many hundreds of subdued and saddened people lined the shore, yet Tokama's sons swam unerringly to Queen Putu and there rendered up their grim burdens. At sight of the two mutilated parts of Tokama's great body the queen's expression of woe changed slowly to one of stern determination, and the sorrow which had filled her gave way to anger that welled up from deep within.

"Kae," she intoned in a voice now low but charged with deadly menace, "in your baseness and your treachery you have offended gods and men. Never again, because of the cowardly slaughter done by you and your underlings, will the race of whales be servants to mankind. One voyage more—one voyage only—shall be made by Tokama's young. It shall be their last for humankind, and it shall be for vengeance!"

On the faces of the princesses Rua and Tahine the tears had dried, and no man, looking upon them at that minute, could have failed to remark their great resemblance to the queen. Brief days ago the lightness of their thoughts and their easy, careless youthfulness had been apparent to all. Now, overnight, they had found maturity. They seemed taller, more poised, more regal, and in each was visible the budding of a queen. Their beauty was no less than before; on the contrary, it burned more fiercely, but it was of a sort as well calculated to destroy as it might be to reward, and at mention of Kae's name one read in each of them a hatred as great as had been their pity.

"When we were children," said Rua to her mother, "you gave us Tokama's sons. If they go out again from Nuku Hiva we must be the ones to guide them."

Putu regarded her daughters somberly. "I had meant myself to go."

"It was because of our entreaties," said Tahine, "that Tokama was sent to death. Can either of us find peace or happiness if we are not allowed to right so great a wrong? Send us to sea, our mother, and we shall not return alone."

Only after severe inner struggle did Queen Putu make answer. "In times of great stress, sorrow, or danger, the feelings which stir within us, even the words we speak, are often not our own. The ruling spirits of the world then possess our minds, our bodies, and what we do is of their bidding. This is such a time, and I dare not oppose your desire to set in motion with your own hands the vengeance which must rightfully be ours. Go—go quickly. Return quickly, and may the gods grant that I have read correctly their wishes."

So it happened that within the hour the sisters were speeding southward upon their twin whales. Side by side they traveled as they had always done before. But how different was now their mood and purpose! Now there was no laughter, no glad shout of sheer exuberance. In truth, the daughters of Putu were free no longer. This was no voyage in which whim and pleasure ruled. The course was set, the goal was fixed, and the whales sensed as fully as their riders the earnestness of their mission. They never paused to sport, to leap and roll and slap the waters resoundingly with their tails. On they drove, straight for Upolu, impatiently buffeting the waves aside as they left league after league behind them. Often the princesses and their mother had ridden in the midst of merrily bustling squalls of the sort that quickly pass, leaving coolness and freshness in their ruffled wakes. It was otherwise on this fateful day. A full-grown, black-centered storm winged them on their way while lightning flashed and the ominous roll of thunder sounded over the desolate slate-grey sea.

"Southward, sons of brave Tokama," Tahine cried above the hiss of pelting rain. "Make haste; bring near the moment when the wreaths now twined round and round our throats may firmly bind Kae's traitorous body."

"Southward, gallant friends," Rua echoed. "Tough sennit lies hidden within the flower garlands that we wear. Speed on; take us quickly to the man who shall find his last imprisonment in their scented strands."

On an early dawn the storm which cloaked the sisters struck upon Upolu. It tore up trees, it flattened houses, and everywhere was howling wind and driving rain and great confusion. In frightened, huddled groups the people gathered, and wherever Kae passed, angry voices called after him.

"Is this the gentle squall by which you claimed your wives would come to you? Is it so the daughters of Putu come, docile, to your arms? Begone, wretched man who led us in evil ways, lest we all die with you. Go down to the sea, and if the women we have wronged are there upon the waves, beg mercy for yourself and for us as well!"

Stunned and bewildered by the sudden fury of the tempest, Kae staggered down to the shore. "Their anger is great," he thought. "One hears it in the wind and in the clashing palms. But all storms end, and then the daughters of Putu shall be mine. He was scanning the ravaged waters of the bay for sign of whale or rider when he heard a woman's voice beside him. "Kae," it said and it was very near. "Kae, we have come for you."

He wheeled and then fell back a step. "Come for me?" he echoed in quickly mounting terror.

Rua and Tahine stood before him, their sea-drenched garments clinging to their tall, slender forms. They smiled. "Yes," he told himself, "they smile—so why am I afraid? Is it because of the hard glitter in their eyes? And they bear flowers, many long *hei* of red blossoms—so why do I tremble? Is it because the color is of blood?"

Gently, caressively, the young women slipped the fragrant flowers over his head, eased them down about his throat, about his arms and legs and ankles. Then abruptly, fiercely, they drew the cordons tight and flung Kae to the ground.

"So," Rua whispered in his ear as she tied him doubly fast, "we bind and wrap you like long fish, a living gift for Putu's priests."

"And so," came Tahine's sibilant breath at his other side, "crimson flowers fold and hide you, a sacrifice to outraged gods."

Together they lifted him and bore him to the water's edge where the two whales waited. Across the head of Rua's mount they laid him. The sisters took their places, and Tokama's sons, with a wide sweep of their tails, whirled and lashed out to sea.

Only then did Kae's fear-constricted throat find voice. "Upolu, my land, my people," he screamed in wild despair. "Let me not die on cold altars far away!" There was no answer. No man ashore made move to follow, yet there were some who thought they heard his cry, faint on the tempestuous wind. Still others, looking off beyond the harbor, imagined they saw briefly the gleaming backs of two sperm whales in the now receding storm; and at least one man, more keen of eye, swore to have distinguished the two superb raven-haired creatures astride the whales.

To Nuku Hiva Rua and Tahine returned, and there Kae was delivered to the high priest of the realm. At the place of debarkation a solemn procession formed. Led by the gaunt priest with the blazing eyes, they marched in slow pomp with the prisoner upon a litter in their midst. Toward the mutter of drums issuing from the inland temple they went, to stretch Kae at last upon the darkened, ever-thirsty stones of the *marae* built to serve the gods. The death chant rose and quivered in the air, then faded.

"O Kae," intoned the first of Putu's priests, "you are about to leave this world, but we who remain behind, and all those who follow us, shall continue to pay the penalty for your sinful deed. Through you we have lost true friends, and whales will henceforth shun the race of men." In his hand he raised the long, sharp knife of split bamboo. "Go, you who spread sacred blood to the four corners of the sea," he cried with quickening pace and rising tone. "Go, and find mercy if you can within Te Po!" The blade fell, and Kae rendered up his dishonored breath.

At dawn the next morning Queen Putu and her daughters made their way through the grey light to stand on the coral border of the basin where Tokama had lived so many years. While the people waited silently, they slipped into the calm waters, and immediately the sons of Tokama swam to meet them. Gone now was all trace of the sternness which had marked the three women when only vengeance filled their hearts. With tears in their eyes they fondled for the last time the sleek sides of the great beasts who had been their faithful steeds and companions.

"Let their way be cleared with the rising of the sun," the queen commanded when she and her daughters stood again upon the shore.

Few minutes passed before the sun's light flared out across the sea, and as it did the gates of the lagoon were swung aside. Twice, thrice, the whales circled the large enclosure, pausing before the opened channel, then swerving back to pass close at the feet of Putu, Rua, and Tahine as if reluctant to accept the gift of freedom.

"Now is the time, my dear ones," said Rua through her tears. "There is the endless trail. Farewell!"

"The moment is here, my loved ones," wept Tahine. "Before you lies the world-wide path. Farewell!"

"Sons of my own Tokama," the queen cried to them, "men have proved unworthy of devotion such as yours. Stay far from land, stay far from roving ships. Seek out your fellows, creatures of your own kind, and never leave them. Our hearts will be near to breaking as you go, but I say to you: take to the waters of darkest blue, take to the bottomless deep, to Moana—the great, friendly, all-

95

enfolding ocean!" As Putu finished speaking, her charges turned their huge blunt heads away from the northern island. Out they rushed from the confining basin to meet the oncoming swells beyond.

Soon they were lost to the sight of those who mourned beside the sea, but a lookout called down from the tallest tree. "They blow! A first blows; a second blows!" There was an interval in which no one moved or spoke; then the same voice came again. "Once more, far off, they blow—the first . . . the second. Far, far off, they blow!"

Long silence followed; then the man descended the trunk of the old palm and slowly walked to the queen and her daughters. Motionless as statues the three women stood, their heads raised proudly, the wind sweeping their hair back as, with straining eyes, they gazed out to sea. The lookout approached and stood before the imperious Putu. "My queen," said he, "the whales of Nuku Hiva are gone forever."

Terii-of-the-Thousand-Eyes

IT was about noon when we quitted Point Venus and turned our faces toward home. The pleasant thought of good food awaiting us helped me to match my step to old Tetua's. With a circlet of green *purau* leaves shading his greyed head, he marched along at a pace I would have been glad to slacken, for the sun was now high and the day had grown warm. But Tetua possessed an infallible means of banishing any sense of weariness. He had but to open his mind, swing aside for me the doors to his other world, and all else was forgotten.

This time, as often before, a small incident of our walk furnished the incentive. We had come to a place where the path left the sea and wandered inland with woods upon either hand. It was a region to which men came seeking firm, straight poles for the supporting rafters of their houses, and as we rounded a bend in the trail our eyes fell upon a single, clean-trimmed shaft of wood lying upon the ground. Tetua stooped and picked it up. He weighed it knowingly in his hands.

"There was a time," he observed, "when this would have been prized material for a splendid weapon. Its girth is right, its balance good. See." His long arm swung back and the natural lance whistled past my head and imbedded itself in the soft earth many yards away.

"A fine throw," I approved enthusiastically.

"*Toa* wood, my friend, is tough and hard. It travels easily."

"But is not *toa* also your word for warrior?"

"There is one word," he agreed, "for a warrior and his spear. Formerly they were one, they were inseparable." He turned to me, smiling, as we started on again. "You think that cast was good? Well, perhaps it might be considered so in these days, when spears are used for nothing more important than the impaling of harmless fish. But listen while I tell you of what a boy of fifteen once accomplished with such a weapon." As we continued through the *toa* grove he began to weave his tale.

There was a period in Tahitian history when the island was divided into many separate kingdoms with as many separate rulers. It was a time of jealousies and strifes, and wars were frequent. Men's lives were in constant hazard, and few were those who then died peacefully of old age. An unfortunate epoch in which to be born, so some might say, yet I think otherwise. For it is in such unsettled, troublous years that people's minds manage to rise above the petty preoccupations which usually loom so large. Life, they discover, when it is threatened and unsure, is an adventure to be keenly, richly savored and experienced to the full. During such eras of turmoil men find within themselves unguessed powers which in days of tranquillity lie dormant and unused. In difficult times the great among us are seen, and it is of one such man, the only son of Paea's king, that I shall speak.

He had not many years, as I have said, and their number was fifteen. His name? I warn you it makes a mouthful, but here it is: Teriitaumatatini. Perhaps it was given to him at birth, in which case the boy grew to fit his name; or it may be that he earned it in later life, and if that is true, whoever bestowed it upon him was a keen judge of character. It means Terii-of-the-Thousand-Eyes. He had, in reality, two brown eyes, but they were of such unusual brightness, and Terii himself was so uncommonly alert, that he seemed to his contemporaries to have many times their seeing power. Terii's vision, furthermore, was of the uncanny sort which, in some mysterious way, senses the approach and the form of things to come; and never was this strange clairvoyance more remarkably demonstrated than on the night his father, King Oropaa, died, with an enemy spear lodged in his broad chest.

Many men were gathered in the house of Oropaa. They sat on the sanded floor in a rough circle and talked of wind and weather and of the fish to be caught on the morrow. Terii and his mother, seated apart from the others, exchanged an occasional word, but for the most part they listened quietly. The time passed, and it was late when at last there came a lull in the conversation. It was not a natural pause, however, but one which was in some way pregnant with apprehension. King Oropaa, who had loved too well the pursuits of peace and had trusted to a security that did not exist, bent his eyes upon the floor. But many of the men looked at each other and asked a silent question. "How can we talk of fishing and everyday affairs; why do we avoid the thing which fills our thoughts?" The silence lengthened, and tension hung heavy beneath the thatched roof of the king's house. Still no one spoke the dreaded word, because the word was "war." In the dark outside, the sea made no more than a muffled whisper on the reef, and the hooting of small beach owls came clearly from far away. At last Queen Mata rose to pour oil into the coconut shells of the dimming lamps, and Terii-of-the-Thousand-Eyes turned to his father.

"May I say it?" he asked.

King Oropaa lifted his kindly, troubled face and looked at the slender lad. "Speak son," he said with a smile of affection. "What is in your mind?"

"This: there is danger in the night."

"Yes," the other nodded solemnly, "and so there is in every night in times when greed and strength go hand in hand."

All knew well to what and to whom the king referred. Scouts had brought the disturbing news. Teva, brutal chief of neighboring Papara, goaded his people on to war; Teva, most feared of warriors, intoxicated his followers with lying tales of injustices, with alluring visions of wealth and ease on Paea. With nimble tongue he wove a spell more powerful than his strong right arm. "Across the borders of Paea," so he raved and shouted, "every swamp is thick with taro, every hill groans beneath its weight of breadfruit, every pen is glutted with fat pig and fowl. Prepare, men of Papara, and we shall seize all that the peasant-king Oropaa has caused the earth to give. Prepare, for though some will die, many more will live amid great riches."

Gravely and with misgiving Terii's father had listened to reports of the gradual incitement of Papara's people, but never had he been able to bring himself to order the uprooting of the pattern of life which, through many years, he had formed for his own people. Above all Oropaa loved the soil, loved to see it tended, fertile, and productive. Nothing would have offended him less than the epithet "peasant-king," if by that was meant one fond of husbandry, of growing, multiplying beasts and plants. So it was that under his leadership the dwellers of Paea had become adept at agriculture, their district the envy of all others. But they were no longer warriors. There was doubtless truth in a saying which fell often from Oropaa's lips to the effect that a man, or a tribe, cannot be all things and that a choice must be made. But it was not all the truth, and today, from the vantage point of many hundred years, it is easy to see where the kindly king made his fatal mistake. Unwilling to assume the burdens, the hardships and sacrifices necessary to form a warrior state, he was not ready to meet the challenge which rose beyond the river on his southern boundary. He ran the terrible risk of losing all.

"Father," Terii insisted, "many nights may have within them the threat of danger, but not in all of them does the darkness lie thick with such oppressive certainty. I feel that death sits listening at the eaves. Before dawn it will be among us; before morning Teva will have struck."

Those within the house stared at the youth, whose prophecies so often had proved true. Had the days for preparation indeed come to an end? Was there to be no tomorrow in which to discuss the advisability of taking youths from the fields and fitting them with clubs and helmets; no tomorrow in which to listen to debate while some pointed out Chief Teva's one redeeming trait—his never-broken word—and so urged treaty or the purchased peace of tribute? Had this time of uncertain peace run its course?

From afar the dying scream of a lone sentry came traveling on the darkness to give each waiting man his answer. Eerily it trembled in the air above the unmoving heads of King Oropaa and his people. Long it hung suspended there, a ghostly, disembodied sound which seemed to cling despairingly to the sweet tropic night and fill each listening mind with a vision of the yawning portals of Te Po. Then it was gone, and Terii's father sprang to his feet and reached for his dusty spear. The king of Paea had no lack of courage, and now, too late, the last of his indecision fell away.

"Rise up," he roared in a voice that roused the village. "Rise up, Paea, and lay hands on whatever weapon you may find. Take spears and axes, knives and adzes, clubs and wooden spades. Take everything which may cleave a human skull, and follow me! It is Teva, who holds nothing sacred save his given word. In stealth he has attacked, cloaking his crime in blackest night. Rise and drive him back!"

The king had reached the door when he found his son close beside him. "Where do you go, youngster?" he demanded quickly.

"With you!"

"Warriors are needed, not boys."

"I can carry a spear," Terii exclaimed. "While others have fished, while others have tilled and planted, I have hurled toa poles at the trees of the upper valley. Give me a weapon; let me go, and Teva himself may feel its sharpened point."

From every side Oropaa's men now came running to crowd the clearing outside the leader's house, but while their shouts mingled with the frightened cries of women and children the king paused still another instant within. He clasped his son against him.

"Your words are brave," said he. "The day will come when you shall hold a spear, but now you have another task, and there is no one else to whom I dare entrust it. Our women and our children must be saved, for in them lies the survival of our name and clan. Take them to the upper valley where you have played at war. Keep them there till the invader's zeal for killing has had time to cool and then, if it seems safe, return. Can you find your way at midnight?"

"As well as if it were broad day."

"Good, Terii-of-the-Thousand-Eyes. You have lifted my greatest fear. Do not tarry to learn how the battle goes. Take your charges and be off. That is my last command."

Before his son could answer, the king of Paea was gone. For a moment he was surrounded by the milling, weapon-brandishing throng of his eager subjects; in the next he had broken free and was racing in the lead for the southern boundary of his realm. Above the war-cries of his followers Oropaa's voice rose in defiance and encouragement. "On, my men! Let Teva's minions feel your anger; roll them back upon the river which they slyly crossed, and let their bodies float seaward to feed the waiting sharks. Be strong, Paea, be strong!"

With his father's exhortations to the willing but untrained defenders still loud in his ears, Terii quickly began to assemble those who were left behind. Like his mother, other women had hastily gathered their most prized possessions and wrapped them in bark cloth. Now, with infants in their arms and others clinging to their hands they formed a straggling procession and left the village, setting off inland. They had reached the foothills when the shouts of the warriors swelled in a confused and jumbled clamor; somewhere beneath the silent palms the battle had been joined. But though the cries of the women and children now mounted in sympathy with those who fought and died below, the vigorous call of Oropaa still was heard.

"*Aue*," rose the grief-filled wails from Terii's little band, "*aue!*" And of all the tongues heard upon the globe no syllables ever held such weight of human misery as can be expressed within those three.

"Peace, my loved ones," Terii urged. "Save your breath for the climb that is ahead."

"Ah, lad," said a middle-aged woman who stumbled close behind him, "of what use is my breath if the man and stalwart son for whom alone I draw it lie bleeding on the ground?"

The boy could make no reply, but an answer seemed to come from far away. "Be strong," it called waveringly, "be strong!"

On through the night they groped their way, the aged, the infirm, the women and their young, and at last they stood at the entrance to the valley in which Terii had once flung spears and imagined himself at war. Here they stopped to look below with eyes that strained and sought to pierce the dark. Terii's mother had put down her bundle and was resting at his side. Suddenly he drew her to him, and with one hand held her head close upon his chest. For long minutes he could not speak, and his fingers moved softly on her hair. There had come a change in the sound of battle, and the note of stubborn hope which had reached up to them sustainingly throughout their march rang out no more. His father's voice was stilled. There were some among the fleeing band of Oropaa's clan who had been scarcely conscious of the repeated cry of their king while it continued, but now its absence left an emptiness that struck home to every one. Even the lamentations ceased, and all stood rooted in despair, incapable of thought or action. Only the grasses stirred, swayed by a gentle current of air which spilled from the valley's mouth to roll slowly seaward like a faint, expiring breath. With what astonishment, then, did they hear anew the same challenging call. Loudly, from within their midst, it rose.

"Be strong, Paea! All is not lost while yet we live. Come, children of Oropaa. In this valley is our security, and in it, too, we must find courage."

Such were the words that roused the dazed refugees from their stupor, spurring them on. But the voice was youthful and it belonged to Terii-of-the-Thousand-Eyes. Holding his mother's arm he led the way.

Although accounts of the gods and heroes tend to vary widely from island to island, the story I now relate is simple history. The coloring of Tahitians is, as a rule, a light brown, but even today one sees men whose skins are of a darker shade, and so it was also in the warring times of which I speak. There is complete agreement everywhere that of all who walked these shores no other was as black as Chief Teva of Papara. The reference is, of course, to the physical aspect of the man, although his character—with the single exception of his abhorrence of a broken word—could equally well be so described. His flesh was of the negroid blackness found in Papua and in the Solomon Islands. It is even possible that the blood of Melanesians ran in his veins since some of our ancestors passed through those regions on their way to a final home in Tahiti, and if such was the case it would go far to explain also his ferocity.

On the morning following his easy rout of the Paeans and the seizure of their territory, Teva squatted on his haunches in the sunlight which spread over the clearing before the once-peaceful home of the slain king. Pigs had been killed and cooked during the night, and, flanked by two of his warriors, the chief was busily gnawing the bones. When, with his strong teeth, he had torn the last shred of meat from a rib, he flung it to a pack of gaunt curs that had come from his own village. With arms resting on his knees, grease-smeared hands dangling, he watched the snarling rush of the starved animals for the thrown morsel.

"*Na reira*," he said with a short, harsh laugh. "That's it. Sink your fangs into your brother, tear the bone each from the other's mouth. Wounds are sauce to the food." Teva looked to the man on his right whose chest bore a long spear slash from which the blood still oozed. "You, Motu—do you not find it so?"

"In this place," Motu grunted, "dogs and men will both grow fat."

"You will have a fine scar," the chief remarked enviously.

"I should have more than that if you had not run the king of Paea through."

"He fought well," Teva admitted, "but we were many, they were few; we were ready, they were not." He wiped his hands on his soiled waistcloth and picked up a lance which lay beside him. "This was his," he said, turning the weapon in his fingers. "It is fine toa wood with grain that is straight and true. But see: it is dull. The oil of Oropaa's palm had not touched it in many a year. That is why we sit here with filled stomachs while his eyes are closed."

"I should like it better," Motu grumbled, "if we had captured more than an empty village. Who is to serve us? Who is to gather the crops and prepare all the good things with which the district abounds? Our own women? They like work in the fields no better than we."

The chief scowled, and his dark face became hard. "Prisoners belong to us, and we shall find them."

"That may be," said the other dubiously, "yet I, for one, have no desire to tramp Tahiti's endless mountains in search of them."

"There you speak like a true man of Papara," Teva snapped irritably. "Lazy in peace, lazy even in war!" A glum silence fell between them, and it had endured some time when suddenly Teva spoke again in different tone. "I think, Motu," he remarked affably, "you may continue to sit in comfort upon your backside. One individual of Paea will suffice to lead us to the others. What does it matter if that one be a boy?"

Unable to understand his chief's words, Motu looked up and saw that Teva was gazing to the far end of the village street. There, walking briskly between the rows of houses and stepping lightly over the sprawled forms of glutted warriors who lay sleeping all around, was a youth who came straight toward the royal dwelling with glance to neither right nor left. An expression of blank surprise spread over Motu's coarse features, and his heavy jaw sagged. "He is unarmed," he muttered, "and walks into our camp as casually as if he went to join a feast." The burly warrior gave his head a shake. "Is it an idiot-boy with such softness of the head that he does not know the meaning of danger?"

"There are others besides idiots who are without fear," the chief said without taking his eyes from the oncoming youth, "and among them are those descended of kings. I recognize the lad, and you can see yourself the belt of red feathers bound about his middle. If he had land on which to stand and rule he would today be monarch. But he has nothing because all that was his father's is now mine."

"Oropaa's son!" Motu exclaimed.

"Terii-of-the-Thousand-Eyes," Teva agreed. But the brightness and the cleverness which won him the name will do him little good today."

As Terii marched purposefully toward his enemy, the warriors whom he passed roused from their heavy slumber, stared momentarily at his straight, unbending back and swinging shoulders, and then, feeling a new tension in the village air, struggled to their feet. Teva, too, had risen, and when Terii stood before him, looking up into the chief's dark, frowning countenance, all the raiders of Papara gathered close about.

Teva fixed Terii with an appraising stare. "It is my good fortune that you are here," he said slowly, "for you will take me where I may lay hands on those of your clan who still live. But tell me, son of conquered Oropaa, what madness brings you among those who have so recently cut down Paea's manhood."

"The sun shines," Terii replied steadily. "It is broad day. Should I then fear to come among men who find courage only beneath the hiding mantle of the night?"

"Oho!" the swarthy leader cried. "It is an insolent young cock with whom we have to deal. Do you think we fear the light of day? I have but to say the word and a hundred hands will reach out to tear you limb from limb."

"Is that proof of courage? No, Teva of Papara, you came by stealth and in the dark to leap upon the backs of peaceful men. It is no victory you have won, and the deed will make your memory black forever."

The chief's face contorted with sudden rage, and he half raised the captured spear which he still held in his hand. Then, slowly, he lowered it and spoke. "Where are your people, boy? Speak, and speak quickly."

"In safety where none shall find them, and there they shall remain till their lands have been restored."

"Then assuredly they shall age and die in the rain-drenched mountains. Do you not know that Teva seizes that which he desires and strikes down all who stand in his way?" The chief drew himself up to his full height. "This land and all it holds I won in battle; it is mine. This village, the house at my back which was once your father's, this spear which his hand once warmed, all are mine, won when I brought Oropaa low. Slaves, too, rightfully belong to me, and you shall lead me to them."

"You will find no guide in me," Terii answered, unshaken by the other's glowering mien. "And what you claim to have won in battle you have taken in slyness and cunning like the marauding tribes of Vavau who, covered by darkness and moving with hushed paddles, creep upon our unsuspecting shores. Are you, who shout so loudly of the glories of war, of bravery and daring, so weak that you must imitate those craven thieves, must use surprise, and strike only the unprepared? Why do you not fight openly?"

The chief of Papara could contain himself no longer and burst out a roar of anger. "May the gods bear witness—those of the sky and the earth, those of the underworld, and those of the lashing sea, as well as any other who may chance to be looking over my shoulder. Listen to the words of this stripling, this coward, who taunts me, Teva of Papara! Fight in the open do you say?" He bent over so that his face came close to that of Terii. "Show me the foe and we shall see who shuns the light of day; show me the enemy and we shall see who goes down in the heat of high noon! Where is he? No man stands to oppose us."

"There is one," said Terii evenly, "for I oppose you."

Teva gave a sharp intake of breath, and his eyes widened in disbelief. "You?" he said, thinking that he could not have heard aright. Then, at Terii's unperturbed confirming word, he shook with uncontrollable laughter. "Oh, ho, ho!" he bellowed, and he fell upon Motu as if in the weakness of his mirth he sought support from his brawny henchman. With both arms wrapped about Motu's thick neck Teva struggled to speak. "Do you hear him? Tell me, Motu of the magnificent scar, do I dream the words which this babe speaks?" Again the chief was carried away by a fit of laughter and was soon joined by all his men, so that the whole village rang with their contemptuous hilarity.

104   At last Teva recovered himself sufficiently to stand erect and to face again the youth of Paea who waited impassively for the uproar to subside. "Boy," said he, "I brought with me no striplings of our own clan to match with you in contests. We are at war, and war is not a game."

"I seek no games," the young prince replied staunchly. "As my father's heir this is my rightful kingdom, and I demand the chance to fight for it."

"The meanest among my warriors would not stoop to battle one so immature," Teva said sharply, all sign of amusement now gone from his face.

"I am not here to challenge the meanest or the greatest of your warriors," Terii insisted stubbornly. "I am here to challenge you."

Angry cries arose from the impatient and increasingly restless men of Papara, who crowded about the chief. "Enough of his babble," they muttered. "Bind him and let his insolent mouth be stuffed with the earth he still thinks his own!"

Yet Teva, though he glared dourly at Oropaa's son, raised his hand and stilled his unruly people. A long moment passed while he debated what to do with the troublesome youth. His natural instinct, and the dictates of common sense, told him to order the boy seized and bound. Then there would be ways to wring from him the secret of the survivors' hiding place. But an unwilling admiration of such unflinching steadfastness in the face of danger caused Teva to hesitate. The silence dragged on, and still he did not speak. Sounds which had once meant peace and happiness and normal living came clearly to Terii's ears: the homely grunting of pigs tethered to stakes or rooting idly in the pens of stout bamboo; the crowing of cocks in the nearby hills; the flutter of wind in surrounding *fara* trees and the swish of small waves on the dazzling beach. He heard these things, but even as he did he knew well that it might be for the last time. The fate of Terii-of-the-Thousand-Eyes, as none realized better than he, then depended upon what went on in the mind of the black chief of Papara.

Abruptly Teva's palm descended with a loud clap upon the broad back of his henchman. "Why should we not amuse ourselves, Motu?" he demanded. "We are not pressed for time; Paea's women and children may be rounded up tomorrow as well as today, and in this obstinate prince I see the possibility of entertainment. Listen to me," he said, turning back to Terii. "You shall have the chance to win back all that your father, in his blindness, lost."

"Hold!" Motu interrupted in concern. "Are you about to risk our victory?"

"I risk nothing," Teva replied with confidence. "As well might he succeed if, like Maui, he set out to trap the sun. At his own insistence I make the proposition, and here it is. You are said, Terii, to have keener sight than any man alive; let it help you today. Choose any one you will among my men. Each of you shall take a spear and throw. Each time your cast surpasses his—if any such time there be—as much land as your spear has covered I will restore to you. That is my word, and my word is never broken." *105*

There were shouts of approval at his suggestion. Jostling and pushing warriors by the hundreds pressed forward, pointing to themselves and calling aloud to Terii "O valiant prince, O fearless giant," they joked, "choose me! See my skinny arm;

no strength lies in it. See my tottering limbs; they barely serve to hold me. Take me, and all Paea will be yours again!"

Terii waited till the noise of their jibes had lessened, then raised his eyes to the chief. "I am to pick an opponent in any man of your clan who now stands on my father's soil?"

The chief made a sweeping gesture which included the entire throng. "Any one. Seek out the feeblest you can see."

"That," said Terii, "is not my intention. I choose the first among you."

"The first! Who is that if not myself?"

"It is none other."

"By all that is holy," the chief exploded, his temper newly flaring, "I begin to think Motu was right when first he saw you swinging into this captured village with such great unconcern. You are mad, and your head is as soft as well-cooked poi, or else you have little desire to regain your native land."

"Let us judge of that when we have done," Terii replied.

Gradually the frown faded from Teva's brow and he shrugged his shoulders. "Very well, foolhardy boy. It was my wish to watch the sport, but it is true that I, too, am of the clan of Papara—as much so as the fisherman who snares my fish, the woman who sweeps my house, or the babes who crawl upon the floor. Although you have tricked me into a promise I did not intend, I will not seek to escape it. Find yourself a spear to suit your size, and we will be finished with this stupid jest."

"You hold the spear I would use."

"This?" Teva whipped up the toa shaft. "More folly! You could not throw such a weapon its own length. Whatever may have been his shortcomings, Oropaa was a man."

Terii reached out and took the spear from the chief who, in his amazement, released it without further protest. "Yes," he said quietly, "my father was a good man, and he will not forsake me now. Are you ready?"

In answer, Teva gave a vicious kick at a mangy dog and shouted, "My spear, Motu, my spear!" Then, weapon in hand, he turned to face his followers. "Fall back! Make way, and give us room!" They obeyed, but as their leader strode out to the clearing with the spindly boy beside him, snickers of amusement were heard on all sides. "Enough of that," the chief barked, conscious of seeming ridiculous in the part he was compelled to play.

"*Haere maru*," Motu urged. "Easy, my chief. Is this not to be an entertainment?"

"All right," he answered testily. "Have your fun if you must, but it is not my custom to act the clown." They had reached the center of the open space which lay before the royal house, and there they stopped, facing toward the Paea-Papara border, with the crowd grouped expectantly at their backs. Teva wheeled to confront his slender antagonist. "Go ahead," he commanded gruffly.

"You first," said Terii.

Customarily the question of who is to start is a matter for protracted discussion among Tahitian contestants. Perhaps it was because he thought it beneath him to dispute with a mere boy, or perhaps it was because he was anxious to finish a business he now regretted having begun, but in any case Teva did not demur. He gave a short laugh in which there was a trace of both annoyance and embarrassment.

"Very well," he remarked indifferently, "have it your way, lad." Without so much as troubling to take a stance, with as much disdain as if he were throwing a bone to his pack of curs, he gave a careless toss to his spear. Its point bit into the ground a short distance away, and, satisfied that no more would be required of him, the chief turned and started for Oropaa's house. He had not gone far, however, when a faint murmur from the onlookers made him retrace his steps.

With as little preparation, and quite as casually as the man of charcoal skin, Terii had planted his father's spear a few feet in advance of Teva's.

"Hmm," said the chief, who had not witnessed Terii's performance, "you do well to lift that weapon, let alone launch it into the air." They went to the two lances and picked them up. "If sufficient strength is left you for a second cast, let fly," Teva remarked condescendingly.

"According to the rules," Terii replied, "the loser goes first."

At these words a scowl crossed the chief's face. Never, since young manhood, had he come out second best in any contest of arms, and even a temporary setback was unpleasant to him. But the next moment he chuckled easily. What harm, after all, to prolong the game a bit? "That is the rule," he admitted without rancor. "Match this, then." Still without taking position, and standing as if he might have been engaged in idle conversation, he drew back his arm. But this time, before releasing the weapon, he gave a more vigorous snap to his wrist, and the spear traveled half again as far as before. "You may take a running start if you wish," he patronizingly informed his young opponent.

Terii did not reply but, mimicking the other's pose of unconcern, flipped his spear two paces farther than had Teva.

A long drawn exclamation of surprise came from Teva's army, and the grin disappeared from the chief's lips as he responded gruffly. "That will do. I tire of this childish sport." And going to his spear he snatched it up. He spread his legs, the left before and the right steadyingly behind, and flung the shaft to a respectable fifty spear-lengths. "Look there with your many eyes," said he with satisfaction. "Match that if you can."

Oropaa's son took his place, balancing himself in the same way as had Teva, and heaved the lance which his father's hands had made to a distance of fifty spear-lengths and three.

"He is possessed," someone exclaimed. "A vengeful ghost hides within his arm."

"Ghost!" Teva snorted. "I will show you the strength of a living arm with a cast to twice as far!"

"Perhaps," Motu suggested, "it would be well to do so. Already you have lost a goodly strip of the land for which we fought."

"Would you have me make a fool of myself?" the chief snarled. "Should I exert all my force as though I were measured with a man?"

"Not necessarily," the stocky warrior replied as he eyed dubiously the lanky arms which dangled at Terii's sides. "Only take care it be not the boy who makes a fool of you."

"Leave that to me, and spare me your advice," barked Teva.

It is unlikely that anyone remarked the faint smile that played on Terii's mouth as they all walked on to the place where the two spears protruded from the soft earth. How stupid Teva's people were! Of course a spirit guided his good right arm. Was not this rich, sun-warmed soil against which his bare feet pressed his father's land? He raised his eyes and gazed down the length of the broad, palm-lined avenue which stretched away before him to the barely discernible glint of racing water that marked the Paean frontier. Was not all this coconut-studded, shadow-washed plain his father's kingdom? Did not each plant and tree and vine speak of that patient man's loving care? Yes, Oropaa's spirit was everywhere Terii looked, in every stone-bordered path, in every lush and marshy taro patch, in every plot of carefully tended yams. All was the work of his father's hand and brain. Small wonder, then, that the slain king should be watching; small wonder that he should lend his own strength to his intrepid son.

Teva came to where the two weapons slanted from the ground and, stooping, wrenched them out. One he tossed to Terii and said condescendingly, "You have not done badly for such an undersized stripling. But this time will be the last. Have at it."

"Was mine the feebler throw?" Terii inquired.

"May the sea dry up and the reef burn!" the chief swore. " 'Feebler throw', do you say? Watch this and see what you call it." He stamped his left foot and his right into place and took a firm grip upon the shaft. "Would you like to know where my spear's point will bury itself?" he demanded.

"I shall see when it stands there quivering," said Terii.

Nevertheless Teva pointed ahead through the aisle of trees. "Do you mark where the two coconut boles grow side by side, twining eel-like, one about the other, till, at their very tops, they split apart in double, lofty plumes?"

Terii nodded. "Yes, I see."

"That is the place; and when I have done you may as well make kindling of the toa spear you hold, for it will never pass mine." Slowly the chief arched his back. The arm which held his weapon extended full out behind him, and the other arm balanced it before. Gone now was all trace of disdain as he bent farther and farther back till at last the butt of the lance touched the ground. "*Tera!*" he cried suddenly.

"There!" His tall, muscular body snapped forward, his long arm whipped over his head, and with the swiftness of a sling-shot stone, the shaft left his fingers. In a graceful arc it rose to reach the apex of its trajectory midway of the embracing trees, then curved downward to stab the earth exactly abreast of the twin boles, ninety spear-lengths away.

Great and uproarious was the delighted applause which then burst from the assembled warriors. Twirling their own spears and clubs they leaped and danced and capered, howling their triumph at the top of their lungs. "The throw of a champion," they yelled. "The throw of a chief! Give up, small son of a vanquished king. Go back to the spearing of small fish, to the tending of fields, to the work of women. Put aside that weapon made for manly deeds and return to things that match your size!" So loud was the din they made that it was heard in the upper valley where Terii's mother and his kinfolk waited anxiously for news of their young prince. Still more clearly it carried to Teva's nearby territory so that even as Terii stepped forward amid a fresh chorus of jeers and hoots he could descry the people of Papara as they came racing toward the river. On the farther bank they halted, all those who, because of sex or age, had been unable to join the night raid, and there they stood with hands upraised to shade their eyes while they strove to learn the cause of such savage and jubilant excitement.

Teva's wide smile again spread over his dusky face. His lips were parted and his strong teeth flashed as he turned to Motu and spoke. "Does that not satisfy you, Motu? Do you still fear to lose your grip on the rich land of Paea?"

Motu was looking gloomily, doubtfully, at Terii-of-the-Thousand-Eyes, who had planted himself in the spot just vacated by the chief, and who, with similar poise and deliberation, drew back his arm and slowly arched his supple back. "I prefer," said Teva's stolid warrior, "to save my rejoicings till the second spear has flown."

Teva was about to make a curt rejoinder, but at that moment Terii moved. In the same way that a sapling bent low over the lagoon to make a snare for sharks uncoils when the trap is sprung, so Terii's slender figure snapped upright. His arm shot through a perfect arc, and Oropaa's little-used spear went whistling from his hand. The shrill sound of its passage on the air seemed to strike every man dumb, and all those who had so recently been shouting taunts and insults remained with mouths foolishly agape as the wooden shaft rose to the level of the palm trees' lower branches. So had their chief's spear done before it started down. But what incredible thing was this? The weapon to which now each eye was glued sped on. It soared still higher—higher—till it grazed the topmost fronds of the coconuts that flanked it on either side.

109

A yell from one of Teva's warriors shattered the silence. "Drop!" he screamed. "Drop, spirit-ridden spear." Others took up the frantic cry: "Fall, fall, fall!"

In its own time the spear pointed earthward and finally sank its hardened point into the ground. No one spoke; all stared. There, by the twining trees lay the weapon of their chief, and there, as far beyond as the length of three canoes, was that of Teriitaumatatini. One after another the many pairs of eyes swerved to fasten upon the son of Oropaa. In wonder and astonishment they gazed, seeking vainly to discover the secret of the thing they had witnessed. How could so reedy, so thin and undeveloped a form as his hold the strength to make a cast that was the envy of every man?

Teva's amazement had been no less than the others', but it was of shorter duration and soon gave way to towering rage. He gave a shake to his big frame and then beat his chest with a clenched fist. "This is trickery!" he bellowed and thrust his distorted cloud-dark face close to Terii's. "It is not your work alone, and you furtively call upon the hidden gods, your ancestors, the winds, or winged things to give you aid."

But Terii answered reasonably. "In whatever I do I call forth my ancestors. How should it be otherwise when it is they who made me what I am? And if the winds favor me it must be that the gods would willingly see righted a grievous wrong."

"The strength of my arm will dictate what is right," Teva growled. Without a glance at the anxious faces of his men he rushed down the field and savagely tore his weapon from the earth. But although each time he hurled his spear Teva now dropped back successively two paces, four, six, and finally ten to make a furious running start, Terii, each time following suit, surpassed him. The day wore on, the heat increased, and steadily the flashing, turbulent waters of the river neared till at last the people lining the farther bank were within shouting distance of the contestants. It was apparent by this time to even the most unobserving among Teva's supporters that the chief was tiring. Perspiration ran down his arms and back and stood out in beads upon his forehead. Long ago he had abandoned the least trace of the superciliousness with which he had begun the contest; long ago he had ceased to patronize his slight antagonist. Many throws back the competition had become a struggle in which the chief fought with all his might to retain his newly conquered kingdom. Yet even now as he leaned heavily upon his spear and eyed the dividing stream, Teva would not concede defeat. He was only dully aware of the grumblings that swelled from his own people, for the sound of his labored breathing was more immediate and loud. Then Motu's gruff voice penetrated his consciousness.

"This is your last chance, Teva. Do not, for want of total effort, lose the land for which forty of our number died."

"Effort!" the chief growled. "Have I the look of one at play? Mind your own business, Motu, and leave this to me. The boy's appearance, it is true, is little different from when we first began, but he must feel the strain as well as I and is surely near collapse. Step aside!"

Teva stalked twenty paces to the rear. Low he crouched, like a beast about to spring upon its prey, his muscles quivering as they waited his brain's signal to unleash his last remaining ounce of strength. With a guttural cry he burst forward, his racing feet thudding upon the earth. At the end of his mad dash his entire body hurtled into the air as if the angrily whizzing bolt he loosed drew him irresistibly after it. In the next instant he crashed full length to the ground, but immediately he raised his head and watched the great spear wing on and on and on. While it was still in mid-flight a tremendous shout rang over the fertile plain—a shout which began with the males of the Papara clan who stood behind their chief, traveled through the air to those others who waited tensely beyond the river and was seized by them and sent rocking back again. From the moment the spear left Teva's hand it was apparent to all, and to Terii, too, that never before in Tahiti had so heavy a weapon sped so fast and so true. The power of desperation was behind Teva's mighty throw; it bore up the brown, tapered shaft, seeming to give it the lightness and fleetness of an arrow of slim bamboo, drawing it above the banana stalks, above the coconut palms, above the still taller breadfruit trees, then guiding it surely downward to fix it firmly, challengingly, on the very bank of the stream, hardly a hand's breadth from the water. A new frenzy seized all Teva's company as with wild shrieks they whirled in frantic dances, beating and pummeling each other with joy.

For the first time Terii felt an uneasy doubt. Almost imperceptibly he shook his head, and silently he spoke his thoughts to Oropaa's friendly, hovering spirit. "My father, I have tried to save the land you loved, but no false pride fills me; I know I am still a boy. Is all that I have gained to slip away?"

Teva came beside him and when the noise was somewhat less, asked: "Will you not admit yourself bettered, king's son? It is no disgrace to concede defeat when success is impossible. Keep your father's spear if you wish. Keep, too, what strength is left you, and we will call the contest closed."

"I may fail," Terii admitted, "but I should be shamed to make no final bid for victory."

The tall black chieftain of Papara looked down on the youthful prince and, despite his former contempt for the boy, made no attempt to conceal his admiration. "I should myself be glad of a son like you," he said slowly. "Make your throw."

Terii, like Teva, walked a score of paces to the rear. He crouched low, and, despite their recent confidence and hilarity, the intently watching warriors were held in an expectant silence. Lightly the youth brushed the palms of his hands over the ground, then gripped his spear. Carefully he found his stance. With right leg flexed, his weight resting against the heel, he slightly, springily raised his body, then let it fall again. And even as Terii-of-the-Thousand-Eyes tested his balance, so also, at that moment, the fate of the whole kingdom of Paea hung in precarious suspension. "The hour has come," he thought. "After this it is done, it is ended.

Wait no longer; let fly." Yet he did not move. "Come!" he goaded himself. "Leap forward!" Poised for action, he remained locked in the tight-coiled, readied crouch, unable, with however great an exertion of will, to command his legs to spring. One may well ask what invisible bonds were these that tied him helpless in such a terrible time of need. The answer is fear—the fear that may descend on any man when he risks all that he holds most dear. Paralyzingly clear in Terii's mind was the knowledge that on him alone depended home, country, even the lives of those he loved.

All at once, from above and far away, there came a single human call. Whirling, Terii looked over his shoulder and through the trees. Quickly his eyes found the lone palm which marked the entrance of the hidden valley where his people waited, and before he turned away he had seen, too, a single figure pressed close to the bole beneath the withering, yellowed fronds. He glanced at Teva, caught the smile on the chief's swarthy face, and knew with heart-stabbing certainty that the upland sanctuary was secret no longer. Now, indeed, was disaster piled upon disaster.

But like the clear, penetrating blast of a conch shell, the cry came again, and with a tingling of his entire body Terii recognized his father's words. "Teriitaumatatini," it called, "*a puai!* Terii-of-the-Thousand-Eyes, be strong!"

Suddenly his dread was gone. With the tearing force with which a shark rips a confining net he burst from his imprisoning doubt and fear. He was free, he was strong, strong in his faith in himself, in his knowledge of his father's presence, in his will to win. Terii raced toward the beckoning ribbon of glinting, swirling water, unconscious of Teva's warriors as they flashed past, unconscious of Motu planted close to one side of the path, and unconscious even of tall, scowling Teva to the other. He was aware only of the fiery surge of his coursing blood, of the glorious, swift rhythm of unleashed muscles and the uplift of boundless, youthful energy which seemed to draw him to the clouds.

Some there are who say that the youth who was soon to become Paea's king took wings that day, and so it may well have seemed. What he accomplished, however, was not done by wizardry. Still, when he threw himself into the air he seemed not to be drawn after his hurtling toa spear, but to soar behind it, impelling it farther and farther, faster and faster. When again he touched the ground it was not heavily, nor did he fall. With agile lightness he found his footing and remained, eyes flashing, head erect, watching the fantastic upward flight of the liberating weapon once his father's, now his own.

"Higher," he murmured fervently, "higher, my lovely spear. Ride the winds, brush the clouds, take hold upon the sky!"

Ever farther back tilted the heads of Teva and his people as with bated breath they followed the ascending shaft. Up and on they saw it go till, high above the river, it paused as if it found there a fragile grip on the shimmering blue. Then, almost perpendicularly, it plunged down. A white fountain spurted from the stream, and the warriors who not long before had swum in darkness the same cold, mountain waters rushed forward to line the near bank as their women did the far. Neither group looked at the other but only at the long spear which bent to the joyous current in the center of the river.

For minutes there was no sound other than the purling of the seaward-hurrying stream. Teva was first to break the dazed silence. Strangely, at this final rout he showed no sign of the uncontrolled rage that had shaken him following his earlier defeats. "Such things," he said calmly, "do not happen without reason. It will be told that I have been beaten by a boy in a sport designed for men, but let no one ever say that Teva feared to keep his promise. Men of Papara, mark well the place where Prince Terii's spear has fallen. That is the boundary between our realms, and there it shall remain." He turned to Motu. "Come, and let all others follow."

Together Teva and Motu plunged into the river and struck out for the opposite shore, and the rest of their band went quickly after. Terii stood alone.

He turned and took a few steps in the direction of Oropaa's village, then halted. Impulsively he wheeled and dived into the clear, spring-fed waters. He retrieved his spear and climbed out again. His mother and his friends and relatives would have seen the retreat of the enemy and might, even now, have left the upper valley. Carrying the toa shaft upon his shoulder, he started with rapid strides for home, and as he went he spoke aloud.

"It is better so, my father. I had thought to leave behind the spear which in your youth you made. Teva will, I believe, keep his word; but though I find life in this world very beautiful, it seems to me most insecure. We shall till the fields you loved, but also we shall keep our weapons bright."

The Cloud Sisters of Lower-Havaiki

AT times I urged Tetua to visit me at my house, which is few miles distant from his own. Always he declined, and his intuitive reluctance is not difficult to understand. As a setting in which to evoke the past and bring ancient gods and heroes to life, my home lacks the proper atmosphere. From without, built as it was by Polynesian hands, it has, to be sure, the appearance of being completely native to the soil. Yet, inside, this simple harmony is lost.

On the desk are South Sea shells, but wood carvings from Switzerland decorate the room as well. Here are large-petaled flowers with which to string a *hei*, but the earthen bowl over whose brim they spill came from Jalisco's kilns in Mexico. Resting on a bookcase are coral fragments from the near lagoon, but beside them lie others from the waters of Japan. There are savage weapons from Nuku Hiva, and machetes from Spanish-conquered Guam. Hanging against a sarong of Javan batik is a charcoal drawing of a deep-chested diver from the pearl shell atolls, but close by are the likenesses of New England kith and kin. A man who has wandered the globe lives among numerous small distractions, and, however little he may care for mere collection, his home holds many odds and ends which betray the paths he has followed, the things he has been or done. My bamboo castle is a place of divided allegiance. Many a memory draws me elsewhere, many a hope and future plan are with me in my house beside the sea, sharing my consciousness of the land in which I presently live.

But at Tetua's—ah, there is utter forgetfulness of the past or future, oneness with the island world. No single thing in all his open, uncluttered dwelling turns the mind down roads already trod, or sets one peering myopically into the vague uncertainties of time to come. As Tetua is of Tahiti, so he who visits him seems to become of Tahiti also.

Surely it was at dawn and sunrise that my awareness of Tetua's proud, high island was most intense. What, exactly, may have been his thoughts and feelings when we stepped from the half-dark of the house to the twilight of a new day, I do not know. Yet it seems to me unlikely that they were very different from mine, for there are times when one man—no matter what his language, tribe, or color—must be much like any other. The hour which brings the marvel of a waking South Sea morning is such a time. It is a brief hour, one of breathless expectancy, and always, while the world about us stirred from sleep, it would find us standing side by side, held by the slowly unfolding miracle. The cool downdraft from the highlands then has ceased. There is a lingering pause before the trade winds spring to life upon the ocean, fanning the island to complete wakefulness, and in that pause is the faint commingling of earth and flower scents with the smell of the salty deep. The mountains lose their color of dreamy grey and, shaking off their drowsiness, come striding closer, closer, as if, like ourselves, they would dash away the last vestiges of slumber by a plunge in the Pacific's marching rollers. The deliberate, leisured sun tops the inland peaks; shafts of light ride down the suddenly bright green slopes; thrice-lengthened shadows of seaside palms shoot over the bay to lie like plumed serpents in stretches of quiet water. Although each tree is freighted with a delirious company of birds that sing aloud their glee, a man may find no voice to express the emotions which then well up within him. Perhaps he is mute, perhaps he does not move, but at no other instant is he more gratefully alive.

On the morning following our walk to Point Venus, when Tetua's eyes had scanned earth and sky and outspread ocean, he turned to me. "Take your swim, Viriamu," he said. "I shall put the coffee on the fire before I join you."

A quarter hour passed, and I was already drying, stretched at full length on the still-cool sands with my hands clasped beneath my head, when Tetua took his place beside me. "Do you read the future in the clouds?" he asked.

"No," I laughed. "At this moment I am quite willing to let the future take care of itself. But I was thinking that, like mankind, those shapes which move across the heavens are of an endless variety, each with a character all its own."

"Oh, yes," he agreed, "they are of every sort and temperament. Some are pompous, bloated and slow-moving, some—airy, gamboling wisps—are children at play. Others are stately women with trailing robes of sheerest milk-white tapa, and there are also those that glower darkly and speak with the rumbling voice of thunder. Our language is rich in words for the different clouds, and many an island babe, especially in former times, was named for them. And that reminds me," said he with a glance over his shoulder to the cookhouse where the fire crackled, "of a story I might tell you while we breakfast."

In an instant I was on my feet and Tetua smiled. "What brings you up so quickly—the thought of coffee, or the tale?"

"Both," I admitted. "One needs the other."

And so, tearing the end from a loaf of bread, Tetua began his story.   *115*

In the land of Havaiki-te-a-raro or Lower-Havaiki there once lived three sisters. All of them were named for clouds. A gloomily unsmiling young woman was Ua, the eldest, and hers was the name of the grey, dripping cloud which holds the rain. Next was stormy-tempered Rau, named for the darkly threatening thunderhead. The youngest was called Mea—a cloud which catches the reddish light of the rising sun. An observant mother had given the girls these names, and while she was alive they fitted each most perfectly. But at the time of which I speak several years had passed since the mother's death, and although Ua and Rau's respectively sullen and ill-natured dispositions had remained unchanged, Mea was not the same. She had ceased to run and frolic as if borne along by gentle breezes such as play across the upper sky; the smile was gone from her lips and so, too, was the glow on her cheeks which had resembled her name-cloud in the dawn. It was as if something stood between her and the sun, taking all the brilliance which rightfully should have been hers. So it seemed and so it was, for Ua and Rau were directly in her path. All clouds are beautiful, but of what use is beauty if it goes unseen? What youth will sing a love song for a maid whose face is hidden or whose charm is all disguised?

One might be moved to ask what manner of father these girls had that he should sit by unprotesting while, month in, month out, his youngest daughter did the work of three. Always it was Mea with her broom of twigs who swept the house in which her father lived, who kindled the oven fires, who baked his fish and pig and poi. It hardly seems possible he could be unaware that from dawn to dark his older daughters lolled in idleness, engaged in no more serious purpose than the bathing and perfuming and adornment of themselves. Yet such was in fact the case, for Reka was a famous warrior whose counsel was much sought after by the country's king. His thoughts dwelt on matters which he considered far more important than the management of his home. With a mind engaged in deciding upon which tribes it might be advisable and safe to wage a war and which it might be best to leave alone, he failed to take note of what went on beneath his roof.

Reka's house stood near the shore at some distance from the inland village of the king, and at about noon one day a messenger from the island ruler came running down the trail which led to Reka's door.

"*Ia ora na!*" he cried as he approached. "King Anuanua sends his greetings."

Reka looked up from where he sat in the shade of the overhanging thatch. "You have news for me?" he inquired, without moving from his comfortable position.

"Not for you," said the youth, "but for the cloud sisters, Ua, Rau, and Mea."

Reka was faintly disappointed. "What can you want of my daughters?"

Before the messenger could reply, Ua and Rau, who had been braiding and perfuming each other's hair, put their sleek heads out the door. "They are asked," said the courier, addressing the dark-eyed, handsome young women directly, "to dance for the king's son. There will be singing and feasting, and all the girls of the realm shall perform before Prince Moe-tapu so that he may choose himself a wife."

Said Rau sharply, "There will be much to do. Mea must beat for us tapa of exceeding thinness, she must crush jasmine to make perfume for our bodies, she must find smallest mountain shells to hang in long strands about our necks. When is it to be?"

"Soon," said the young man, "so soon that Mea will have no more than time to make the dress that she herself will wear."

Rau had come out of the house and now stood, proud and tall, before Anuanua's messenger. "Is it likely," she asked in a voice which carried the chill of blanketing rains from the southern pole, "is it likely that Prince Moe-tapu would care to look upon a child so plain and lacking in all charm? Mea will have no need of other garment than the coarse brown stuff she daily wears. Her place is here at home. Now tell us, boy, when will the drums begin to throb?"

Taken aback by the heartlessness of Rau's tone and words, the youth was unable to reply immediately, and he stared in dismay first at the two disdainful girls and then at their father, who, as soon as he learned there was no question of war or other affair of weight, appeared to have lost all interest and was gazing placidly out to sea. "The time," the messenger replied at last, "is tomorrow at sundown; the place is the ground before Anuanua's dwelling, which many dancing feet have pressed before." Hurriedly, then, he started off; but on his way he passed the outlying cookhouse and paused a moment, listening to the sound which came clearly through the leafy walls. Someone was rapidly rubbing a coco shell against a sharpened, pointed grater, shredding the firm white meat of the nut from which to wring sauce for the midday meal. The king's young envoy hesitated. Surely, he thought, that would be Mea preparing the food for her idle family. Could it be that two women so haughtily beautiful as were Ua and Rau had a younger sister who held no interest for a man? Unable to resist the temptation to see for himself, he stepped quietly to the back of the shelter and peered through a chink in the fronds.

The girl, who bent over a large wooden bowl filled almost to the brim with a cargo of milky white, could have been sixteen, but hardly more. She sat astride a three-legged bench with the grater held firmly between her knees, and as she turned the nut in her hands, scraping the inner surface of the shell, her tangled hair fell forward, half covering her supple arms. The single length of rough cloth which was fastened above her breasts was bare of all design or decoration. She wore no flower, no amulet of polished wood or bone, and although the king's messenger could see slim legs which seemed made for dancing, he saw also a mouth pensive and sad, eyes large and somber. Dawn-Cloud—was that indeed her name? Then surely it was bestowed in jest and mockery. Disappointed, and now confirmed in the judgment of the older sisters, the youth turned away. Anuanua's feast would lose nothing by this girl's absence.

In going he must have made a sound, because Mea paused and listened. Footsteps? Perhaps a lover? So any other girl would have thought. But Mea dismissed the

117

idea immediately. Such things might be for Ua and Rau, but not for her. She gathered up the grated coconut and wrung out the rich cream into three bowls which she placed on the floor. She added half a calabash of raw fish, yams, and plantains, then stepped to the door and called, "*A mai tama'a.* Come and eat."

It was Reka's privilege as a male and a warrior, and a famous one besides, to dine first. He got up with alacrity and was soon helping himself to the good things which Mea had assembled. When he had finished, Ua and Rau promptly took their places beside the spread banana fronds, while their younger sister waited. Customarily, after a leisurely repast, Reka's elder daughters went directly to the house, where they stretched out languidly upon their sleeping mats; but today they walked first to Mea.

"Eat quickly of the scraps which we have left," said Ua. "There is work to do, and you shall be busied the long night through. Make dresses for each of us in which to dance before the prince and king."

"Make them fine and make them light," Rau commanded. "Make them soft and sheer. We must appear enchanting in Moe-tapu's sight so that he will take one of us for wife."

Mea could not suppress a quickening of the heart at her sisters' words. There would be feasting, much singing, and, best of all, endless dancing. What would she not give to be able to forget her sorrows, to fling aside all care and leap nimbly into the dancing ring, to lose herself in the joyous, intoxicating rhythms of the *'ori?* She was far from any idea of captivating Prince Moe-tapu, whom she thought lumpish, lazy, and unexciting, and if anyone had mentioned such a thing she would have considered it both impossible and absurd. But just to dance! By some look or gesture she must have betrayed her unreasonable excitement, for Ua gave her a frigid glance.

"Does your face brighten, child? Does a glow of color touch your cheeks? Be done with foolish fancies! We will not be shamed by one as plain as you, so think not to go beyond your home."

"Do not anger us with silly daydreams," Rau snapped with the hint of lightning in her eyes. "Get quickly to your feet and be about your tasks."

Without further speech they left her. Mea, the faint suggestion of the dawn-cloud quite gone from her features, rose to do as she was bidden. And as the rapid, steady tapping of her mallet rang through the drowsy afternoon as she worked upon the moistened mulberry bark, her hopelessness had never seemed so clear, her unhappiness so great. The fact that even as she worked events were in the making which were to change vastly her fate and fortune was, quite naturally, no consolation since she could not foresee them. She was no wizard, no *tahua*, this girl of loveliness still unguessed by all save her jealous sisters, and, like most of us, she could do no more than plod forward through the narrow world her eyes were given to behold. As you have seen, this world, in Mea's case, was bounded by two dark clouds. Yet even at that moment, when those shadow-casting shapes loomed highest and most imprisoning, forces were at work which would soon alter her fate.

In the land of Upper-Havaiki, Kahu-kura, only son of King Uri-toa, was suddenly seized by a strange malady. He was at this time about eighteen years of age, and although there may still have remained a certain boyishness in his bright-eyed, handsome features, his body had the height and the firmly muscled form of a full-grown man. Never in his life had he had a day of illness. But on the afternoon, and at the very hour, that Mea, many leagues away, bent to the arduous task of cloth-making, Kahu-kura first noticed the trouble with his ears. He had been diving for fish at a place in the lagoon not far removed from his home, and after a pursuit of several minutes beneath the water he pinned a plump, red *iihi* against a coral ledge and then burst to the surface with it firmly impaled upon his spear. He swam to his canoe, removed the fish from his spear, and was about to dive again when, abruptly, he stopped and gave a vigorous shake to his head. He listened intently, then pounded his ears with his palms and listened once more. The sound was still there.

He called to his father, who sat on the shore with several of his friends telling stories of things done and seen and heard.

"Who is beating the drums?" Kahu-kura shouted.

The group on the beach looked out to him in surprise. Briefly they consulted in tones which failed to reach the young man. Then the king cupped his hands to his mouth. "Shake the sea water from your ears," he advised. "The temple drums are silent; the hula drums are put away, and there is no sound louder than the crickets' chirping."

Kahu-kura smiled. "You make sport of me. There are drums. They are faint and far, but clear."

The king frowned slightly and, rising, walked to the edge of the lagoon and beckoned to his son. "Come here and let me look at you," he commanded.

Kahu-kura drew himself into his canoe and, taking the paddle, pushed in to shore. "Has deafness come upon you all?" he asked good naturedly as he stepped out.

"We are not deaf," said his father, and, drawing the youth to him, he peered first into one ear and then the other. "Well," he remarked when he had finished his inspection, "I see nothing—neither bug nor louse nor ocean brine. Now, have done with such a childish game; it does not become your years."

"Father," said Kahu-kura earnestly, "I have no desire to play at games. I hear a drum, and now I perceive that it is not upon our island. It beats from out at sea in the direction of Havaiki-te-a-raro, and I think it calls to me."

An expression of concern now appeared on the king's face. "Miru," said he to one of his companions, "I fear my son is ill or else bewitched. Summon the priests and the medicine makers and let them seek a cure."

So it was that the best minds of the kingdom were soon assembled. Many were the fingers which poked inquisitively into Kahu-kura's ears, many were the charms which were hung about his neck. Many also were the spells and incantations which were mumbled, spoken, and intoned. All was to no avail. Finally King Uri-toa saw that the devices of even his wisest men were without effect, and he proclaimed what all had then begun to fear. "Son," said he, "this may be a day of happiness or sorrow. Which, we cannot tell. One thing only is clear: a spirit has found lodgment in your body and will bend you to its will. Harken, obey, and thus the drumming in your head may at last be stilled."

"That I shall do," the youth replied, "for now the throbbing message bids me put to sea. I must follow and find, for good or ill, the place in which it rises. I feel strongly drawn away, yet perhaps it is not, after all, a drum I hear. The sound is more like that of wood on wood than the hollow note of taut shark skins. Such a sound the women make when beating tapa cloth, yet whereas their mallets rise and fall in dull monotony, this secret song of mine is quick with life and yearning. Will you believe when I tell you in what persuasive, fascinating language it speaks to me? It is in rhythms of the hula!"

"We must believe since it is you who say it," the king answered, "even though such things surpass our understanding." Then he addressed the crowd which had gathered on the strand. "Wait here, people of Upper-Havaiki, while my son and I go to our home for a last word before we part."

When, a few minutes later, they stood within their house, the king reached up and detached the cord by which a bulky package was suspended, safe from damp and insects, beneath a rafter. "This, Kahu-kura," he explained, as he carefully unfolded layer after layer of protecting tapa, "is the cape I wore when I was made ruler of this land. Never since has it seen the light of day, and you will find the red feathers —tail plumes of wild ducks from the high mountains—dimmed with age. Other kings have donned sacred crimson cloaks in symbol of their sovereignty, but not such a one as this." There was a soft rustling as Uri-toa shook out the garment so that it spread about his feet and lightly trailed upon the sandy floor. "This cape, my son," he continued, "is more than *tapu*: it is charmed. Lash it to the mast of your canoe, and whether the winds blow from north or south, or even cease to blow at all, your craft will forge on to the goal you keep in mind. I have no other gift, and I ask only that this thing of beauty which our ancestors plucked from the sky may keep fresh within your memory a father's love and so, perhaps, lead you back some day."

Uri-toa placed the winged cloak over the youth's shoulders. Briefly they embraced, pressing noses side to side, and then together walked down to the shore. There Kahu-kura made fast his feathered sail to the slender upright spar which rose a little forward of amidships. He seated himself in the stern and grasped his paddle. The customary farewells were exchanged, even as they are today when a man sets out from his island home.

"Friends and relatives, remain behind."

"Kahu-kura of the crimson cape, go."

"Louder now in my ears the spirit drumming rings," the young prince answered. "I am ready; I shall go."

With his own hands King Uri-toa launched his son's small outrigger onto the calm waters. No breeze stirred, yet there came a fluttering in the red feathers at the mast as if they were again inhabited by the wild fowls from which they had been seized; and the canoe sped out to sea toward what adventure no man knew. Through the remaining daylight hours it continued, through the starlit night as well, and not until the next afternoon did Kahu-kura again catch sight of land. Never in all that time had the strange, compelling signal ceased its steady pulsing; but though it still came in heart-lifting, dancing rhythms, it seemed to the voyager that the percussive message held also overtones of sadness and of wordless longing for the very joys its lilting beat suggested.

"What can it mean?" Kahu-kura asked himself. "This island which I near is surely Havaiki-te-a-raro, and Anuanua is its king. But who calls me here, and why?" Unable to find an answer, he allowed his canoe to sail on where it would, and in this manner he skirted the coast for some distance, till at last he was borne to a beach of smooth round stones. He dragged the outrigger to the safety of a grassy bank, removed the remarkable sail, folded it, and tucked it under his arm. Where to, then? His eyes roamed irresolutely the jungle-clad terrain which stretched before him. And what of the ghostly, luring rhythm—had it ceased to lead? Suddenly Kahu-kura stood stock-still. No longer did it echo in his head. The tapping of wood on wood rang sharply on his ears, not from within himself, not like the faraway sound of dreams, but real and close at hand. In an instant he was running toward it, leaping the fallen trunks of trees, tearing aside the tangled vines, startling into the air flocks of angrily scolding birds, and sending armies of ungainly land crabs scuttling for their holes. He crashed through a thick brake of sagging, top-heavy elephant ear and burst into a little clearing, then came to an abrupt halt. The place was hardly larger than the floor of a modest dwelling. Like a room it had bounding walls, walls of growing jungle green, but Kahu-kura remarked them not; like a room it had a carpet, not of sand, not of woven mat, but a carpet of sweet lush grass, and this, too, he did not perceive. There was a gently flowing spring, and the roof was all of blue, yet Uri-toa's son remained quite unaware of every thing save one.

She knelt beside the bright, pebble-bottomed pool, the four-sided tapa beater, silent now, still half raised in her hand. Frightened and surprised, she looked at him with big and somber eyes.

Slowly and very quietly, as if he feared to dispel the lovely vision which he had found at journey's end, Kahu-kura came toward her, and Mea, unable to move or speak, awaited him.

"Who are you?" he breathed when he was close to her. "By what name are you called?"

Reassured by the gentleness of his tone she lowered her arm and placed the grooved beater on the board beside the mound of foam-white tapa which she had made. A faint smile trembled on her lips. "You will think it strange. My name is Mea."

"Dawn-Cloud!" he exclaimed in pleasure. "It is a happy choice, and such you seem to me."

"Do I?" she asked in wonder. "Not since my mother held me as a child has it been thought."

Kahu-kura sat beside her on the grass. "Are the people of this island blind?"

"Blind?" she echoed, bewildered.

"Have you not suitors by the hundred?"

Mea had imagined that she had forgotten how to laugh. Yet suddenly, at his question, she was doing so, and was herself startled by the merry sound which rippled from her throat. How could it be? Was the lack of all admirers, before so deep a sorrow, become a matter of no consequence? But there was no time now to solve so perplexing a problem. "Suitors?" she said. "I have not one, and it must be of my sisters you are thinking. Ua and Rau are sought by all the youths, although they want Prince Moe-tapu only. It is for him they go to dance tonight."

"And what of you, Mea? Do you also wish for Moe-tapu?"

She shook her head.

"But you will dance?" he persisted.

Again the negative shake of her lovely dark head.

"Then for what," he demanded, "are the robes I have heard you beating through all the night and day?"

Mea turned away and, with eyes once more shadowed, gazed into the limpid depths of the little spring. "They are my sisters' things," she murmured, "not mine; they are for Rau and Ua, not for me."

Kahu-kura placed his father's cloak on the ground beside him and took both her hands in his. "Mea, look here to me. I know now why I have come across the sea. It was to go with you to Anuanua's feast and there to dance with you. I know now," he continued confidently, "why you called to me, why I heard and why I took to my canoe."

The glow was bright on Mea's smooth brown cheeks, and sun tints played within her eyes as beneath Kahu-kura's glance her naturally joyous and happy spirit came wakening to life. "No youth of Havaiki-te-a-raro," she thought, "has lips like these that smile at me, no son of my island speaks with voice so warm and moving, none have hands whose touch is like caresses in a fleeting dream. His nearness sets the world alight, filling me with hopes and promises which I never dared conceive. And yet there is mystery in his words."

"I did not call," she whispered, "although I surely would have done so if I could have reached your ears."

"There is an inner language," Kahu-kura replied, "which travels farther and more clearly than any spoken tongue. First, I think, it reaches silent, watchful gods who then lift it on the winds and send it where they will. In such wordless speech your message came to me; it took me from my father and brought me here to you. So listen while I tell you how we shall face each other in the hula when the flares are brightly burning and revelry is high."

"I should love to hear you tell it," said Mea wistfully, "although it cannot ever be."

"Not be! For what reason should it not?"

She ran a hand over the plain, work-roughened material which clothed her. "Like this? Could I go to a feast dressed as I am?"

"No," he laughed, "but why should you? What of the tapa which lies there fresh from off your board? It looks worthy of a queen."

"No one in our country," Mea admitted with a hint of pride, "makes finer cloth than mine. But you forget; that is for my sisters, for Ua and for Rau."

"By the clouds of rain and thunder from which they take their names!" Kahu-kura exclaimed. "Are they then incapable of making dresses for themselves?"

The girl did not answer, and in her silence and the slight trembling of her lower lip Uri-toa's son read much that he had not guessed before. When she reached down and grasped again the carven stick with which she thinned the fibrous bark, he took it from her hand.

"There is still much to do," she protested gently, "and already the sun is halfway down the sky."

"Mea," he said abruptly, "will you do one thing for me? Will you, for the rest of this day, forget your sisters, forget all that troubles you, and do only as I say?"

She looked at him doubtfully. "What would you have of me?"

He got to his knees and bent over the tapa board. "First, lie here upon the grass while I finish what you yourself have begun."

"But that is women's work," she protested.

"Do not the priests beat out bark to clothe the temple idols?"

"Yes," Mea hesitated, then with a laugh stretched herself on the soft green carpet and cupped her chin in her hands. "You may tell me when you tire," she remarked considerately.

"Tire!" he scoffed. "Is it likely that one who swims the deep lagoons, who hunts the mountain boar and sails alone the dangerous ocean, would falter at such a task as this? Do you not know who I am?"

Said Mea, reasonably, "How should I?"

With wooden beater upraised the young man paused. "What?"

"I have not heard you say."

He grinned broadly and the corners of his mouth curved up his cheeks. "That is true," he admitted, "and it is unlike a man of our race to forget to sing his own praises. However, it is not too late to begin." The mallet descended and a rapid tattoo rolled out into the little glen. Kahu-kura raised his voice, and this is how he chanted to the rhythm which he beat upon the slowly forming cloth:

> Behind was Havaiki-te-a-nia,
> Before, the applauding waves;
> Astern was Kahu-kura,
> Mea was ahead!
> Then cried Kahu-kura
> Over the foaming sea,
> "O what land is it,
> What land is looming up?"
> Havaiki-te-a-raro,
> Where lies the Dawn-red-Cloud!
> Again cried Kahu-kura
> Over the curling waves,
> "Draw, sail, that my canoe may run.
> Draw to sea and draw to shore,
> Draw, that my canoe may run!"

In this way Kahu-kura described his recent voyage, but it was no more than a simple introduction to the story still to come. He told the exploits of his youth and childhood, even of his infancy; he told the romance of his father and mother and gave their history; he went on to aunts and uncles and all his family. During the waning hours of the day the chant continued as he moved unerring backward through the generations to deeds of those long gone but familiar as his own. While the song still spoke alone of Kahu-kura, Mea had remained alertly attentive, but by the time he was dealing with the manner in which a great-great-grandfather had surprised a giant turtle on the beach, her eyes had slowly closed. Of this he was quickly aware, and though he smiled, the repetitive chant kept on, lest by sudden silence he should waken her. Only when the last strip of bark was of the smooth consistency of cloth did he lay aside the beater and let drop the far-from-ended narrative.

Immediately Mea sat up. "*Aue!*" she exclaimed in distress. "I fell asleep."

"It is good," he replied, gathering up the finished tapa and placing it in her lap. "You are rested?"

"Yes, Kahu-kura." She eyed him speculatively for a moment, then asked impulsively, "Why are you named for a flaming cloak?"

He touched the faded feathers of the once bright garment at his side. "I have never before been sure, but today I think it is because my happiness will come to me so clothed. Be quick now, Mea. Carry the tapa to your sisters. Then bathe yourself and return to me before the sun has set."

"Never will they permit me to leave so soon."

"Then come without permission," he said almost angrily. "This is not to be a night when rain or thunder clouds hold the center of the sky. It shall be yours, Mea, yours alone if you will do each thing I say."

The girl rose with the white material in her arms. "I could wish no more," she told him, "if we went no farther than this quiet spring, but whatever you ask of me I shall be unable to refuse." Going to the inland side of the small forest clearing, she parted the green wall and slipped through. Immediately the tropic plants closed behind her, and Kahu-kura was left alone.

No sooner had the leaves set trembling by her passage stilled, than Kahu-kura himself, taking an opposite direction, set out through the jungle and, going from plant to plant, began gathering the largest of the island's flowers, great red flowers whose full-blown, backward-curling petals exposed long, nodding stamens with pollen-crusted tips. They were not plentiful, and he had made a rough circle covering much ground before he was back again at the starting point with the number he desired. There he ripped a long ribbon of pliant *purau* bark and, seating himself once more by the tapa board, rapidly strung the brilliant blossoms to form a festive *hei*. He lightly dipped the finished double strands in the spring and laid them, fresh and cool and bejewelled with glistening drops, upon the dark green grass.

"*Nehenehe*," a voice murmured. "Oh, beautiful." And he turned to find Mea close beside him. She stooped and, picking up the *hei*, buried her face in its sweet fragrance. "It is the breath of our bright islands," she said, lifting her eyes to his.

He put out his hands and slipped the garland over her head. "Yes," he agreed, looking into her shining countenance, "and I see before me the most lovely flower this soil has ever grown."

If Anuanua's messenger—or any other dweller in the land—could at that moment have beheld the radiant girl, he would have spoken likewise. Directly from the stream in which she bathed she had come. To her bare arms and shoulders, to her waist-long, night-black hair, sparkling drops of water still clung as if she had run through showers of sun-filled rain. Even on her brows and parted lips was a dew which glowed like the spring-drenched blossoms at her throat and breast. So, at Kahu-kura's coming, had Mea stepped from the shadow of her older sisters to stand thus disclosed in all her natural, vibrant charm.

For a moment Kahu-kura remained silent, staring, enchanted by the joyous miracle he had so quickly wrought. Then he gathered up his father's cape and took Mea by the hand. "Beloved," he said in undisguised excitement, "already you are beautiful beyond compare. But we have not done, and we must hurry." He led her back along the way he first had come and released her only when they stood upon the shore beside his small canoe. Full in their faces shone the setting sun where it rode upon the distant waters. Over all the sky which the great god Tane, in the beginning, so laboriously raised, the sun spread its vivid, luminous color; over all the world from which Tane, in the time of glorious creation, banished the teeming, murmurous confusion of endless dark and first admitted light, it sent its ruddy glow. It suffused each floating cloud above, each white-capped wave beneath, each evening-quiet frond of palm, each grain of powdered coral on the silent strand.

Kahu-kura unbound the feather cape. With a sweep of his arms he flung it high up into the air. "O dazzling wanderer of the heavens," he cried, "pause one instant in your flight and touch with flame the red cloak of a king!" While his words still rang, the regal garment caught the distant fire and then, brilliant, shimmering as if every feather had been steeped in burning red, descended slowly, bird-light, to his outstretched hands.

"Ah, Mea," he exclaimed in great delight, "I see what the gods have done for you: again these plumes are crimsoned as when first the wild ducks winged them across the blazing sun." With a deft movement he slipped Uri-toa's magical cloak about the girl's waist, made it fast, and leaped back to admire with astonishment the success of his own inspiration. The trembling *mo'ora* feathers rippled from her hips, streamed down her thighs to flutter about her bare and nimble feet. Seeing her flashing smile, the last trace of sadness now vanished, Kahu-kura wondered momentarily if it could be an earthly creature now so gladly facing him, or whether a passing breath of rising air might snatch her up, to place her in a proper home among the freely, gaily drifting shapes of heaven.

Then from far inland the drums of Anuanua broke out in a swift staccato rhythm. The festival had begun. On the beach by Kahu-kura's canoe Mea gave a sudden clap of her hands and, caring for no other audience than the man she loved, began the hula later seen by many eyes.

At the same time, Ua and Rau left their home and, walking leisurely in order to attract more attention by a late arrival, started off to the place of celebration.

126

Clothed in the fine garments which Mea had begun and Kahu-kura finished, they sauntered along with chins held arrogantly high, well pleased with their appearance. Yet, as usual, the words they exchanged were bitter.

"Did you notice her when she brought the tapa?" asked Ua. "In some way she was changed, and I had the impression that silently, secretly, she laughed at us."

Rau passed reassuring fingers over the flower circlet on her hair. "I felt the same and should have boxed her ears. There will be time for that tomorrow."

"But where can she have gone? You don't suppose she means to follow us?"

The second sister laughed contemptuously. "Be sensible, Ua. How could she? Do you expect her to come clothed in nakedness?"

"I do not know what to expect of this night," Ua replied, "but I fear it brings nothing good. Do you forget how, when we put the blossoms behind our ears, red ants came out to walk upon our faces and bite our cheeks?"

"No," said Rau angrily, "I do not forget, and for that, too, Mea shall feel my hand."

They came into Anuanua's village and walked down the path between the deserted thatch dwellings toward the crowd which already had gathered outside the house of the king. Anuanua sat at the head of the long carpet of food-laden banana leaves which was reserved for the men, with his son, Moe-tapu, at his right, and Reka, his foremost warrior, on his left.

"One of us will have this fat prince for a husband before another dawn," Rau muttered under her breath as they approached the trio, "and thus both of us will be assured of riches for the rest of our lives."

"Hold your tongue," Ua advised, "lest others read your words."

The king looked up at this moment, and a deceivingly gentle smile promptly appeared on each girl's face. "Oho," exclaimed Anuanua jovially, "my son shall have no lack of beauties from whom to select a *vahine* for his own. But how is this, Reka? Do not three daughters sleep beneath your roof?"

The father of the cloud sisters nodded. "There is a third and youngest."

"And why is she not here?"

"Why? For the reason that we forbid . . . " Rau began.

Before she could go further the elder girl's fingers closed on her arm, the nails biting into her flesh. "Mea, poor child," Ua purred in a voice soft as lightly falling rain, "is dull and unattractive; she has no liking for festivity and prefers to stay at home."

Anuanua showed his surprise. "Is it so? In most families the youngest is the first to come and last to leave where there is dancing and singing. However, Reka, you have no cause for complaint. The two young women who honor our feast have charms to spare for six. And I have not failed to notice also," he added, "how fine are the robes they wear. Diligence at the tapa board is sign of a good wife."

Ua and Rau had been glancing demurely through lowered lashes at Moe-tapu, who simpered back in his doltish way, but now the sisters left the men to take their places at another festive mat of green fronds which had been arranged for the women. Torches of bamboo with oil-soaked coco husks rammed down their hollow upright ends were set alight by scores, and, though dusk now hung heavily round about, the air in Anuanua's village glowed a cheerful red.

All Havaiki-te-a-raro well knew the purpose of so grand an entertainment, but, unwilling to be denied the pleasure of making a speech, Anuanua got to his feet. "My people," he proclaimed, "Moe-tapu is now a man and needs a wife. Somewhere on this island a girl has grown. She may be known to him or she may not. Tonight she shall come forth and by her dancing speak to him. My son, as his girth testifies, is formidable at table, but though he feasts, his eyes will not be closed. In the hula he shall find his bride and by subsequent more careful examination confirm her as his choice. Enough. I have done. *Tama'a maita'i.* Eat well."

The shouts of approval were loud, though brief because of the abundance of steaming, savory food which lay so temptingly near. Many hands reached out to grasp the red bananas, the yellow bananas, the little fish and big, the pig and the fowl. Others took hold upon the drums to continue the rolling, rumbling music which Mea and Kahu-kura could hear on the shore of the lagoon. "*A'ori*—dance, dance!" The cries came from everywhere, and presently, in answer to the repeated summons, a girl moved out into the open, her body swaying, her feet tapping lightly the bare, torchlit ground. A second followed, then another and another, till more than a dozen supple young figures were weaving in and out and about each other in the convolutions of the hula.

The king beamed broadly. "That is right," he called to them. "Play your game, girls of Havaiki. The night is young." Then turning to his companion he demanded "What do you say, Reka; if you were my son's age, would you be content to choose only one among so many quick-limbed young *vahine?* For myself, I would take the lot!" Anuanua laughed uproariously at his own jest, but although Moe-tapu gave an occasional glance to the dancers, his attention, for the most part, was concentrated on the head of a large fish which he gnawed with obvious relish. Very nearly an hour must have passed before the prince, who was by that time sitting replete and heavy lidded, opened his eyes and showed signs of interest in what was going on.

Two tall girls of even height and equal slimness had entered the dancing space. In perfect measure, in perfect unison, like twin *'aito* saplings which bend their slender lengths to the same light breeze, they fitted their steps and gestures to the rising and falling cadence of the drumming music. If their dancing lacked something in warmth, if it held a suggestion of cold calculation, it was nevertheless of a sinuous grace which surpassed all that had yet been seen. Prince Moe-tapu did not raise his posterior from its comfortable, solid seat against his heels, but the slight craning of his neck showed that he was now fully awake. Anuanua, quick to detect this faint sign of animation on the part of his offspring, gave Reka a vigorous nudge.

"Watch now," he advised. "I think Moe-tapu feels a stirring in his breast and that your own daughters are the cause of it."

Reka would have preferred to return to the discussion of a coming campaign, which had been thus interrupted, but, in obedience to the king's wishes, he glanced at Ua and Rau and then at Moe-tapu. "Yes," he agreed, "perhaps there is to be a union of our houses."

"Ua," called Moe-tapu with unaccustomed energy, "Ua and Rau. Come here to me; let me press the nose and hear the speech and look into the eyes of both of you."

The drums were silenced as Ua sat at one side of the prince, and Rau at the other, but so great was the buzz of excited comment which immediately swelled up that the volume of sound was hardly lessened; and a moment later, when Rau bent languorously close to Moe-tapu to set her wreath upon his head, when Ua brushed his cheek in putting a flower behind his ear, the cheering and applause were such that the wildest music would have gone unheard.

It was the signal for which Kahu-kura, standing with Mea in the darkness beyond the village outskirts, had waited. There was no need for caution, yet in his excitement he was whispering as if they were in danger of discovery. "Do you read that noisy jubilation the same as I? It means the prince has found the companion whom he thinks the fairest in the land. What surprise awaits him when he learns his great mistake! With what alacrity will he cast his choice aside! Are you ready, Mea? In another minute the singers will take up their chant, and the drummers will outdo themselves in celebration both false and premature. Accept the music as your own, and dance as you have never done before!"

There was a tremor in Mea's voice, and even in the darkness her eyes flashed. "Yes," she replied, "I am ready, and I shall dance for a noble prince; but his name is Kahu-kura, and I wear his crimson cloak."

"When you have done," he said eagerly, "return quickly here to me. Before morning we must be far at sea."

A shrill, sustained falsetto note reached them, coming from the leader of the singers. When it seemed human lungs could hold the piercing tone no longer, the entire chorus burst into a heavily rhythmic minor chanting. In quick succession came the feverish rattling of sticks on blocks of wood, the rapid, fluttering pulse of small, finger-stroked drums clasped between the knees, the boom of giant drums resounding to the impact of calloused, opened palms. Women's voices caught up the soaring melody and carried it, frenzied, higher still, while men of Havaiki-te-a-raro, seated cross-legged, elbows on knees, hands cupped before their faces, rocked forward and back to the sound of their own deep voices, in an all-pervading, throbbing background to the sacred chant called *ute*.

"That song is made for you!" cried Kahu-kura. "Breathe it, Mea; let it fill your heart and soul. Out, out into the village and forward to your triumph!"

Mea needed no urging. With a bound she reached the middle of the narrow path which led to the scene of revelry. Between the deserted, stilt-raised dwellings she sped on hurrying, dancing feet. To Mea it seemed that all the night was laden with tangible, caressive friendliness. It drifted out from the silent houses which had sheltered youthful lovers, laughing children, and the serenely quiet old; it hovered on the dim green roof of arching palms; it permeated the garland-scented air. What a different world since Kahu-kura had come to share it! His magic cloak swirled about her legs, brightening as she approached the forest of torches which surrounded Moe-tapu and the two sisters of rain and thunder clouds.

Mea was midway to the song-transported crowd when there came a faltering in the upraised voices. All at once the entire company became aware of Reka's youngest daughter. Every eye turned to watch the astonishing apparition, and each reflected the same trembling flame. In that second the complex structure of the *ute* faltered, shattered, and the singing voices fell silent. But for a second only, and in the next, a roar of delight came from the many hundred throats. Here was hula such as had been glimpsed in wind-swept grasses, in tumbling waves, cascading falls, in nodding palms and leaping fires, but never before in living flesh. Beat the drums! Sing out! Sway and clap and stamp that the most distant gods may hear the great rejoicing!

With redoubled fervor they caught up the throbbing, dizzying chant, and on its tumultuous crest Mea was borne onto the dancing-ground. The flaring torches caught her in their ruddy glare and once again the feathered skirt was turned to crimson flame. Twice round the bared circle Mea danced—danced with every fibre of her body, lips slightly parted as if she kissed the night, brown legs flashing through the splendid sheath of swirling feathers. Twice she passed before Moe-tapu, the second time so close that the flying fringes of her skirt fanned his cheek.

Sharply the prince demanded of Ua: "Who is this being in whom I see all there is of beauty in the wide green world? Who is she, what is her name, and why has she been hidden from my sight?" Ua's hands were clenched. She made no reply, and the son of Anuanua whipped about to her sister. "Speak! Who is it makes your charms fade to the color of cloud rack in a winter sky; who is it has set all our senses reeling? And why," he asked, seizing her by the wrist, "do I see hatred in your eyes?"

"Do you not know," Rau stormed, "that this girl, who by trickery turns your stupid heads, is the little drudge who cooks our food and sweeps our floors? She is the despised daughter of Reka to whom a soft-headed mother gave the name of Dawn-Cloud."

"Mea?" Moe-tapu's mouth formed the syllables soundlessly. Then he roared them forth. "Mea! Ah, name of loveliness, name of promise, name for me to call a wife!" Angrily he threw Rau's arm from about him and struggled to his feet. "So this is the youngest daughter, who takes no pleasure in the hula, who holds no attraction for a man. Away from me, sisters of deceit, away before I tear out your lying tongues!" He followed his impetuous words with blows of his open hand. Terrified, their heads bowed in shame, the two cold-hearted girls fled stumbling through the massed singers, tearing their fine raiment, bursting the threads of their garlands, strewing the crushed flowers behind them. And still the prince shouted after them. "Fold yourselves in black disgrace. Swim out to sea, sink down, hide in dark waters, and never return!"

Moe-tapu gave a shake to his shoulders as if he would throw off the memory of so evil and great a deception. Then he turned to the dance floor. "Now, Mea," he cried happily, "there comes a man to match you step for step." He leaped into the circle of flickering light. The chanting rose in a final delirious crescendo, and the formerly apathetic prince did his best to follow his elusive, flaming love; but as well might he have tried to capture the blue, fleeting spirit-fires which dance through midnight woods. Only when the *ute* came to its close on a deep, humming note like a long-drawn sigh of ecstasy, did Moe-tapu near his desired one. In the brief silence that followed, he remained in the half crouch on which the hula ended, while his breath came hard and perspiration rolled down his fleshy back. If he had not hesitated a fatal instant, he might then have put out a hand and touched her; but before he could do so she had risen and, lightly as a butterfly in the breeze, was running back down the house-lined path from which she had come. Once he called out. "Mea! Wait for me!" But there was no answer. She had disappeared into the shadows where the dimming torches failed to reach.

Moe-tapu walked slowly back to his father. "I have lost her," he said disconsolately. "I have lost her, and now I shall never marry."

King Anuanua rose to signify that the festival was over. "We have seen a miracle this night," said he, "but do not yet begin to moan, my son. A bird of heaven has danced before us, and she will not fly away."

Unfortunately for Moe-tapu, however, his father was mistaken. At that minute Mea stood on the shore where the full moon shone, and Kahu-kura was beside her. "Many faces there surrounded me," she was saying, "but it was yours alone I saw. Many eyes, I think, were watching me, yet I felt only yours."

"In my own land," Kahu-kura replied, "we shall dance together and speak our love." He pushed his canoe down to where the waters lapped on smooth round stones. "Wait here," he told her. "There is still one thing to do."

He went a little way down the beach to a blooming *purau* tree and came back with two of its large flowers in his hands. "You are tired," he said, removing the bright red blossoms which adorned her hair and throat. "These flaming things

131

lead not to rest." He replaced them with those of creamy yellow. Next he removed the skirt from about her waist and, as he had done once before, tossed it high. But this time as it rose into the soft, tropic air Kahu-kura looked out, not upon the setting sun, but upon an ocean where the moon's light trembled.

"O darkly beautiful sea," he intoned, "may these feathers glow softly with your color of dreams." The cloak fluttered back to Kahu-kura's hands, and it was silvered blue.

Again he put it about her. "Now," he said gently, "it is luminous night in which I fold you. Sleep, Mea, sleep."

He gathered her up and placed her within the bow of the canoe; then, taking his paddle, he pushed quietly out from shore.

The Dragons of Dark River

HAD it not been for the fat brown lizard, I should almost certainly have taken my leave of Tetua on that very morning. Not that I was in the least eager to do so, but already, it seemed to me, my visit had exceeded a decent duration. As usual, I was comforting myself with the thought that it would be no final parting, that I would return again, and that my companion, sighting my canoe from afar, would be there, waist deep in the sea, waiting to draw me up to shore. But who could be sure? Are the gods less capricious today than in the times of Kahu-kura, Tafai, and bold Rata? Tetua was not young . . . .

Such thoughts were in my mind as we sat in the open doorway through which pass side currents of the vigorous trade wind that sweeps the Bay of Matavai, and words of farewell had actually risen to my lips when, with a little plop, the lizard fell out on the mat between us. For a moment he remained motionless save for the flickering of paper-thin lids over minute, beady eyes; then, having apparently gotten his bearings, he darted across the floor, up the wall, and onto the converging rafters, where, in a corner of the roof peak near the grey spider's web, he rejoined his brothers.

Both of us had followed the little reptile's unerring return to his usual hunting ground, and Tetua smiled.

"At your home, Viriamu, have you a *mo'o?*"

"Have I a lizard?" I laughed. "A dozen families of them have adopted me, I think. Often in the evenings one drops onto my open book."

"That is good," Tetua nodded. "Today they are small and harmless, and a house that has no *mo'o* is an unlucky house."

It was at this point, of course, that I pricked up my ears and forgot all about my intended departure. "Small and harmless?" I repeated.

"Have you seen them otherwise?"

"Never."

"Well, then. They are no longer anything to fear. They no longer grow to monstrous size nor tear men limb from limb; and although they are still clammy to the touch, their breath does not come hissing from their nostrils like chill wind rushing through holes in the south horizon. Men, it sometimes seems to me, have grown small, and so, without question, have the beasts with which they once heroically struggled."

"Do you mean to say," I asked, again glancing up at the tiny, but rather grotesque creatures which inhabited the roofing thatch, "that men once fought with lizards?"

"With giant lizards. Certainly I do," said Tetua emphatically.

As anyone who is interested in the ancient lore is likely to do, I had come upon mention of Tahitian dragon myths in many an old book or manuscript, and, of all the legends of a fascinating people, none had aroused my curiosity more. How did it happen, I wondered, that in an island which is known never to have harbored reptiles larger than the humble house lizard, stories exist which speak of gaping-jawed, long-tailed animals whose blood was cold, whose hides were armor-hard? Were they a memory come echoing down the generations since Polynesians first left a vaguely guessed homeland in which rivers teemed with savage crocodiles? But such speculations are for the literal minded; they do not interest Tetua. He has no need to look beyond the islands to find the site of any event he may recount. And who am I to suggest that a tale of his is transplanted from some land many thousand miles away?

"It may be," Tetua conceded equably, "that the great *mo'o*, the serpent, and other now unseen species were never plentiful. If they had been, it is more likely that my own race, rather than theirs, would be extinct. But if they did not once live and breathe, I should hardly be sitting here talking about them. True?"

"Quite."

"True also," he added, "that one cannot speak of the deadly *mo'o* without being reminded of that brave Tahitian, Vei of Taiarapu. You must know of him already."

This I denied, and Tetua shook his head a little. "You still have much to learn, and who can say how many days are left me to instruct. Listen, though, and Vei shall be added to the number of our heroes whom you have come to know." My interest aroused, I waited eagerly for him to begin.

Probably there is no time when a man, especially if he be young, is more fully alive to the world about him than just before he enters battle. So it was with Vei on an early morning when the warriors of Patea, chief of Taiarapu, were assembling for attack. Never in all his twenty years had he known a dawn of equal freshness, one in which the air that filled his lungs sent such a joyous tingling of expectancy throughout his tall, sturdy frame. And never before had realization been so keen of how friendly, how much his very own, was the half-moon-shaped village with its long row of houses, some large, some small, some with new roofs of fresh brown thatching, others rain weathered and grey, all following the gently curving shore.

Close to where he stood was Patea's house, most imposing of the lot and, to Vei, best known of all the dwellings. How many nights had he slept, like a member of the family, on the mats within, how many times had he passed, with the freedom of a son, through the wide doorway of the chief—the chief who was himself without male issue. To one side was the big *'uru* tree in which as a child he had climbed, balancing on the outer limbs to pluck the ripened breadfruit and drop them into the baskets which Patea's two daughters held out below. Nearby were the paths along which he and Ro'o, his dearest boyhood friend, had raced upon their stilts. But time had hurried by, the stilts were thrown away, other children clambered in the trees. Vero, older of Patea's daughters—his heart quickened at the thought of her— had reached nineteen. Her sister, Marita, was little younger, and Ro'o was a proud warrior, senior to himself. Proud, yes; too much so, perhaps, but such is often the way with those of noble birth.

Noble birth! Vei frowned, and for a moment a shadow passed over the otherwise glorious morning. Who would have thought, in the days of sailing toy canoes over the minnow-filled shallows, of shooting with bows and arrows, that the accident of birth could be so all-important? If someone had told him then that as he came to man's estate a rigid barrier would rise between him and the playmates to whom he had been as a brother, Vei would have refused to believe it. Now he was grown; now he knew.

Leaning upon his long spear which he had planted in the ground before him, he watched the hurried yet affectionate partings which everywhere were taking place. Young men, about to set off to war for the first time, embraced their anxious parents. Seasoned fighters tossed up their children with joking, reassuring words. Nearby, Ro'o, wearing the belt of red feathers which signified his rank, clasped Patea fondly; and quite rightly, for was not the chief his uncle? Next he pressed his nose to Marita's, and then, while Vei's hands gripped hard upon his lance, he did the same to Vero. And why not? Were not the two girls Ro'o's own cousins? Oh, lucky man to have such relatives as they; lucky man to have relatives at all! For Vei, as you may have guessed, had none. No mother came to wet his cheek with her warm tears, no father laid hands upon his shoulders to murmur words of courage in his ear.

First discovered as a babe lying in a green basket of plaited palm leaves hidden in the bush, he was reared by Patea's broad-bosomed, kindly wife. He had heard rumors in plenty of his origin. Some held him to be the son of an aristocratic woman of the *'arioi*, that sacred society of entertainers to whom children are forbidden; and for father they gave him the noble chieftain of a distant clan. But others, whose gossiping voices were just as loud, claimed that he came of *menehune* stock, that he was the offspring of common laborers. Nevertheless, despite such disagreement, there was no one in Taiarapu who would not admit that the young man's bearing and deportment spoke eloquently of good blood, and even now as he waited,

135

aloof, while his fellows were briefly gathered to their family groups, he had the unmistakable air of one made to lead, not follow.

Vei's courage had no need of bolstering; he could do without a father's last injunctions to face the foe and not give ground. Without looking at her directly, he was keenly aware of Vero's every move and gesture as she said goodbye to Ro'o, and although, in truth, the girl's manner with her cousin was most casual, even bordering on impatience, to Vei's imagination it appeared otherwise. To think that not many years ago, when he was still a boy, he and Patea's daughter had walked freely hand in hand, while now stern *tapu* forbade him to so much as speak to her unless he was addressed. "But can such thoughts change the ancient customs?" he asked himself angrily. "Forget this love which is not only mad but impossible, and put your mind to the coming conflict."

Ro'o and Patea were leaving to join the band of warriors who gathered by the shore, and Vei wrenched up his weapon with quite unnecessary force and started after them. He had passed the chief's house when a voice stopped him.

"Vei," it called, "*a mai*. Come here."

Marita! He turned and went quickly to her. Keeping his eyes on the younger sister, though Vero stood close beside her, he said, abrupt in his surprise, "You are crying, Marita. Is something wrong?"

For a moment she made no reply, then sobbed, "I weep because Vero weeps."

A sudden, wild hope sprang up in Vei's breast. He tried to tell himself that the idea which had entered his head was put there by a mischievous spirit bent on adding ridicule to his other sufferings. But the hope remained. He allowed himself a glance at the girl who filled all his waking thoughts. Tears quivered on her lashes, rolled down her cheeks. A mere glance he had meant to take, yet seconds passed while he gazed into her brimming dark eyes.

"Tell me, Marita," said he, unable to turn away but with wit enough remaining to address the younger sister. "Tell me, why does Vero cry?"

"Because great sorrow fills her."

"And why should she be sad?"

"*Aue te aue*," Marita wailed and in the excess of her own grief poured out far more than Vero herself might have dared to do. "It is for you, Vei, that her bright tears fall. It is for you she will tremble till the fighting's done, and then, if you do not return, she will surely die from loving you!"

"Oh," Vero protested in dismay, "Marita, you go too far!"

"Has she said an untrue word?" asked Vei.

136 Vero's eyes were bent on a small, carved image which she held. Then, with a slight shake of her head, as if she thus dispelled her tears or, perhaps, brushed aside all caution, she looked up again. "How can I deny a thing which has been clear to the sharp-eyed, sharp-tongued old ones of our village for many months? Should

I hide from you the truth which others quickly learned? Hear it from my mouth and think me shameless if you will: I love you greatly, and so, I think, I always have."

"Must one be shamed by love? Ah, no, Vero, it is cause for untold happiness; and if before I looked forward gladly to this day, when young warriors may prove themselves as fighting men—or else as loud-sounding drums which hold windy emptiness—now my joy is doubled. I have much to say, and much more still to ask of you, but all can abide the outcome of the battle when the gods, and I myself as well, have seen if I am worthy. Dry your tears and wait for me."

Quickly Vero stepped close to him and made fast to the belt of his loincloth the little wooden image; and Vei, looking down, saw a miniature replica of the massive idol which ruled over the inland temple. "Let 'Oro, Lord of Wars, watch over you," the girl prayed fervently. "Let him put strength into your arms and bring you back to me."

"No man shall wrest this from me," Vei soberly replied. "It may be that the talisman wields a potent charm, yet I think there are times when a woman's power may be as great." He raised a hand as if he would have touched her, as if he might have wished to feel the soft texture of her hair, but then he let it fall. The time was not yet come when he could permit himself such pleasure. He turned resolutely away and went to join his comrades.

It is unnecessary to detail the events of the bloody battle which that day took place along Tahiti's shore, because this story deals with perils far greater than men alone provide. Enough, therefore, to say that Patea's warriors blundered into their enemy's ambush and were threatened with annihilation, when a single youth among them burst with savage fury through the tightening cordon of the enemy and gained their rear. With whirling club he raced among the confused attackers, shouting loud his challenge and, heedless of their numbers, thoughtless of the danger, put them all to rout. Vei, for it was that stalwart lover, had left his fellows far behind in his mad rush to victory. When at length they came up to him they found him bending over his fallen enemies, methodically slicing off their ears with his bamboo knife. According to the approved custom, he spitted his trophies on a stem of a coconut leaf and tied it about his middle.

"By all the gods," said Ro'o, who had been staring at the havoc Vei had brought about, "you have no less than twenty pairs of ears, and you bear no single wound."

"I bear a charm that no man can withstand," smiled Vei.

"Indeed you must," the other agreed with envy in his voice, "and the red-stained belt you've gained, though it is not made of royal feathers, will bring hardly less honor. The ovens shall be kindled, the feast shall be long. Patea's gratitude will be unbounded."

During all the night which followed, the seaside village of Chief Patea was, as Ro'o predicted, the scene of tremendous celebration. Gifts of pigs, of fruits and

137

lands, were showered upon Vei so that he was suddenly become a man of wealth. Patea made a fine and lengthy oration praising Vei's exploits. Yet Vei, though not unappreciative, was little impressed by all the lavish gifts, and of Patea's speech he heard next to nothing. Not once in all the evening had his eyes left Vero's face, and it was only when Patea was reaching the end of his eulogy that Vei suddenly gave him full attention.

"A man whose prowess has been shown so great," the chief declaimed, "should not be without descendants in large numbers. The blood of conquerors must be passed on. Vei shall take a wife whom I myself will select for him."

Vei and Vero were now openly smiling at each other in their happiness and confidence of what the chief intended. In the next instant their expressions changed to blank dismay.

"I cannot," Patea pursued, "give one of my own daughters since Vei's parents are unknown. But because we have seen his true nobility, the bride shall be one who is near the royal family, and her name you will learn in due time."

The chief sat down and lifted a coconut to moisten his throat after so long a discourse. It is unlikely that he remarked the despair on Vero's lovely face or the tears which started afresh in her younger sister's sympathetic eyes. And, although he may have thought it strange that Vei rose and left the assembly with so little ceremony, he could have had no inkling of the rebellious thoughts which stormed in the young man's brain.

It was a night without a moon, and low-lying clouds blotted out the stars. Occasional lightning flickered across the southern horizon, and at each passing the fitful fire left the darkness more intense. It was a night fitted to the blackness of Vei's mood. Was it for this, he asked himself, that he had plunged headlong into battle? Had Vero's charm and Vero's love made him strong only that he might find her more unattainable than before? So it seemed to him as he walked distractedly, heedless of the path he took, leaving behind the village where they had spent their happy youth. There was a continuous muttering of distant thunder which had, to Vei's ears, the sound of low, ironic laughter. Did not the same prankster spirits which had first caused him to lose his heart now mock him with that sardonic rumbling? "See," Vei imagined them to jeer, "see what we have done for you: you are a hero now, and in reward you shall be bound to a woman you neither love nor know. Do you still dream of Vero, whose tears once fell for you? Would you free yourself from so disastrous an infatuation? Then take 'Oro's image from beneath your *maro* and cast it into the sea. Plunge after it. Swim out from Taiarapu and Tahiti. And do not turn back."

138

Vei had reached a desolate section of the coast to which men seldom came save when they sought the giant turtles that swim to shore to bury huge eggs in the warm, protective sand. He stopped beneath a gaunt *fara* tree whose bare branches held isolated leaf clusters over the dark water. His hand found the little carved figure beneath his loincloth, and his fingers closed about it. "Swim out, not back," the tempting spirit voices echoed, but suddenly Vei raised his arm and shook a clenched fist at the flickering lightning. "Never," he cried, "never shall I part with her. No man, no spirit, no laughing fiend who hides in the night skies shall stop me!"

"I am ready, Vei," said a quiet voice at his side. "I will go with you, anywhere."

He whirled in surprise. "Vero! Why are you here?"

"To be with my *tane*," she said simply. "To be with my man."

He looked down at the dim oval of her face. "But do you not fear Patea's anger?"

"Yes," she admitted, "I do; yet my fear of losing you is greater still. Take me, Vei, take me with you."

"But where," he groaned, "where in all the world can we go?"

"We must listen," said Vero softly, "to the night owl's cry, to the speech of *fara* leaves whispering above our heads and so, perhaps, find an answer to our need."

"As well," he replied despondently, "might we find an answer in the silence of the slumbering lagoon."

"And why not?" she asked, ignoring the irony of his words in her hope to lessen his discouragement. And before he could stop her she had slipped into the quiet water and was swimming away from shore. For a moment he remained watching the bits of phosphorus which the movements of her body sent swirling, then, suddenly forgetful of the impossible obstacles which threatened their happiness, he gave a laugh and plunged after her. Out over the tranquil, coral-bounded lagoon they swam, the man following the girl but never quite overtaking her, and their splashing startled into the air little schools of flying fish which skittered away to disappear in the night. It was not till they were midway to the reef that Vero rolled onto her back and waited for him.

"When you were a boy," she said with still rapid breath, "you never caught me, nor can you do so now."

"No," he replied, his brief elation quickly leaving him, "I fear the gods intend that you shall always slip away beyond my reach."

From where they lay the shore was an indistinct blur of grey, and only a faint glow of torches far down the strand showed where Patea's people still celebrated an indifferent hero's splendid deeds. Inland, all was utter blackness where the rugged mountains pushed up their crests to heavy layers of cloud, and, as if the intensity of the night had crushed her brave attempt at lightness, Vero was silent. She found Vei's hand and held it in her own, but the minutes passed and neither could find any word to say.

Then, floating close beside him, she began to speak. "Oh, Vei," she murmured with her eyes still on the empty and deserted heavens, "where are our neighbors in the sky? Surely in the sun or moon there must be a resting place for such as you and me. Why can we not step into their distant safety as did Hina, goddess of the moon, long ago? Could you not carry me up the webbed ladder of her trailing hair?"

He smiled sadly. "That I would, most willingly, if the path was one for earth-bound mortals; and there alone, I think, might we be secure. In no village of Tahiti can we hide; our secret would travel faster than the wind.

"My loved one," Vero asked suddenly, "did you ever slake your thirst within the sea?"

"No," he exclaimed, astonished at her question, "never, of course."

"Then do so now, for I think we have been brought to a strange miracle."

He watched in amazement as Vero put her lips to the lagoon. Then, cautiously, he bent his head and tested with his tongue. The water was fresh! He drank, and it was sweet and cool as a mountain spring. Hurriedly he passed a hand across his face and dashed the water from his eyes. "Do you know what we have found?" he demanded. "This is Vai-po'iri which gushes from the bottom of the sea to brush our limbs with its cold hands."

"Dark River," said Vero slowly, "the same of which the bards are always chanting, the same which roars through the dragons' caves and then rushes down to the hidden underworld."

"Yes, yes," he agreed in mounting excitement, "you have heard the songs: Dark River, peopled by the great ferocious mo'o that devour all but the heads of incautious victims who step within their deep, forbidden caves. Here it bursts up from the underground and spews forth the naked skulls of those who looked upon its monster-infested waters. And you were right, Vero. The lagoon speaks to us, answering the question which I asked in vain. It tells of the only place where we shall be safe from prying eyes."

"Oh, no!" the girl cried in horror. "It speaks of death alone. Do not listen, Vei. Come away, come away before your mind is quite bewitched." With strokes made frantic by the terror which Vei's words inspired, she swam for shore. More slowly he followed her, and as he went he formed his plan. Perhaps he was in truth to some degree bewitched, for no one altogether sane could have entertained so wild a scheme. Yet if now Vei's thoughts seemed quite mad, it was the greatness of his love which made them so—that, and the lack of an alternative.

Coming up beside here on the beach he pressed her against him trying to warm her with his body and to still her trembling. "Wait for me," he said and he stroked her sea-wet hair. "By midmorning I shall have reached the caves, and if I succeed in winning us a refuge you will see me before the sun is down. It is not long."

"Not long!" she exclaimed, throwing her arms about him. "Do I not know from the day just past how hours can seem like years?"

"Those who stay behind often need the greater courage. But remember that I still wear the charm of 'Oro."

"*Aue*," she moaned, " 'Oro protects warriors who battle in the sun's bright light, while you would pit yourself against the creatures spawned within Te Po. His power does not reach the underworld."

"However that may be," he replied, leading her back toward the now sleeping village, "I carry his image because Vero's hands have fashioned it, and perhaps it is she, too, who will bring me life and victory where other men have died."

When they came to Chief Patea's house no glimmer of light showed through its walls. "Go quietly," he whispered. "Lie down and look for restful sleep."

She put her cheek close to his. "I shall not find it, Vei, till you are by my side." She slipped within, and Vei walked to his own house where, noiselessly, he picked up his battle-axe and spear.

A few minutes later, unseen, he left Patea's village. He went slowly, his feet feeling their way, the spear balanced on his shoulder and the long-handled axe with rounded blade of tough, burnished shell swinging in his right hand.

Soon the murmur of a broad river reached his ears, and he came to the sloping bank. His hand found the gunwale of a small outrigger canoe used by fishers of fresh-water shrimp, and he stretched himself beside it. He could go no farther till break of day, so he crossed his arms behind his head, determined to find sleep even as he had advised Vero to do. But, like Vero, who stared into the blackness held within her father's roof, he remained in semi-wakefulness. And there, lying prone by the stream, while he awaited the slow passing of the hours, Vei fought— as anyone approaching desperate adventure must—his most terrible battles. Reality could never equal in frightfulness the visions which flitted through his mind. He saw himself confronted by the awful foe, trying to raise his arm, to bring his weapon's point to bear; and he saw himself unable to move. He would try to shout, try to break the numbing spell, and no sound would issue from his lips.

Finally a faint greying of the eastern sky delivered Vei from such torment. Tossing his weapons into the canoe, he lifted the vessel and placed it in the lazy current which only a short distance farther on made conjunction with the sea. Grasping the stubby paddle with its half-split blade, he set off upstream. Often before he had ridden in the same battered little craft when his mission had no other end than the capture of succulent, long-legged shrimp, when his heart was light, and a song came readily to his lips. On this momentous morning Vei did not sing, but, grateful for even so simple a task for his muscles, he swung the paddle vigorously and felt his spirits rise. Trees about him soon took shape, the entire *141* winding valley brightened, doves and parakeets and purple swallows darted back and forth above his head; the river beneath him wakened, too, and, flowing between narrowing banks, quickened pace to set up a lively rustling where it foamed white in rocky shallows. He was far into the interior when a shaft of sunlight broke through and set the green wilderness ablaze.

Suddenly Vei could contain himself no longer. He was young, and, as is the way with youth, his blood took fire with the breaking day. Standing in the stern of the canoe he whirled the blunt paddle about his head as if he cut through an invisible host of enemies. "Demons of Vai-po'iri," he shouted, "slink back into your dank and slimy holes. A man comes to drive you from the earth!" He seated himself, and with rapid strokes regained lost distance, then leaped up again to shout defiance. "Creatures of the howling caves, flee to the shades of Te Po and leave the world for those whose blood is warm. A warrior comes to make an end of you!" Birds by the thousand swarmed into the air as his voice rocked back and forth between the valley's converging walls, and for an instant he stood watching and listening in satisfaction before pushing on once more against the increasing swiftness of the current.

It was not bluff or pretentious boasting, this calling out in loud defiance. It was the usual manner of a Tahitian who goes against great odds, and by those echoing, scornful words his daring, already mounting with the rising sun, was drawn up higher still.

"O dragons of frigid breath, depart and draw your scaly lengths behind you. Scurry down Dark River's blackly winding tunnels." The paddle descended resoundingly upon the water. "Vei is here to rend and stab and slay!"

The point at which shrimp fishers and all prudent men turned back was now far behind, yet Vei continued to forge more rapidly ahead. There came a sharp bend in the stream and beyond it the channel was choked by the buttressing roots of somber *mape* trees which grew on either side. Flinging down the paddle, Vei leaped to the bank and drew out the canoe. He caught up his weapons, and for an instant he stood alert and listening. The friendly, sunlit stream beside him tumbled over the thirsty roots, sending a sound like liquid laughter into the air. But the woods reverberated with another sound which told the poised warrior that he had neared his goal. It was the hollow, muffled rumbling of another stream, and it spoke of clashing waters struggling deep within the ground; of Vai-po'iri plunging through the secret dark on its tortuous subterranean journey to the sea.

At a half run he started toward it, threading his way between the hoary *mape* trees. Abruptly the woods thinned and he was wading through tall grass across a field which led against the steeply rising northern side of the valley. On the wall-like cliff tangled vines and creepers masked the soil with a solid blanket of green, but they failed to hide the single wide, rock-rimmed opening. He gained the threshold, swept aside the trailing vines, and plunged within. Only then, when the thunder of the underground river hammered at his ears, when darkness filled his eyes, did he come to an unwilling halt.

"Out, devils of the night," he cried, "out, and let me see the foe!" Just perceptibly the obscurity lessened and he called again. "Away, black-robed things which make me blind. Sink back to night's reservoir in Te Po's abyss and let me have broad day!"

Broad day did not come, yet Vei's eyes made out the down-slanting path which stretched before him, and he set his feet upon it. Slowly, steadily, step by careful step he descended, bare soles gripping the chill wet slope of basaltic rock, deeper and deeper into the fearsome underworld. "Ah, Vero," he thought, as he strove to pierce the thick, oppressive gloom, "if I do not return, think not to follow in these forbidden regions of rightly stern *tapu*. Remain where you can look into the far-extending sky in which Mahana rolls back the dark each day and shows to you the faces of your friends. Stay there, beloved, and if your *tane* fails let him be forgotten!"

The tunnel emerged into a huge central cavern from which countless others led away in all directions into the dim unknown. Vei stared about him at the dismal labyrinth and knew with a tightening of his chest that even if no worse enemy appeared, a man might, once confused, wander for all eternity in such a bewildering maze as this. He looked back the way he had come to find the entrance shrunk to an opening the size of a child's balled fist. Overhead there seemed no limit to the height of the tenebrous chamber, for though the surrounding walls arched inward, they passed from sight long before joining to form a vaulted roof. From the dome of everlasting night great roots, thick as a large man's thigh, felt their serpentine way down toward the bottom of the pit.

"Banyans," thought Vei, "banyans, seeking the black waters of Vai-po'iri. Where they find a clutching hold, there the angry river runs." Grateful for even such sinister-appearing guides he groped on. Down, ever down till the chink of light behind was gone, till no other world existed than the shadowed one in which he wandered. "But what, Vei, has become of your defiant shouts?" his thoughts continued. "Has your courage no need of such support? Yesterday when you charged in battle and slew a score of men your cries were heard far round about. Why do you now go grim-lipped and silent?" Perhaps he himself did not know why, but one can guess that as he neared the clamorous torrent he feared, amid so great commotion, to hear the smallness of one man's lonely voice.

He crossed a ledge of stone and stopped when cold spray whipped across his feet and ankles. Clinging to the root of a banyan tree whose leaves must have been dancing in the breeze somewhere high in the world of sun and air, he peered over the brink of a short, sheer cliff to see greyly foaming waters a dozen feet below.

With eyes gradually grown owl-like in their ability to penetrate the murk, he made out, upstream, the funnel-shaped opening through which Vai-poʻiri spewed into the caves. The stream's course within the cavern was brief. Almost at his feet, in a dizzying vortex, it dropped from sight. Vei pushed himself back onto the ledge and propped his battle-axe and spear against an enormous boulder of a height more than twice his own which balanced there on rounded base. He removed his *maro*, rewound it securely about his waist, then put out his hand for his spear. Suddenly he froze motionless. A loud, protracted hissing reached his ears. Clutching the spear he spun around.

On the opposite bank something stirred. A long segment of what had seemed part of the rocky shore slowly detached itself and with deliberate, crawling movement approached the stream. By the river's edge it stopped with baleful eyes upon the tense, waiting man, and there Vei saw it in all its frightfulness. Little wonder that men trembled at mere mention of its name; little wonder that for ages past such beasts had drawn their cold, hissing breath unmolested within these damp abhorrent caves. Two tallest spears laid end to end would not have reached from the enormous slit of its fearful mouth to its barbed and forking tail. Spasmodically the great jaws fell open, exposing heavy rows of bladelike teeth and a black gullet down which the largest mountain boar could have slid with ease, then came together with a grinding clash. Interminable minutes passed while the man and the moʻo faced each other across the river of darkness. At last Vei's taut nerves and thumping heart could endure no more. Something snapped within him, and, forgetful of any fear he may have had of the inadequacy of his young voice, he gave a terrific shout and lifted high his spear.

"Foul thing that shuns the light, come and die upon my lance's fire-hardened point! Come—and feel the strength of one whose blood is red and warm. *A mai, a mai!* Come, come!"

While this outburst still echoed through the caverns, the moʻo slid into the stream. So swiftly that it appeared not to swim within the hurrying waters but to glide over them, it gained the near shore and lunged up the cliff. An instant later the blunt snout shot above the crest, and with furious clawing and scraping of its talons the moʻo gained foothold and reared aloft. Its mouth yawned wide and with a roar it lunged at the young Tahitian. Down plunged Vei's spear straight into the gaping maw, down till the weapon was swallowed to its entire length. No creature ever lived on the earth above which such a blow would not have felled; but though the reptile had been struck deep within its vitals, instantly it hurled Vei back and pinned him against the unsteady boulder by which his axe was laid. Frantically he strove to free himself, to push aside the cold weight which pressed him to the even colder stone; yet while the breathing of his terrible antagonist came in racking gasps, as if the moʻo slowly drowned in its own dark blood, its strength ebbed no more swiftly than did Vei's. His senses reeled and spots of fire had begun to dance before his glazing eyes when a hissing signal of compounded danger spurred him back to full consciousness. Twisting his head he looked below to see a second hulking shape appear in the black waters of the pool and dart for the steep shore.

With strength born of terror Vei wrenched himself free, escaping the vise in which he had been held. Momentarily the dying reptile clawed the slippery face of the boulder, then crashed down to lie prostrate and unmoving. Chest heaving, Vei snatched up his axe and whirled to find the second mo'o almost upon him. It had gained the ledge, and Vei had only time to see that it was double the size of the first great lizard when the creature charged.

With battle-axe upraised Vei waited till his foe was almost upon him, then leaped aside. As the mo'o rushed past, Vei brought the weapon down with all his might. There was a clash like stone on stone as the cutting edge of shell struck armored scales and glanced off harmlessly; yet the blow goaded the monster to heightened fury, and for a second time the caves reverberated to a maddened dragon roar. Instantly the mo'o wheeled and dashed open-mouthed for the Tahitian; again Vei narrowly escaped to deal his unavailing blow.

Back and forth the reptile stormed, barely failing at each thunderous attack to sink its jaws into human flesh. But Vei's feints and dodges inexorably slowed, and the battle-axe swayed unsteadily in his hands. Vei's strength had nearly reached its limit of endurance when next he swung his weapon. The gleaming, polished axe head descended. Once more it glanced impotently from the tough shield and came to rest at Vei's feet. And there, this time, it remained. With expressionless eyes the youth stared at the nicked and dented blade.

Always its charge had carried the mo'o beyond its prey, and always no more than seconds passed before it had recovered and turned. Now the powerful, forked tail lashed out and swung the whole great creature round; the squat legs sank almost from sight within the heavy body as it prepared to spring. But Vei gave it no attention. Heedless of all else he continued to gaze down, as if fascinated, at the battered weapon whose blade still rested on the ground before him.

Suddenly his head tipped back, his mouth opened, and peal after peal of laughter went ringing through the caverns. Laughter! At the ridiculous, apparently useless axe he held—that proud weapon which had slain twenty men in mortal combat only to become as absurd as a child's toy? At himself? At fate? Or was there in that outrageous mirth an echo of the sound to which Vei had listened on the night just gone, a sound which came from the low horizon where lightning shimmered and unseen spirits made audible, rumbling sport of hapless man? Yes, certainly it was back into the faces of the very gods that Vei laughed. Elemental forces of destruction have never been held at bay by a man's magnificent ability to deride their towering strength or by his own small means. Sometimes, however, to those who endure when all seems lost, there comes—often in a manner mysterious and unexpected—a final victory.

The moʻo advanced, slowly at first, one webbed, claw-tipped foot put forward, then another, as if suspicious of those sounds of outrageous mirth unknown till then in the underworld. Nearer it came, nearer, till the distance between them was cut in half; then, sure of its prey at last, it lunged forward with a deafening roar. Vei was wrenched back to reality. His grip tightened on the axe handle. He was about to lift the blade aloft so that he might swing it down as he had ten, twenty times before. Too late! Too late to raise his weapon, too late even to leap aside. The moʻo was almost upon him when it reared, exposing the dirty white of its underside, and Vei swung his battle-axe in the only way he could. From his feet, from the ground, he brought the damaged but still-sharp blade up from the ground, swinging it with all his remaining strength in a sweeping arc. Into the soft, bloated belly it bit its way and then drove on, ripping, slicing through the sole unprotected part of the otherwise invulnerable beast. Higher and higher the blade plowed its grisly path, laying open the moʻo from end to end. Only when the battle-axe struck the massive jawbone did it come to a shattering halt and the haft splinter in Vei's grasp. Its work was done. The king of dragons collapsed amid its own entrails, writhed briefly on the cliff edge, then slid over the brink to plunge into the turbulent pool below.

Vei leaned weakly against the great boulder while he watched with curious detachment the last agonies of his terrible enemy. He saw the waters of Vai-poʻiri stained a still darker hue, he heard the approaching raucous blowing of countless others of the same hideous breed, and he saw four, six, ten of the blunt snouts forge their way up into the down-rushing spillway. Without weapon of any sort, he stared as the newcomers pounced upon their disabled, mortally wounded fellow.

"Look while you may, Vei," he told himself dully, "for soon it will be done. Soon your time will come. Wash from your thoughts the rash and impossible plans you made. No single man shall ever exterminate the demons from Te Po; but one can choose to die rather than crawl back to those he loves in abjection and defeat."

Deliberately, and for the second time, Vei removed the waist-cloth from about his middle; then carefully rewound it as a warrior invariably does before he sets out on perilous adventure. So Vei prepared himself to meet bravely that last great adventure which must come to every man. But as he smoothed the *maro* about his loins his hands touched a piece of wood which hung on short sennit cord beneath a fold of the tapa. He brought it forth, and there, lying in his open palm, ʻOro's big-eyed, square-skulled image gazed up at him. Vero's handiwork, Vero's love were in that small, symbolic carving, and Vei's fingers moved over it caressingly.

Perhaps it was a trick of the feeble light in that land of gloom, but far more probably it was the magic which lies implicit in the ancient religion of Tahiti: beneath Vei's glance the idol of the god of war became blurred, 'Oro's frightful features dissolved, merging, fusing into another shape. Vei blinked, and then saw clearly. A thing of beauty was cupped within his hand, and it was Vero's diminutive, perfect likeness.

"Find happiness," he said, addressing the tiny effigy softly. "Find happiness and forget."

The response struck swift and urgent on his ears and in the first words was an impatience touched with anger. "Happiness!" came Vero's voice. "All that I shall ever have is locked in you. Act, Vei! You cannot destroy the mo'o horde, but you may trap them in their sunken river where they shall never again be seen."

"How?" he cried, looking at the figure in his hand, but once more it was only 'Oro that he held. "How?" he demanded of the invisible, oppressive ceiling from which the banyan roots curled down. No reply reached him save his own frantic, waning cry as it was thrown back and forth from wall to wall. For a moment—certainly the longest in his life—he groped for the elusive answer which, with now furiously mounting hope, he knew must be there if he could but grasp it. Then it came. He knew. The boulder—the unstable boulder balanced on the ledge above the single opening through which Dark River tumbled past the dens of unnumbered lizard-giants to its final exit in a faraway lagoon. Topple it over, hurl it down, Vei, upon the contorted, twisting reptile mass which clogs the boiling stream; but hurry, for their feast is nearly done. Hurl it down and close forever the single door through which such ugliness may reach the outside air!

Dropping to his hands and knees, he slid far beneath the boulder, wedging himself between the ledge below and the rounded bulk above. Back flat against the stone, he gave the ancient battle cry. "Brave ancestors, *tauturu mai!* Give aid! Bold forebears who passed to me the gift of life, come near! O my fathers, dwell within my body and together we shall move this mountain!" Vei gave a mighty upward heave. Shudder after shudder ran through his frame as with hammering heart he strained to force himself from the ground. The fabled Ru could hardly have exerted greater effort when he sought to raise the sky, only to have his eyes suddenly bulge from their sockets, his back become hunched, and his intestines fall away to settle on the horizon of Bora Bora. "*Tauturu mai,*" Vei gasped. "Noble ancestors, send me strength!"

Do not question that his ancestors heard; never doubt that they were near. A tremor shook the awakening rock. The tremor grew. There was a grating crunch as the base of the boulder ground against the ledge. Its vast inertia at last overcome, the huge boulder slowly tipped, then of its own momentum began to roll. Freed, Vei sprang upright to see the great mass he had set in reluctant motion lunge suddenly forward and topple into the spume-filled air above Dark River. Straight for the whirlpool, in which the gyrating tangle of dragons thrashed and fought, it plunged. With a crash which rocked the mountain overhead and must have been felt to the very center of Te Po it drove into the black-lipped hole down which Vai-poʻiri flowed, stopping it, damming the river for all time to come.

No man has since laid eyes upon a living giant moʻo. Whether they still exist along the borders of the river's lower channel it would be difficult to say. However, the rock with which Vei imprisoned them may be seen today, although not in its entirety. Only its upper surface shows. When the river's age-old outlet was shut off the waters quickly rose. Where the noisy torrent formerly passed, a lake was formed, and soon it covered all but the boulder's rounded dome. At that level the waters found other, unrestricted outlets and came no higher.

Thus the voices of both Vai-poʻiri and the lizards which inhabited it were at the same time stilled; and the place where Vei fought became a quiet, secluded grotto much favored by young lovers through all the intervening years.

First to find happiness by the shadowed lake were Vei and his beloved. It was after nightfall when he brought her to the sanctuary he had so newly won. There he spread coconut fronds to make their couch and strung candlenuts to make them light. Vero was terrified when first she saw the great lifeless body of the moʻo sprawled upon the ledge with its jaws locked upon the end of Vei's spear. But her fear was brief and soon gave way to wonder and admiration and pride in her tane's victory.

"Tell me, Vei," she entreated, "tell me all about it."

This Vei did very willingly, and it was nearly morning when he had finished. "You have walked far, Vero," he said at last, "and you are weary. Now you should sleep."

"I would rather listen to you endlessly," she smiled. "But one thing puzzles me. When we came here tonight, why did you compel me to walk while you rode in the canoe?"

"So that your footprints might be seen."

"Oh," she exclaimed, starting up in alarm, "I shall be followed!"

"Certainly you will," he agreed calmly. "And it is time that I was going, for I intend to be of the searching party, close to your father's side."

"Then it is the end," she faltered.

"No, Vero, no more than the beginning. It is not right that we should be forever banished to the wilds like those who have committed crime. We have done no wrong and should be free to love and marry and live in the world of sunlit day. And so, before many hours more, we shall be." Gently he silenced her questions and her protests and laid her head back against the green palm leaves. "For the present do not ask me how. Close your eyes, and when you wake again you will understand."

Before she could reply he was hurrying toward the cavern's entrance and the small canoe in which he had come. No one was stirring in Patea's village, and first cockcrow had not yet sounded when he gained his house and stretched himself upon his mat to wait the break of day.

Hardly was it light along the shore when an anguished cry was raised. "Vero is gone!" From house to house the alarming news traveled, each family taking up the word and passing it along. "Vero has disappeared!"

Smiling his satisfaction, Vei rose. He tied a length of stout cord about his middle, then walked to Patea's house. There an excited crowd was already gathered. They were all talking at once, each eager to express his ideas about the mysterious disappearance of the chieftain's daughter. Patea put an end to the confusion when he caught sight of Vei and called out to him. "And you, Vei, have you word to say?"

"A small one," he replied.

"Speak it," the chief commanded.

"When last I saw Vero, she was on her way to hunt for river shrimp."

So Vei put them on the trail, and by midmorning the searching party had passed the bend in the stream—the spot where prudent fishermen turned back—and continued on, following the upward-leading footsteps. Now some began to drop behind, murmuring scarcely plausible excuses. But though Patea saw with growing dread the direction in which his daughter's steps were leading, he pushed resolutely on. Vei walked beside him and did his best to make his face show the same concern and horror which was increasingly plain upon all others.

Only when they stood aghast before the entrance to the caves did the chief give way to complete despair. "*Aue*," he groaned in agony, "what now is left to me! The one for whom I lived is captive to the lizard-fiends and lost forevermore." In abandoned grief Patea seized the shark-tooth ornament which hung about his neck and repeatedly struck his brow with it until blood flowed down his aging cheeks.

Vei stayed his chief's hand. "Wound yourself no further," he advised, "until the truth is known. Select a man to enter here and bring your daughter back to you."

Patea looked about the circle of his warriors, but as his eyes fell upon them, each, even highborn Ro'o, turned his face away. "No, no," Patea replied at last, "leave me to my sorrow. Were a warrior of mine to step within these shunned and *tapu* caves he would prove himself sprung from the finest stock in all the land. But I cannot ask or hope for the impossible."

Vei leaped to the entrance of the tunnel which led down to the lake where Vaipo'iri once had cascaded. There he turned and faced the chief. "I take you at your word, Patea," he declared. "A daughter I shall restore to you—but she shall also be my wife."

Guided by the flickering light of the candlenut tapers, he hastened down the path he had first so blindly followed. He knelt at Vero's side and wakened her. "Come, my love," he whispered. "We are prisoners no longer and are free to live where we will beneath the open sky."

"Free?" she asked, unbelieving.

He laughed joyously. "Come and you will see."

Quickly he ran to the fallen mo'o, lashed it firmly with the cord he had brought, and hoisted the ponderous head onto his shoulder. Then, with Vero at his side, and dragging the inert body of the lizard behind, he started back. Arrived at the mouth of the cave, he heaved his repellent burden through the opening. It fell to the ground and rolled to the feet of Chief Patea and his astonished followers. For a long moment all eyes were riveted on the slaughtered monster; then they were raised to Vei and Vero, both unharmed, standing in the cave's entrance. The young lovers came forward, and Vero ran to her father's arms.

When at last Patea released her, it was to lift the circlet of pointed sharks' teeth from about his neck. "Vei," he declared, "my daughter is come back to me, bringing with her a conquering hero in whom I find a son." His voice lifted in a shout of thanksgiving. "May you live to follow in my place when I am gone."

"*Ia ora na!*" the warriors chorused. "May you live, Vei! Slayer of dragons, may you live!"

Proudly Patea dropped the brilliant white emblem of chieftainship over Vei's head.

In Parting

I WAS homeward bound, far out on the broad, majestic Bay of Matavai. The little canoe rode easily the deep, slow Pacific swells which swept over the sunken chain of reefs where Nona once had fished, finally to curl green and white on black volcanic sands. There was no sound save the gentle slapping of the outrigger, a whisper of breeze, and the murmur of small whirlpools which the paddle stirred to transient life on the sun-bright sea. To this faint accompaniment Tetua's parting words echoed back to me.

"Come again," he had called from where he stood on the curving strand. A breaking wave had raised its voice between us; then I heard him distantly once more. "Soon, Viriamu! None of us lives forever . . . !"

Very true. Thanks to Maui's splendid failure, none of us does. And who would have it otherwise? Yet, like Maui, I could not help wishing that, for the friend I left behind and for myself as well, time in which to continue sharing the Polynesian past and present might go on—if not forever, at least for a generous while. Or long enough, in any case, to allow for other returns, that I might once again harken to the last of Tahitian bards, the last brave teller of his people's wondrous tales.

In sudden decision that the next such return should not be long delayed, I swung the paddle vigorously, and in response the canoe surged forward over Matavai's untiring, heaving breast.